The Traitors of Camp 133

The Traitors of Camp 133

A Sergeant Neumann Mystery

Wayne Arthurson

The Traitors of Camp 133
© Wayne Arthurson 2016

Published by Ravenstone
an imprint of Turnstone Press
Artspace Building
206-100 Arthur Street
Winnipeg, MB
R3B 1H3 Canada
www.TurnstonePress.com

Turnstone Press gratefully acknowledges the assistance of the Canada
Council for the Arts, the Manitoba Arts Council, the Government of
Canada through the Canada Book Fund, and the Province of Manitoba
through the Book Publishing Tax Credit and the Book Publisher
Marketing Assistance Program.

This novel is a work of fiction. Names, characters, places and incidents
are either the product of the author's imagination or are used fictitiously,
and any resemblance to actual persons living or dead, events or locales, is
entirely coincidental.

Printed and bound in Canada by Friesens for Turnstone Press.

Library and Archives Canada Cataloguing in Publication

Arthurson, Wayne, 1962–, author
     The traitors of Camp 133 / Wayne Arthurson.

(The Sergeant Neumann mysteries ; 1)
Issued in print and electronic formats.
ISBN 978-0-88801-587-7 (paperback).--ISBN 978-0-88801-588-4 (epub).--
ISBN 978-0-88801-589-1 (mobipocket).--ISBN 978-0-88801-590-7 (pdf)

     I. Title.

PS8551.R888T73 2016   C813'.6   C2016-902598-5
                                               C2016-902599-3

To Auni and Vianne.

The Traitors of Camp 133

Lethbridge, Canada

June, 1944

1.

Mueller looked to be kneeling in the corner, praying. But the truth was his knees were inches off the floor. A rope hung from a coat hook and was wrapped around his neck.

Sergeant August Neumann stared at the body for several minutes. He watched it, looking to see if it would twist as some hanged bodies did, but it was wedged so tightly into the corner and the rope was so taut that there was no leeway for movement.

The body was in the northwest corner of a small classroom. Neumann stood near the teacher's desk, about three metres from the body. Without moving his feet, he leaned to the left and then the right, trying to see the face. He could not.

"Pretty impressive," he finally said, speaking German.

"Impressive, Sergeant?" asked Corporal Klaus Aachen, the young soldier standing next to Neumann. "It's horrid, if you ask me."

Neumann turned. Aachen was a head shorter than the sergeant who stood at least six-and-a-half feet and weighed 200 pounds. However, due to his stocky, muscular frame, one would never call Aachen small.

"You consider this horrid, Corporal?" asked the sergeant. "Weren't you in Stalingrad?" Neumann stepped closer to the body and inspected the rope.

"Just for a few months. Then I got wounded. When I recovered, they felt I had been a good enough patriot so I didn't have to go back," Aachen said, furrowing his eyebrows.

"This place is better than Stalingrad, I'm guessing."

"Stalingrad was a hell-hole. But in this camp I feel like I'm wasting away, unable to fight." Aachen stared down at the ground.

"It may not be pleasant here, but the Canadians are decent hosts. Better than the Russians, I suppose," Neumann said. "If you'd stayed in Stalingrad you'd be dead and Russian children would be using your frozen body as a sledge. Or you'd be surviving on snow and grass while the Russians worked you to death in a Siberian camp."

Aachen nodded. "Don't get me wrong, Sergeant, I'm pleased to be alive. And I don't wish to go back to Stalingrad or even into battle again. But many of my friends and family are still back there, fighting and dying, and I just feel ... I don't know ... empty and angry that I'm stuck here, unable to help them."

Neumann placed a hand on Aachen's shoulder. "You're a good German, Corporal Aachen. I feel the same way every hour of every day."

The two men went silent for several seconds, looking at the body.

"Stalingrad, eh?" Neumann said, breaking the silence. "Is that where you got your..." Neumann trailed off, tapping at the upper part of his chest, just below the neck.

Aachen looked where Neumann was pointing and then down at the same spot on his body. There was nothing there. His face reddened slightly. "My Cross. Yes, I got it in Stalingrad." His voice became almost a whisper. "It was ... nothing."

"Nothing?" Neumann's voice was loud, but pleasant. "One of the highest honours the Fatherland can bestow on our soldiers and you call it nothing."

"I didn't mean nothing," Aachen sputtered. "I just, well, it was an honour, but I don't believe I deserved it."

"Of course you deserved it, Corporal Aachen," Neumann said, slapping the younger man on the back, his big and meaty hand creating a loud thwack. "The Führer would not bestow an honour on a young man such as yourself if you did nothing. You must have done something."

Aachen opened his mouth to speak, but was at a loss for words.

Neumann again grabbed Aachen's shoulder and gave it a quick shake. Not many people could move Aachen in such a way, but the sergeant was one of the biggest men in the camp. "That's okay. You don't have to explain. Some things we just don't like to talk about. I understand completely, I can tell you that. But never again dismiss your actions as nothing or I will kick your ass, you hear me? You did something and the Führer and your country rewarded you for honour and bravery. You don't have to explain it, but you have to accept it, understand?"

The young soldier nodded, his freckled and pimpled face again turning red. "Yes, sir."

"Good," said Neumann with a clap of his hands. "So tell me, Corporal Aachen, why do you, a veteran not only of Stalingrad but also of Tunisia, a winner of the Iron Cross First Class for bravery under fire, find this scene horrid? You no doubt have seen worse things than this. Probably worse things than I have seen. I've heard many things of Stalingrad, most of it horrible."

"Stalingrad." Aachen sighed. A faraway look came over his face. While Aachen was barely twenty-two and had a face like a school boy, he did not look young at this moment. He seemed almost ageless, his eyes dark as if they had witnessed the Wild Hunt, that mythological group of ghostly huntsmen that foretold of death and catastrophe.

"Nothing can describe the horror of that place," Aachen said softly. "The Russians were animals; the terrible things they did, not only to us, but to many of their own citizens, were incomprehensible. Did you know, Sergeant, that they only had enough weapons for one in five Russian soldiers to have a rifle?"

Neumann nodded. "I've heard that. I've also heard it was one in ten."

"Whatever the number, they would send every single one of them into a charge and those who didn't have a weapon would have to wait for one of their comrades to get shot and then fight with the other Russians to get his weapon. Or somehow make it all the way across to our lines without getting killed, find some way to kill one of us with their bare hands, and then steal our weapon. It was a bloodbath."

"The Ivans are crazy."

"Completely," Aachen said with a nod. His voice became a whisper as he continued. "But we Germans, and forgive me for saying so, Sergeant, but there were things we did in Stalingrad that made me wonder if we Germans were any better than the Russians we were fighting. It just seemed so senseless."

"War can seem that way. Especially in the heat of battle. But you still haven't answered my question: why do you consider this a horrid scene when you've seen much worse?"

Aachen shrugged like a little boy who had been caught doing something mischievous by an adult. "You expect terrible things to happen in battle. You expect death and blood and horror, expect seeing your friends shot or blown to bits as all hell rains down on you. So while Stalingrad was terrible and so was Tunisia, as you know as well, Sergeant, you expect it and very quickly aren't surprised by it. You don't like it, nobody likes it, not even the Russians, but it's just part of the landscape of war.

"But this," Aachen pointed at the body, "this is just waste. Captain Mueller was a well-respected person in the camp. A lot of people looked up to him and to find him like this, hanged by his own hand, is pathetic."

"So you believe this is a suicide, Corporal Aachen?" Neumann asked, a flat tone in his voice. "You believe that Mueller has taken his own life?"

"What else could it be?"

Neumann shrugged. "I don't know. You could be right; it

could be suicide. Mueller was respected and well-liked, but many respectable and well-liked men have killed themselves without warning, confounding their friends and family. But during the time between the wars, I learned not to speculate too much. The facts will usually point the way in the end."

"So what do we do now?"

"Now? We leave and go about our business."

"We just leave Captain Mueller here?"

"For the moment, yes. Mueller is dead; he won't mind," Neumann said, turning and walking away from the body towards the exit.

Aachen stayed back looking at Mueller. "But shouldn't we inform the Canadians? They would probably like to know about something like this."

"If we tell the Canadians directly, people will suspect that we are informers and we'll never be able to do our jobs," Neumann said, standing at the door looking back at Aachen. "Maybe we'll find some way to get the word out through more indirect means."

Aachen stood there for another moment and then walked to the door. Before they left the room, Neumann grabbed Aachen's shoulder and stopped him. He turned him so they faced each other.

"Let me give you another piece of advice, Klaus, as one soldier to another. As one veteran of the African campaign to another. And as your former squad commander," Neumann said, placing a hand on each of Aachen's shoulders and squeezing hard. "Forget Mueller for a moment and think about what you said about Stalingrad. I understand what you said about the senselessness of it; I've seen my share of battle, in this war and the previous one. We all do things we aren't proud of and wonder what the point of it all is. At least those of us who still retain our humanity.

"But let me caution you. Not all soldiers are as open as me, especially officers. And especially officers who have feelings of inadequacy because they were captured by the enemy and placed in a prisoner-of-war camp. So be careful when you talk about Stalingrad. Be careful not to mention certain things about it because to some, that could be interpreted as a traitorous action. And even though we're in a prisoner-of-war camp, not able to fight for the Fatherland, we are still at war and you know what they do to traitors during the time of war. Do you understand?"

Aachen nodded slowly, eyes wide with fear.

Neumann nodded back and then relaxed. He let go of Aachen's shoulders and dropped his hands. He smiled brightly as if there was nothing wrong in the world.

Good," he said, giving the body one last glance. "Let's get the fuck out of here."

2.

Neumann and Aachen stepped out of the classroom building. There were no clouds in the wide open sky and the sun shone almost directly above, reflecting off the pale prairie and creating an intense glare that made them squint. Aachen brought a hand up to shade his eyes, but still couldn't stop squinting. Neumann climbed down the steps and Aachen quickly followed behind. They walked along the well-trodden path between the classrooms and the group of large barracks about 100 metres to the southeast.

The camp itself was no more than one square mile in area, filled with buildings of varying sizes, including barracks, messes, classrooms, workshops, and two of the largest recreational halls in Canada, each of them able to hold up to 5,000 people at once. Surrounding the entire camp were three types of fencing. First, an inner perimeter similar to fencing around a ranch—three lines of barbed wire, about three feet high—surrounded the camp. Twenty metres outside of this fence was the main camp fence, a five-metre-high fence of criss-crossing barbed wire topped by another three-foot-wide barbed wire that extended into the camp like a ledge. Another five metres outward was an identical fifteen-metre-high fence with the same extension at the top, but at every five metres along this fence was a high pole from which hung a light that was kept on. Farther out, spaced 200 metres apart, were the watch towers, each one continually manned by at least four Veterans Guards armed with a Enfield, as well as a fifty calibre machine gun.

In the five-metre space between the two high fences, many of the guards and their dogs patrolled the camp day and night. The twenty-metre space between the smaller inner perimeter fence and the larger fence was no man's land. No prisoner, no scout, no guard, no civilian, no dog was allowed on that strip of land, except when it was cut with a large tractor once a week in the summer. If a prisoner climbed over the inner fence and stepped into that strip, they could be immediately shot, no questions asked. That, however, had never happened since the camp opened. Prisoners had crossed the line but the Canadians preferred to order them to go back. Most times that was enough, but a few times, warning shots were required.

The only time a prisoner was permitted to cross the line was to retrieve a football accidentally kicked into the no-man's area. Yet before they chased down the errant ball and risked getting shot, they had to wave a handkerchief to get the attention of one of the watch tower guards. Only when the guard waved back with their handkerchief could the prisoner climb the fence. And even then, there were always a couple of rifles trained on the prisoner retrieving the ball.

And because the camp was set out in the open prairies of southern Alberta, there was a constant wind that flared into buffeting gusts, blowing dust all around. Aachen grunted with disgust.

"Is that a remark about my decision concerning Mueller's body, Corporal?" the sergeant asked without breaking stride. "Or is there something else on your mind?"

"It's just this wind. I hate it."

"Is the Rhineland a windless place?" Neumann asked with a chuckle.

"Of course not. We have plenty of wind back home. But usually just refreshing breezes on a hot day. Or warm gusts to blow and melt the snow way. The wind here is ..." he paused "...relentless is the only word I can think of. It just never seems to stop. I believe I'm starting to develop a lean in my step because of it."

Neumann chuckled again. "We had plenty of wind like this in North Africa—hot and dry, full of dust and grit—but you never complained about it then."

"That's because when the wind blew in North Africa, it grounded any planes that could strafe us and prevented artillery from targeting our position. The wind here just seems pointless. It only makes everything feel hotter and I have no idea how these people can plant anything because most of the earth seems to blow away."

"You're just going to have to get used to it, Corporal, because there's a good possibility we're going to be here a long time."

"You really think so? Even after the invasion in France?" Aachen said the final word quietly, even though there was no one remotely nearby.

"I've learned never to make predictions about the end of a war. When I was in the last war, not much younger than you, every year we all thought we'd be home by Christmas. But I spent a lot of Christmases in a trench hoping it would get a bit colder because that might kill the rats. Of course, the cold only made the rats hungrier and bolder. You learned pretty quickly to not fall asleep with your boots and gloves off, even if you were in a warm location."

"But begging your pardon, Sergeant, that was a different kind of war—more of a battle of attrition."

"War is war, take it from me, Corporal."

"Yes, Sergeant, I understand … but only to a point. In your war the enemy never landed over a million soldiers and almost 150,000 vehicles in less than a month."

"You really have to stop reading the magazines the Canadians give us, Klaus. They are designed to diminish our morale."

"Still, this is no small matter, the invasion."

"Of course it's no small matter. It's a major invasion of the continent, a bold move by the Allies. But they've been in France for a month and they haven't even taken Caen yet. That's a long way from defeating us. A very long way. And you shouldn't be hoping for such a thing."

"I'm not hoping for defeat, I would just like to finally go home for good."

"You have something against taking my orders, Corporal?" the sergeant asked, smiling.

"Of course not, Sergeant. I would take your orders all the time. You can come home with me and continue to give me orders after the war if you like."

"Be careful what you wish for—I might take you up on that."

"You would be very welcome in my home. Very welcome. My mother would cook you a great meal and my father would offer toast after toast, forcing you to drink every time. He makes his own brew out of potatoes. It's the worse thing I've ever tasted in my life."

Neumann smiled, slowing down his walk, imagining the scene. "That would be quite wonderful, Aachen. I can picture it now. Getting drunk with your old man. Would he allow you to join in the drunken debauchery?"

"Of course. Now that I'm a decorated veteran, he couldn't refuse me. But it wouldn't be that kind of debauchery. My father is a surgeon so it would be more of a slow decline."

"Ha! Slow decline, yes. Sounds like my kind of fun. Aachen, I do believe I will come visit you when this war is over."

Aachen sighed. "It just would be nice to decide for myself when and what I would eat, what time I would go to bed, and have the freedom to walk anywhere I damn well please."

Neumann put his hand on the corporal's shoulder as they walked. "We share the same sentiments, Klaus. Although returning home after a war can be very challenging to say the least. Germany has changed since we left. A lot of people have killed, civilians included. And I think some may not like how we handled the Jews. I didn't mind the ghettos but those camps we've heard about … not something I'd have ordered."

Aachen looked about quickly. "I'm not sure it's wise to talk about such things, Sergeant," he said with a whisper.

Neumann grunted. "You're probably right. But the Germany we return to may not be the same Germany that you remember."

"Well, I'm not the same person that I was before I left, either."

The two men stopped talking once they arrived at the barracks, a group of thirty-six clapboard two-storey buildings that looked like they were built in a month or less, and probably were. These buildings were arranged in six rows of six running north to south and in the middle of each row was a slightly smaller building, the mess where the prisoners who lived in that row ate.

Neumann and Aachen continued walking along a two-metre-wide lane between the barracks, the wind lessening. Although the buildings were just long boxes with a series of regularly-spaced single-paned windows on each of the two floors, there were a myriad of murals painted on the outside walls. The murals were of varied quality, some primitive, others beautiful and imaginative, with many levels in between. The subject matter also varied from depictions of various German landscapes, rivers, hills, and mountains to streetscapes of major cities like Berlin to images of German village life. They also included scenes or replicas of posters from popular movies and portraits of people who were probably friends, family members, or comrades of the artists. Some weren't even murals at all, just walls painted in a seemingly haphazard rainbow of colours. There were not, however, any overt murals of military or Nazi symbolism; the Canadians had banned such displays, except for on flags at funerals or special occasions.

To improve on the lack of beauty of the structures, the pathways between the barracks were lined with gardens, some designed to provide sustenance and filled with strict rows of vegetables, most only green shoots at this time of year, while others were merely decorative, the colours of budding flowers randomly distributed.

There were also prisoners everywhere, and almost every single person, save for a few like Neumann and Aachen, wore a uniform of blue, each one with a large red dot, almost half a metre wide, on the back. The official explanation was that the red dot made it easier to spot a prisoner in case he escaped, and any escapee who tried to rip out the dot would be left with a large hole in the back of their shirt, rendering them unable to blend in with the civilian population. The unofficial version was that the giant red dot on the back of the uniform provided a good target for the Veterans Guards to shoot at. All the guards had shoot to kill orders for anyone trying to escape.

There were prisoners strolling along the paths in large and small groups, couples, or just walking alone. Other prisoners were leaning against the walls, chatting amongst themselves and quietly enjoying the sun and a cigarette. Every barrack entrance had a cluster of prisoners around it, like a group of adolescents near a schoolyard. Most of these prisoners were smoking, some joking amongst themselves, a few playing a game of cards, and others just standing about.

German prisoners weren't the only ones around the camp. Small groups of unarmed Canadians soldiers called scouts patrolled the inside of the camp, interacting with the prisoners on a friendly basis but also keeping an eye out for any problems such as radios or signs that someone was digging a tunnel. Scouts were also tasked with spreading Allied propaganda which is why the majority of prisoners didn't spend much time talking to them unless they were forced to. The scouts were unarmed because weapons of any kind were not allowed in the camp.

In many ways for Aachen and Neumann, it was like walking through a small German village, except that all the buildings were recently constructed, the village was surrounded by fences topped with barbed wire and search towers, and every search tower had a squadron of enemy soldiers with orders to shoot to kill anyone who got within three metres of the fence. All of these guards had served in the First World War and had volunteered to fight in this one, but were deemed too old for the front lines. Instead, they were assigned to guard the growing number of German prisoners coming over from the European theatre. And even though the Veterans Guards were much older than most of the Germans they were guarding, the prisoners didn't take them lightly because Canadians had a reputation for being tough soldiers, even amongst the Germans. And these Veterans Guards had been hardened by the horrific battles of the previous war.

Also unlike a real German village, a good number of the residents were indolent, content just to while their time away. There were plenty of opportunities for work—every non-commissioned prisoner was required to do a stint of mess duty every day as well as military parade drills a couple of times a week—and there was no lack of recreational and educational diversions. But there was always a large number of prisoners who preferred doing absolutely nothing productive once they had been captured and placed in a camp. There were, of course, others who tried to keep themselves occupied and in this part of the camp, at the barracks, they included prisoners washing the windows of the barracks, hanging wet laundry, sweeping dust from the well-worn paths, or working in the gardens, their backs bent over so that the red dot on the back of their uniform was pointing to the sky.

As Aachen and Neumann weaved their way through the series of laneways between the barracks, the sergeant glanced at all the gardeners. After several minutes, he came upon a grey-haired prisoner who was kneeling in a flower garden. He was placing what looked to be a small sandbag along the edge of the garden, using a spoon to pile earth onto the sandbag in order to create a little mound that acted like a barrier between the garden and the prairie. Neumann stopped behind this soldier, stood at attention, and cleared his throat. Corporal Aachen also snapped to attention as the older soldier looked over his shoulder. He glanced up at the two men standing in front of him, shading his eyes from the glare, trying to recognize who was summoning him. After a moment, he smiled and set down his spoon near a pile of more sandbags.

"Sergeant Neumann, what a pleasant surprise," the older prisoner said, slowly pushing himself to his feet. He grunted painfully as he did so. Though he was probably the same age as Neumann, he looked at least a decade older. His hair was grey and thinning, except in his ears, and his skin was mottled with liver spots. His eyes were alert, but sunken in his head, and he had a slight paunch hanging over his belt, which made his stoop seem more prominent.

Neumann saluted the gardener in the Wehrmacht way, right hand to forehead. A second later, Aachen repeated the gesture. Both of them stared straight ahead, making no eye contact. The gardener casually returned the salutes and then reached out a hand. Neumann relaxed slightly, looked him in the eye, and stuck out his right hand. The gardener grabbed it and shook it vigorously.

"It is very good to see you again, Neumann. It's been a few weeks. You're looking very well."

"You as well, General Horcoff."

Horcoff released Neumann and waved the comment away. "Bah, you're just saying that because I'm a superior officer. I'm old and in this place I'm getting older. The Canadians have provided us with many things to make our lives comfortable, but a well-furnished cage is still a cage. There's nothing for me to do except dig the dirt. It's giving me a sore back and I'm getting fat."

"We're all getting fat, General. It's all the food these Canadians keep feeding us. The only one not getting fat is Corporal Aachen. Something in his metabolism keeps him the same size he was in North Africa."

Aachen didn't respond at all to the sergeant's statement but when the general turned to him and slapped a hand on his shoulder, he blushed. "Corporal Aachen," the general said with a bright smile. "Always great to see you, as well. You ready for your match? Ready to show those submariners what the Wehrmacht is made of?"

"Aachen was born ready for this kind of thing," Neumann said, responding for his subordinate. "When he's not following me around the camp, he's training. Lifting his sandbags, throwing medicine balls around, running around the camp like he's late for dinner."

"Ha. I hope you don't mind me borrowing some of your weightlifting sandbags, Corporal. I know you need them to build your strength, but they're very good for keeping weeds out of my garden." The general pointed at his little barriers. "The weeds are relentless here, but I hope to defeat them, much like the way I hope you'll defeat that Neuer fellow. He may be big, but he's no match for our Corporal Aachen. No match."

Aachen blushed more deeply but said nothing and did not move from being at attention. General Horcoff slapped the corporal on the shoulder again. He then turned to Neumann. "While it's good to see you, Sergeant, I'm assuming that your presence here is not a random meeting."

"The general is as astute as ever."

"So what is the real reason behind you coming to my garden?"

"It's Captain Mueller," Neumann said in a quieter voice. "He's dead."

"Mueller? Which one is Mueller?"

"Captain Mueller was a tank commander in the 501st Panzer Division. Used to be a mathematician as a civilian so he became a teacher here in the camp."

"Ahh, the Bolshevik."

Aachen flinched at the statement, but recovered before the general could notice. Neumann, however, did notice, and he stepped between the general and the corporal. "I wouldn't technically call him that, sir. He was more interested in helping the younger and less-educated soldiers improve themselves so they could find better positions when the conflict ends."

"While I understand and support the idea of young soldiers bettering themselves, it still sounds like Bolshevism to me. There is an order to things, Sergeant. An order to humanity. And to encourage people to rise above their station can be unwise, which is what I heard Mueller was known to champion."

"Be that as it may, General, the important fact is that Mueller is dead."

The general rubbed his chin with his hand. "Yes, yes. And despite his political leanings, he was known as a strong commander and strategist. He fought well. It's a shame to hear of the death of such a comrade." The general paused and pursed his lips. "Any idea of the cause of his death?"

"Hanging. Aachen and I have just come from viewing his body. We came upon it during our morning rounds."

"Suicide then?" Horcoff asked with wide eyes.

"At first glance, yes, but with further examination, I'm saying no."

"What!?" Horcoff hissed. He looked about and whispered, "Are you saying Mueller was murdered?"

Aachen's response was also one of surprise although more restrained. He broke from his pose to turn and look at the sergeant.

"That is what I am saying," Neumann said with a nod. "And that is why I first came to you."

"Are you absolutely sure?" Horcoff asked, squinting.

Neumann nodded. "First off, his hands were tied."

"Yes, that would give it away. No one can hang themselves with their hands tied."

"Well, they can and they have, sir. I have seen it myself many times in my years between the conflicts. There are a few techniques in which the hands can be self-tied before the hanging."

"Why on earth would anybody wish to do that?"

"People are very complicated, sir. Especially those who wish to kill themselves. Those who self-tie are wishing to prevent themselves from backing out of the task at the last minute."

"Plenty stupid if you ask me," the general said with a scoff. "Nevertheless, your experience tells you that Mueller did not tie his hands himself?"

"Correct. And the way he was hanged, with so many knots, I'm saying there was probably more than one person involved, at least two, no more than four, in the actual hanging. I'm not accounting for if there was anybody else in the room, either as a witness or directing the task."

"Are you sure about that?"

"Quite sure," Neumann said with a nod. He gestured toward Aachen. "The corporal here is the strongest person I know in this camp. He is also quick for someone of his weight, but even with those two qualities, there is no way even for him to be able to tie the rope in the way it was tied around Mueller and pull on the rope so that he could be hanged in the way it was done.

24

Unless he was unconscious. This was a either a coordinated action by a group of people or by a very determined person who caught the captain off guard, subdued him somehow, and then had plenty of time to hang him."

"Any idea which people?" the general asked.

Neumann shook his head, but then looked about to see if anybody was listening. He stepped closer to Horcoff and spoke quietly. "To be completely honest, General, I believe Mueller was killed because there are others who believe the same that you do about him."

The general waved his hand and did not lower his voice to Neumann's volume. "I may have not agreed with some of his political leanings, but Captain Mueller showed many times that he was a loyal German, loyal to the country, loyal to the Führer. He was a strong commander and an excellent strategist. And for me, that's enough."

"For me too, and no doubt for Corporal Aachen as well. However, there are those in the camp who would not see things that way."

The general stepped back, another look of surprise on his face. "Are you saying what I think you are saying?"

Neumann nodded.

"Then this is something other than just murder, Sergeant," the general said, striking his fist into his hand. "This could be an affront to the leadership of the camp. We cannot allow things to go back to the ways of the SA and their Brownshirt thuggery. We cannot intimidate and assault people willy-nilly because we don't like the way they talk or what they read. There must be a process in place. We are not anarchists."

"But the question is what shall we do about it? If things are resorting to the ways of the SA, we cannot confront them head on. That would only create more chaos and violence."

The general paused and glanced at his garden. He reached down and pinched off the head of a flower. "I see your point, Sergeant," he said quietly, bringing the flower to his nose and smelling it. "We must be subtle in our approach. Very subtle."

"Which is another reason I came to you first. I needed to know if I should pursue an investigation into Mueller's death or allow people to believe he killed himself."

The general smelled the flower once again, then he crushed the petals in his hand and tossed it to the ground. "Considering the situation, I believe an investigation is warranted, although it would have to be a very careful investigation. If there is a group operating using the tactics of the SA and they discover what you are doing, they could come after you."

"I can take care of myself, General, you know that."

"Yes we all know how you can take care of things," the general said, but didn't elaborate. He stepped away from the sergeant and focused his gaze on Aachen. "However, you remember how the SA operates; if they can't get at you, they'll try to get at someone close to you. We are well past our prime, but it would be a shame if something happened to our young corporal here."

For the first time since they found the general in his garden, Aachen broke protocol and spoke. "It is my duty as a loyal German soldier to give my life in support of my superiors."

The men paused but then the general laughed and slapped Aachen on the shoulder. "Well said, Aachen, well said. If I had

had more soldiers like you in North Africa, we would not be here in this camp."

"Begging your pardon, General," Aachen said with steel in his voice. "You had thousands of soldiers like me in North Africa. We did not lose that battle because of them."

The two older soldiers froze in surprise, and this time it was Neumann who responded first. He turned on the corporal, the anger seething in his face and posture. His hands curled into tight fists and he stood over the much shorter corporal.

"Corporal Aachen! How dare you speak to the general in such a way!" Neumann shouted, spittle flying from his mouth across the corporal's stoic face. "You have committed a gross act of insubordination and if you think that our experience in North Africa will allow me—"

"—Sergeant Neumann!" shouted General Horcoff, instantly stopping the tirade. Neumann slowly turned to look at Horcoff. "Leave the corporal be," the general said in a quiet voice.

"But sir, he was disrespectful. He spoke out of turn."

"I said leave the corporal be," the general snapped, his tone quiet but commanding.

Sergeant Neumann moved to attention. "Yes, General."

Horcoff moved to stand in front of the corporal. "Corporal Aachen doesn't deserve your anger; I do." He put both hands on the young man's shoulders and gave him a smile. "This bright young man is correct. There were thousands of strong and loyal German soldiers fighting in North Africa. Brave men, wonderful men, men who gave their lives in our fight or were wounded or captured, not because of the mistakes they made, but the mistakes we made, those of us in command. It was wrong of me to blame my men, when a lot of the blame hangs on me."

"No one blames you, sir," the sergeant said, still at attention. "We just underestimated the Brits and Amis, especially after the early days."

Horcoff shook his head. "We didn't think they would regroup so quickly, although Rommel had an inkling that would happen. He wanted to push further but no one listened to him. Our men loyally followed our orders and fought bravely but in the end we lost the battle and here we all are, stuck in a prisoner-of-war camp in the wilds of Canada. At the very least this camp is clean and open to the air, unlike those horrid, closed ships that we crossed the ocean on."

"Yes, sir, that trip was an ordeal."

"Being stuck with those Italians and their smells is a memory I'll never forget. Horrible, disgusting people. Guess our only consolation is that when Germany prevails and the Leader sees our camp and how well it is kept, he will know that we are still honourable Germans."

The general stepped away from the corporal and pointed at Sergeant Neumann and then at his flower garden

"That is why I garden, Neumann. That is why I spend all this time digging in the dirt, growing flowers. So that when the Führer comes to our camp after Germany is victorious and releases us from this prison, he will see that despite our surrender, we didn't wallow in pity and capitulation, and we didn't allow our camp to fall into disrepair. We kept our pride and honour as Germans."

He moved closer to Neumann and leaned to speak quietly into his right ear. "And that is why you must investigate this murder of Captain Mueller. When our Führer removed Rohn and his SA from power, he was telling everyone that we Germans are not thugs and anarchists intimidating communists and old Jews on the street. We are men of honour, men of purpose, who will do things with a proper process as a great nation should. And we must prevent anarchy from returning, even here.

"So investigate this murder, Sergeant Neumann. Do so with discretion, but find out who killed Captain Mueller and bring them to justice. Honourable German justice, if you get my meaning."

Sergeant Neumann stiffened to attention and snapped a quick Wehrmacht salute. General Horcoff quickly responded with a sharp one of his own.

Neumann turned on his heel and strode away. "Let's go, Corporal," he snapped as he walked past Aachen.

The corporal also saluted, got one from the general in return, turned 180 degrees on his heel, and followed the sergeant.

The general watched them walk away. He sighed, then turned to look for his spoon. When he found it, he slowly lowered himself to his knees and began digging. He started to whistle, but then stopped himself and looked around.

After a moment, he went back to silently digging.

3.

Both Neumann and Aachen broke their marching stride after a few steps and began to walk normally. They walked several metres along the trails between the barracks, and even though they were side by side, it was obvious that the sergeant was leading the way.

They passed several prisoners toiling in their gardens and walking along the paths. The prisoners greeted them politely, several wishing to begin a conversation with the sergeant, but Neumann politely waved them away, telling them that he would find them later. A corporal who had served in the same company as Neumann and Aachen, however, was able to flag them down. Neumann waved him over.

At just twenty years old, Corporal Dieter Knaup was tall and muscular with a bright face and an easy smile, although his many pimples made him look even younger than he was.

He bounded over like a faithful puppy when he saw Neumann beckon him over.

"Hello, Sergeant Neumann. It's a wonderful day, isn't it?" Knaup said, his head nodding rapidly with each word. "Great to see you as well, Klaus. I hope the training has been going well. I'm really looking forward to your match. It's the talk of the camp! Everyone's excited, and we're all pretty sure you'll easily defeat—"

"—Knaup, please," Sergeant Neumann said, raising his hand to cut off the young corporal.

Knaup froze, his smile vanishing into a worried frown. He stiffened, almost to attention, his head still nodding slightly. "Yes, Sergeant. Sorry, Sergeant."

"Don't apologize, Knaup. I called you over for a reason."

"Yes, Sergeant?"

Neumann pointed at Knaup. "Do you know Doctor Kleinjeld?"

Knaup nodded quickly. "Yes, he's the one who treated my frostbite this past winter. I lost part of a toe, but he managed to save my foot."

"I want you to go find him and give him a message."

"Yes, Sergeant. Message to Doctor Kleinjeld."

"Tell him that he needs to take a look at Captain Mueller in Workshop Number 4."

"Right. Captain Mueller in Workshop Number 4." Knaup rubbed the back of his head. "What's wrong with Captain Mueller?"

Neumann flicked the back of his hand. "Just give the doctor the message," Neumann said more sternly.

Knaup immediately stood at attention."Yes, Sergeant. Sorry, Sergeant."

Neumann looked over at Aachen and rolled his eyes. Aachen shrugged but said nothing. "I also want you to accompany the doctor when he goes to see Captain Mueller. And to follow any orders the doctor may give you. Whatever he requests, you do."

Knaup nodded. "Yes, Sergeant. I will do as you ask."

Neumann then stepped forward until he was only a few inches away from Knaup. He held an index finger up and pointed at the corporal. "And one final thing, Knaup, and this is very important," Neumann said quietly. His finger jerked towards Knaup with every word he spoke. "You give this message directly to Doctor Kleinjeld. You don't pass it on to his assistant or a nurse or anyone else. Only Doctor Kleinjeld gets the message. Understand?"

Knaup's face turned pale. He nodded once, very slowly.

"And you tell no one about this message. Absolutely no one. When I release you, you don't stop and visit and you don't answer anyone's questions about where you are going. You go straight to Doctor Kleinjeld, give my message, then go with him and do whatever he tells you. These are direct orders. Do you understand me, Corporal Knaup? Do you understand the importance of what I'm asking you?"

Knaup blinked several times, his mouth hanging open. He looked over at Aachen, but Aachen said nothing.

"Don't look at Aachen, Corporal Knaup. I'm the one giving the orders here," Neumann said. "Do you understand my orders?"

"Yes, Sergeant," Knaup said after a couple of seconds. Then he shook his head. "I mean, no, Sergeant. I'm sorry, I really don't know what you mean, but I can tell it's very important. So I will do as you ask. I will pass your message to Doctor Kleinjeld. I will go with him and follow his orders. And I won't tell anyone anything."

Neumann stepped back and smiled. "Good man, Knaup. You've always been an excellent soldier." Neumann slapped him on the shoulder.

Knaup's face tightened again. He gave Aachen another glance, but quickly looked back to the sergeant. Knaup stiffened to attention. "Yes, Sergeant. Thank you, Sergeant."

"Okay, go along now. Go find the good doctor," Neumann said, stepping back and waving his hand at Knaup.

Knaup paused and then walked away without looking at Aachen or Neumann. His stride quickened as he moved away, becoming a half run as he turned the corner.

4.

After Knaup left, Neumann and Aachen continued on their way. Aachen glanced up at the sergeant. "So, when were you going to tell me your theory about who killed Captain Mueller?"

"What are you talking about, Aachen? I already told you."

"You told General Horcoff. I just happened to be standing there when you were doing it."

"And where else would you be when we are making the rounds? I knew you would hear what I told the general. You don't expect me to repeat myself all the time."

"It just would have been good to know what you had planned."

Neumann laughed. "Relax, Corporal. We're in a prisoner-of-war camp. No one's shooting at us anymore, so there's really no need for me to go over every plan with you before I do something. Although I do promise that if we ever get the chance to

34

attack a position again, I will make sure I apprise you of my plans before we do so."

Aachen grunted. "At the very least can you tell me where we are going, now?"

"Of course. Mueller lived in Hut 14 so I'm going to talk to his hut leader, Staff Sergeant Heidfield, to see if there were any concerns."

"You're not going to tell him about Captain Mueller, are you?"

Neumann said nothing for several steps. "I don't know. We'll see how it plays out. Heidfield's decent to the fellows under his command, but he's a bit of a rogue, so we have to watch what we say to him."

Every hut housed 800 men in row after row of wooden bunk beds. But since it was the middle of the morning, a couple hours after the first count, there were only about fifty men scattered about playing cards, writing letters home, mending clothing, taking showers, and just hanging about. There was still the noise of conversation, water pipes creaking, and the wind battering the walls and windows, but compared to the times when the hut was completely occupied, when it was full of the sounds and scents of 800 German soldiers living in a bunkhouse the size of a small school, the place was practically peaceful.

Neumann and Aachen walked through the rows of bunks, looking for Staff Sergeant Nico Heidfield. They found him in the middle of the row nearest the south side wall. Heidfield lay on his lower bunk, dressed only in a shirt and underwear, reading a small book. His head was resting on a pillow at the foot of the bed so as to get more light from the window.

Sergeant Neumann sat on the bunk next to Heidfield's saying nothing, waiting for the hut leader to finish what he was
reading. Aachen stood near the window, but in a casual posture,
leaning his left shoulder against the outside wall as if he was just
waiting for a bus to arrive. Part of Aachen's shadow fell on half
of Heidfield's book.

The hut leader ignored the shadow for as long as he could
and then he sighed deeply, reluctantly dog-eared the page he
was reading, shut the book, and set it on his chest. He stretched
like a man waking up from a nap.

"Sergeant Neumann," he said, elongating the name as he
stretched. "If you're looking for something to drink, you're out
of luck. A scout found our still a couple days ago. He took it
away with some of his scout friends. Come back in a week and
we'll be up and running again."

Though Heidfield was a staff sergeant, outranking Neumann,
he was a lot younger, only a few years older than Corporal
Aachen. And he looked young as well: tall, blond, and blue-eyed
with a spot-free boyish face, straight teeth, and a movie star
haircut parted on the left with the hair swooping to the right,
slightly longer than regulations allowed.

Neumann smiled and leaned his hand on the mattress of the
bunk he was sitting on. "Sorry, I gave up drinking your homemade stuff once I had a taste of the brew you and your boys
made on the ship transport over here."

Heidfield responded with a bright smile. "Oh that was good
stuff," he said, rubbing his hands together. "I can't believe what
we accomplished in that disgusting place. Amazing ingenuity.

Even some of the Canadian merchant boys bought stuff from us. The pinnacle of my career, that brew was. Something I'll never forget."

"Neither will most of us on that ship. Which is why I'll pass on any offers of brew you make to me. Even if you open the most prestigious nightclub in Berlin—"

"—and I will, no doubt about that," Heidfield said, quickly turning onto his side, allowing his book to fall to the floor. He pushed himself to a seated position and waved his hands frantically, as if conducting an invisible orchestra. "It will be the hotspot of the city, I can guarantee you that. Anyone who is anyone in Berlin will want to come to my club. The movie stars, the politicians, the rich kids with money, the big-shot power brokers, they will all want to come to my club. And only a few will get in because there will not be enough room for all of them."

Aachen shook his head while the sergeant gave a sarcastic chuckle. "Well, count me out because like I said, I will never sample your brew again after drinking the stuff you cooked up on the cruise."

"But you will be welcome anytime, Neumann. Anytime," Heidfield said slapping the sergeant on the knee. "A man of your integrity and standing will have carte blanche at my club. Whatever you desire will be yours for the asking."

"As long as I don't have to drink what you serve."

Heidfield ignored the jibe, turning to point at Aachen. "And you as well, Corporal Aachen. You've made me a lot because of your skills on the mat. So if you ever get to Berlin after the war and come to my club, you will never have to wait in line. Never."

Aachen said nothing and turned to look out the window.

Heidfield smiled at him and then faced the sergeant. "So if it's not brew you want, Sergeant Neumann, how can I help you? Wishing to make a bet on Aachen's match? I'll admit that it's a bit unorthodox, but I'll take your bet. The odds are against Aachen at the moment because everyone thinks Neuer is bigger and stronger, but that only works in your favour. Well, in mine as well because worse odds against Aachen provides a better payout for me."

"I'm not here to bet on Aachen."

"Then why are you here?"

"I'm here because I need to talk to you as the hut leader."

Heidfield laughed openly, his face bright and joyful. He slapped Neumann on the knee again. "Then you have come to the wrong place."

The staff sergeant bent down to pick up his book and leaned back on his pillow. He continued chuckling as he started reading again.

As he did, Neumann leaned forward and spoke. "I don't understand. What's so funny?"

"I am not the hut leader of this space," Heidfield said, pointing at Neumann with his book. "I was voted out a couple days ago."

"Voted out?"

"Well, technically they voted someone else in—some sergeant who was just transferred over from Medicine Hat. Real serious type. Has a huge taste for the colour black, especially in clothing, if you understand my meaning."

"When did this happen?"

"Oh, he got here a week or so ago."

"No, no," Neumann said with a wave of his hand. "When did they vote you out?"

"Couple of days ago. I had just finished taking a shit and a group of prisoners came up to me, real grumbly types, all sweaty and tough, telling me that I was no longer the hut leader. And when I told them that the men had voted for me, they said there was another election."

"There's not supposed to be another election for three more months."

"That's what I said. I told them the Canadians were very picky about when we're supposed to have elections for hut leaders, that they wanted to teach us the importance of democracy and elections." Heidfield pointed with his book again and winked. "Like we've never had elections in Germany before, eh Neumann? I mean how do you think the Leader got into power in the first place?"

"Never mind that, what else did they tell you?"

"They got all huffy and bruisy when I mentioned the Canadians and told me if I knew what was good for me, I would accept that there was another hut leader and shut up and walk away—which I did. Not because I was intimidated by those SS guys; most of them, except for one or two, looked to be political types, desk riders or command adjuncts who never saw a second of combat and wanted to be evacuated, but didn't manage it before the Tommies took over."

"How many of them were there?"

"About six. Maybe seven. I wasn't counting."

"Do you know the name of the sergeant who replaced you?"

"Konrad, I think. Big ugly man—a bit like you Neumann, no offence. Although unlike you, I hear he's not very pleasant at all. Doesn't care what the men want. And like I said, really loves the colour black." Heidfield winked at the final statement.

"And you say he just got transferred from Medicine Hat?"

Heidfield nodded, looked at his book for a few seconds, and then rolled on his side again. "I don't know what this is all about Sergeant Neumann. I have no idea what you and Corporal Aachen are doing here and to be honest, I don't really care. I don't care if this black suit aspirant is the hut leader now. In fact, I'm actually very pleased that it's no longer me. I didn't campaign for the job—didn't want the job—but since the boys voted me in, I figured that I might as well take it to help them out. But now that they voted me out, or whatever happened, I can relax and wait for the war to end. Maybe even make a few extra marks that I can somehow smuggle back home."

Heidfield lay back on his pillow and returned to his book, saying nothing more.

5.

Back outside the hut, Neumann stood a few feet away from the entrance near the edge of one of the laneways. He reached into the front pocket of his uniform. Out came a packet of cigarettes. He pulled one out and put it into his mouth. Then he put the packet back and starting padding his pockets, looking for his lighter.

After several seconds of this, he looked over to Aachen, who had tucked himself against a wall to escape from the wind. "You have a light, Corporal?"

Aachen shook his head. "I can't smoke until after my match."

"Ahh, good man," the sergeant said, padding his pockets again, his frustration mounting. After a few more seconds, he snatched the cigarette from his mouth, crumpled it in his hand, and tossed it to the ground.

"Fuck," he said. "What a fucking waste."

"Are you talking about the cigarette or something else?" Aachen quietly asked.

Neumann turned on the corporal with the intention of berating him for insolence, but quickly stopped himself. "Dammit. How could something like that happen?" he said, shaking his head. "How could a group of thugs elect one of their own as a hut leader without me knowing about it?"

"It's a big camp," Aachen said softly. "One man can't keep track of all the goings-on."

"I should. That's my job."

"Well, did you know that a scout found Heidfield's still and destroyed it?"

Neumann tilted his head to the side. "No. I was unaware of that."

"There you go. Another thing you didn't know."

"This is not helping. I should have known about that as well."

"Then why didn't you stop Mueller from being killed?"

"Because I didn't—" Neumann started to say and then he stopped himself. He stepped back, leaned against the building, then looked at the ground for a moment. He sighed deeply.

"Right. Thank you, Corporal Aachen." Neumann collected himself, pulled out the packet of cigarettes again, and put another one in his mouth. This time, after putting the pack away, he found his lighter in his back pocket. He lit the cigarette and took a deep drag. "Still, I believe I should have known that there was a new hut leader in Hut 14," Neumann said, blowing the smoke out as he spoke. "That's a big change."

"Like I said, it's a big camp. You can't know everything."

"But a new hut leader; I should know that."

"Well, Staff Sergeant Heidfield said it was only a day or so ago that this happened."

"But it should have been noted to camp command. Somebody on the administrative side should have been aware of it." When Neumann spoke of camp command, he spoke of the Germans who commanded the prisoners in the camp. Since there were over 12,000 prisoners in this camp, it was almost impossible for the Canadians and their Veterans Guards to run the camp. Since the Germans already had a command structure in place, it made more sense for them to oversee many of the administrative and logistical operations of the camp, including internal security. For the most part, the place was essentially a German military camp enclosed by barbed wire.

"Unless no one in administration knows about it," Aachen said. "There is a possibility that because of the way they elected their new leader, they may be reluctant to inform command and the Canadians of the situation."

"That's very true," Neumann said, pointing with his cigarette. "But there is another possibility."

"What's that?"

"Someone in command or administration does know about the new hut leader and they are preventing the information from being spread about." Neumann thought for a moment, then stuck his cigarette in his mouth and clapped his hands twice.

"Right. Okay, Aachen, let's go." His voice was filled with purpose as he strode away.

It took Aachen a second to realize the sergeant was moving and a few more seconds to catch up and start walking alongside him.

"Where are we going now?" Aachen asked as they made their way through the laneways between the barracks.

"We're now going to resume our duties from before we got sidetracked with Captain Mueller."

"The chef in Mess 3."

"That's right. We're going to talk to the chef in Mess 3 about the discrepancy in his supplies."

"What about the new leader in Hut 14? What about the fact that someone could be withholding information about that change?"

"That might be important, but we should just do what we are supposed to do."

"What about Captain Mueller and Doctor Kleinjeld? Should we go see if he's dealt with the body yet?"

"In time, Aachen. In time. First we have to deal with the chef."

"But the chef has nothing to do with the new leader in Hut 14. Nor with Captain Mueller."

"Of course he doesn't. But that's what we've been ordered to do and I really think that at this moment in time, we should be seen doing what we have been ordered to do."

Aachen stopped for a moment while the sergeant kept walking. He looked up; a haze due to the harsh brightness of the sun almost obscured the blue of the sky.

After several steps, Neumann stopped and looked at the corporal. He slowly walked back to stand next to Aachen.

"General Horcoff is right," Aachen said. "There is a power play of some sort in the camp."

"There's always some sort of power play going on in the camp," Neumann said putting a hand on the young man's shoulder. "That's how the military works. Those in command jostle for authority and influence, trying to get their plans and ideas put into practice. It's happening in this war and it happened in the Great One."

"But Mueller may be dead because of it."

"Thousands upon thousands of soldiers are killed each day because every command decision made in every battle is the result of these struggles for power in the upper echelon. Millions upon millions of men, women, and children are dead in this war because of the same thing. Mueller is only one man and in all that, he barely even counts."

"It's just that—" Aachen started to say, but couldn't finish.

"I know, Corporal. You want it to all make sense. You want there to be a purpose to it all, especially since you've given your life to it. But this is war and war never makes sense. It only kills people."

"So what do we do?"

"We do what we've always done in the trenches. Keep your head down and try not to get killed. Which is why despite what has happened with Mueller and what General Horcoff has said about investigating it, we have to go talk to the chef. No matter what is happening in the camp, those are our orders for today and it's important that we appear to be following those orders."

"Right," Aachen said with a nod. "We shouldn't rock the boat."

"Correct. Rocking the boat will only cause it to tip over and we'll all drown," Neumann said, removing his hand from Aachen shoulder. He took one final drag of his cigarette and tossed it into the path. He ground his boot on the burning ash. "However, there's nothing stopping us from leaning in the boat to subtly alter its direction."

Aachen gave a quick nod and smile to his sergeant. "Okay, let's go talk to the chef."

"Good man," Neumann said.

They resumed their walk.

"Is there anything I should prepare for?" Aachen asked. "Will there be any surprises in our discussions with the chef, like with General Horcoff?"

"I don't think so," the sergeant said with a shrug.

"So the typical procedure."

"That's what I'm thinking, although be prepared for the possibility of improvisation. So far it's been an unusual day and I'm not sure how the chef will respond to our inquiries."

"Like I said, the typical procedure."

The sergeant paused in his steps for a moment, looking to say something to the corporal. But when he saw the feigned look of innocence on Aachen's face, he rolled his eyes, shook his head, and continued on. The corporal fell in step beside him.

They were several metres away from Mess 3, which was located almost directly in the centre of the barracks quarter of the camp. It was a relatively large building—an open warehouse able to seat and feed 800 soldiers at a time with an industrial kitchen at the back. However, when compared to the large housing structures in which the soldiers actually slept, it seemed much smaller.

There were two entrances to the mess, a set of double doors on the south wall and another matching set of doors for the kitchen on the north side. Since it was the end of a breakfast shift, a good number of prisoners were milling about, either standing or sitting on the steps leading to the doors, or in an area about a three metre radius from the doors. Most of them smoked and a few carried bits of fruit.

The sergeant stopped and turned to the corporal before they got within earshot of the loitering prisoners.

"You probably know this already, Corporal, but I must stress that we cannot make any mention of Captain Mueller when we talk to the chef or to anyone else we may meet on the way. Do you understand?"

"Of course, Sergeant," Aachen said with a nod. "That goes without saying."

"I know, but I felt I had to say it." Neumann turned to the door and adjusted his uniform. "Okay, let's go to work."

The two soldiers walked to the mess. Since all of the prisoners knew who they were, they cleared a path for them, but in a casual manner. A few of them greeted the sergeant by name or rank, treating him like he was the village policeman, which, in a sense, he was. One or two greeted Aachen, asking if he was ready for his match, and once word of the match came along, the prisoners became more interested in the pair, peppering Aachen with questions and suggestions on how to win.

"Come on boys, let us through. Just because most of you have nothing better to do, some of us have duties we need to accomplish," Neumann said waving his arms at the crowd. "And stop touching Corporal Aachen's muscles to see if he's strong enough. You don't want to be responsible for him getting hurt before the match, do you? Your friends aren't going to be appreciative if you're the cause of that."

The crowd instantly backed away at those words, giving Aachen as much room as possible. One prisoner even opened the door for the two, escorting them in like a doorman at a fancy restaurant.

With the crowd out of the way, the two walked into the building. Even though it was after nine and the sun had been up for more than three hours, the building was dark. There were very few windows in the mess and most were covered with a thick film from cigarette smoke plus the grease and grime from the cooking.

The building was mostly one large room filled with long wooden tables with benches on each side. Even though the third and last breakfast shift was over, a large number of prisoners still lingered, picking at the remnants of breakfast from the big bowls in the centre of the tables in which the food was served, or smoking from their now endless supply of cigarettes courtesy of the Canadian government and the Red Cross. There were also others completing their required daily KP, picking up the debris, putting away bowls, cups, and utensils, and wiping the tables.

A number of the prisoners inside noticed Neumann and Aachen and shouted some encouragement to the corporal but most kept their distance. There was something in the way the two walked through the mess that told the bystanders that it would probably be better for them to remain bystanders. Some prisoners even got up and left the mess; trouble was best avoided.

Neumann and Aachen made their way through the mess, weaving in and out of the tables and a couple of times separating and taking divergent paths. But in the end, they managed to arrive together at their intended destination: a table at the back of the mess next to the door of the kitchen.

Five prisoners sat at that table—four of them on one side, all tall and skinny. They were also all eating, scooping out scrambled eggs from a large bowl and grabbing slices of toast from a large pile on a plate next to the bowl of eggs. Two of them also held cigarettes in their mouths while they ate, dropping the ashes into another bowl, beside which sat a pack of Canadian cigarettes.

Neumann and Aachen ignored these four and focused on the POW that sat by himself on the other side of the table. By contrast, he was shorter but almost the same width as three of the other men sharing his table. He also wore the white mess uniform, but had a brown sweater draped around his shoulders, like a male opera singer relaxing at his favourite watering hole after a performance. And though his face was fat, full of jowls, and covered with spots, he had a pencil-thin moustache above his full lips which seemed to be pursed in an expression of annoyance. His face was red and glistening, as if he had just exerted himself. Unlike the four workers across from him, he had no bowl of food in front of him, only a small, empty soup can which he used to catch the ashes from his cigarette. He calmly smoked using the French technique, puffing on the cigarette, and then allowing the smoke to leave his mouth so he could inhale it through his nose.

The sergeant sat down on the bench next to this prisoner while Aachen remained standing at the edge of the table. "Captain Splichal. I knew I would find you here. Resting after another meal served. Quite frankly, I don't know how you guys do it. Feeding thousands of men three times a day, seven days a week. Must be exhausting."

If Splichal was surprised to see Neumann and Aachen, he didn't show it. He only leaned back slightly, took a drag from his cigarette, and blew the smoke to the ceiling.

"It's no different than feeding the same amount of men in North Africa, except that there are no Tommies trying to bomb the shit out of my kitchen. That's always a good thing. And the food's a lot better here," Splichal said. His voice was low and slow, as if he had been a boxer in a previous life. "Especially the beef. I don't know what they do with the cows out here, but this is the best beef I've ever eaten, better than the time I worked for that hotel in Frankfurt. You can't get beef like this at home."

"No one's had beef back home for years," said the sergeant. "Most people can't even get horse meat anymore."

"You think I don't know that?" Splichal said, taking another puff of his cigarette. "I got a sister living in Berlin; she keeps sending me letters. Not only are all the horses gone, but so are the pigeons, the crows, and all the other birds. Most of the cats are wisely in hiding and soon people will be looking to their dogs, if they haven't done so already. I was just saying the beef is really good here. You can't find beef like this anywhere in the world. If I was cooking for the Führer, I'd serve him this beef."

"The Führer is a vegetarian," the sergeant said. He reached across the table, grabbed a cigarette from the pack near the bowl, and brought it to his mouth. He was about to reach into his pocket when one of the skinny kitchen workers leaned over with his lighter. The sergeant turned towards the flame, lit his smoke, and nodded to him.

"Yeah, but he still allows meat to be served at his table for those guests who are not vegetarian so this is what I would serve them. Although it's a long way to the Führer's kitchen from here."

"A very long way," the sergeant said. "Listen, Chef Splichal, you and I both know I didn't come here to talk about what you would serve to the Führer."

The chef nodded and then waved his hand at the four prisoners on the other side of his table. Without a word, they all got up and left, going into the kitchen through the doors behind the chef. "So, tell me why you are here."

"There is a concern with pilfering in your kitchen."

The chef laughed, his whole body shaking. "You've got to be kidding. Pilfering? You are worried about pilfering? Do you realize that this is the Wehrmacht you are talking about? There is always pilfering in the kitchen. It's like gravity—it's always there and you can't make it go away no matter how hard you try."

"Well, there is pilfering and then there's what happening here at your kitchen. Every other mess in the camp pretty much has a pilfering rate around two to three percent. And that's normal—that's the gravity you're talking about. But your kitchen is a lot higher than that. According to supply, your rate is around…" the sergeant turned to Corporal Aachen. "…What was that number again, Aachen?"

"Sixteen-and-a-half percent." Aachen was stoic, standing at a tense at-ease position, looking ahead at the wall.

The sergeant turned back towards the chef and gave him a smile. "Sixteen-and-a-half percent."

"That can't be right," the chef sputtered. "I run a tight kitchen."

"Well, the corporal is never wrong about the numbers. He's very serious about things like that. He's very serious about many things. You've probably seen his matches, haven't you."

The chef looked at Aachen and nodded.

"Then you know how serious this young corporal can be. But that's only the half of it." The sergeant leaned in more closely. "Did you know that he was in Stalingrad for several months before he was shipped over to North Africa? He was a sniper there, one of the best. Took out ninety-three Ivans in three-and-a-half months. Almost one Ivan per day. Isn't that right, Corporal?"

"No, sir. That is incorrect. I did not shoot ninety-three Ivans in Stalingrad."

The chef raised his eyebrows at that, and Neumann slowly turned to face the corporal, giving him a questioning look. "Are you sure, Corporal?"

"I'm quite sure, Sergeant. I did not kill ninety-three Ivans in Stalingrad," he said, his voice monotone. He paused for a second and then blinked. "I killed eighty-seven Ivans."

"Ha," Neumann blurted out with a clap of his hands. "Told you he was serious with his numbers. He doesn't even want to take credit for an extra few Ivans. So the pilfering of sixteen-and-a-half percent is correct. And by my count and supply's, that's way too high."

The chef ignored the sergeant and turned his attention to the corporal. "Aachen, I know you have a birthday coming up, and as per our custom, we will be preparing a cake for you. Unfortunately, we only have two flavours available, chocolate or vanilla. Or maybe there is something else you would like. I'm quite sure I can get something for you to make your birthday more special."

"I don't think the corporal is interested in any cake you have to offer. He's got a big match coming soon. He can't be eating cake."

"Ah yes, the match. I can't wait for that," the chef said, smiling only with his mouth. "There is a lot riding on that match of his and not just Wehrmacht pride. I hope he's not denying himself too much, though. It would be a shame of he got injured some-how before the match. A terrible shame."

The chef stood up to leave. "And, Sergeant, I will take your comments about pilfering into consideration, however, if you excuse—"

The sergeant cut off the chef by placing a big hand on the fat man's shoulder. He squeezed hard, causing the chef to wince and then pushed the man back to a seated position.

"Sit down, Chef. This is very important and I need to have your immediate attention."

"In case you have forgotten because I don't wear a uniform," the chef said with mock indignation, "I am a captain and you are a sergeant. You cannot manhandle me in this way."

The sergeant laughed and reached out to pluck the cigarette from the chef's mouth. "You may officially outrank me, but I am the Head of Civil Security in this camp and Corporal Aachen is my assistant. I don't report to you. I report directly to the commander of this camp, and it is that commander who has sent me to discuss the pilfering problem with you." He narrowed his eyes and scooted closer to the chef. "Besides, you, me, Corporal Aachen, and everyone else in the camp knows that I'm no ordinary sergeant, am I right?"

Splichal's face started to turn white.

The sergeant leaned in, placed his hand around the back of the chef's neck, and slowly brought him close so they were only centimetres away from each other. The chef was starting to sweat.

"You do know what I'm talking about, Captain Splichal?" He said the last two words very slowly, enunciating them clearly.

The chef nodded quickly.

"Tell me what I'm talking about."

A look of panic came over the chef's face and he started to breathe heavily. He looked about, looked at Aachen, but the sergeant squeezed his neck and shook him. "No one's going to help you, Captain Splichal. No one. Because they all know who I am. You do too, so that gives me the right to manhandle you any way I fucking well please."

The chef stammered but could not form words. His started gasping, he eyes growing wider by the second.

Sergeant Neumann gave him a soft slap on his cheek. "Besides, you don't want to end up like Mueller."

Corporal Aachen gasped out loud and broke out of his stance to give the sergeant a look of incredulity. But Captain Splichal didn't notice the sound, nor the movement. His face turned even whiter, his eyes wide, questioning. Neumann smiled brightly and released the chef from his grip. The fat man fell back, almost tumbling off the bench. He grabbed his chest, panting heavily, as sweat dripped from his forehead.

"Mueller? What happened to Mueller?" the chef asked once he caught his breath. "Which Mueller?"

"Captain Mueller. Tank Commander back in Africa. Became a teacher when he got here. Taught a lot of boys about mathematics and sciences—even Aachen here took a class. Isn't that so, Aachen?"

Corporal Aachen was so surprised that he couldn't respond. But no one was paying attention to him. Chef Splichal was staring intently up at Sergeant Neumann who now had an unconcerned look on his face.

"What happened to Mueller?" the chef whispered loudly, almost a hiss.

"Mueller is dead," Neumann said. "The corporal and I just came from viewing his body. Hanging. Not a pretty sight."

"He killed…" The chef started to say but then his voice got caught in his throat.

The sergeant shook his head.

"But who would kill Mueller? He was harmless."

"Word is he was a Communist," the sergeant whispered into the chef's ear. "And if there's one thing command doesn't like, it's a Communist. And pilferers. In fact, they hate pilferers more than they hate Communists. Only Jews are hated more than pilferers, but it's pretty damn close."

The sergeant then stood up and leaned all of his six-and-a-half feet over the chef. "There is pilfering going on in your kitchen. A lot of pilfering. And it has to stop. Today. I don't care how you do it; it just has to stop. Because if it doesn't…" The sergeant trailed off and smiled calmly. "Many take a dim view of those who steal from their own soldiers. Do I make myself clear, Captain Splichal?"

The chef nodded quickly, his face full of fear.

The sergeant turned towards Aachen and gave him a quick slap on the chest. "Okay, let's go, Corporal. We're done here."

It took Aachen a couple of seconds to break out of his shock before he shook his head and followed the sergeant through the kitchen door.

6.

They walked through the kitchen which was full of steam and bustling soldiers cleaning up the debris from the last meal and preparing the ingredients for the next one. They ignored the bustle and the odds shouts of encouragement towards Corporal Aachen and his upcoming match and walked out the back double doors that also acted as a receiving area. There were more soldiers milling about this area, smoking and talking; there was rarely a place in camp for someone to be alone.

The sergeant stopped and whispered in Aachen's ear. "I know by your silence you've got something to say, Corporal." Neumann began to quickly walk as he continued. "But I prefer if the next part of our conversation is unheard so let's move to a more open area, shall we?"

Neumann headed north, through the lanes between the barracks, through more gardens, more prisoners working in gardens, past more murals and more soldiers just hanging about, enjoying the heat of the summer. Aachen followed a half step behind.

It took several minutes before the two of them made it to an open area halfway between the classrooms, long, one-story structures just north of the barracks, and the two halls, the largest structures in the camp. Able to hold almost 5,000 prisoners at one time, the Halls were also the largest of their kind in western Canada.

But the soldiers were far enough away and the wind loud enough that Neumann and Aachen were free to talk without anyone eavesdropping.

The sergeant turned to face the corporal and held his hand up to stop the younger soldier from speaking.

"I know what you are going to say, Aachen. I know I told you not to mention Mueller to anyone and then I go and use it in our discussions with the chef."

"I was completely shocked that you brought his name up, Sergeant," Aachen said. "You had already made your point about pilfering and easily put down his pathetic attempts to threaten and bribe us at the same time. Can you believe he thought that knowing my birthday would scare me?"

"Small-time criminals like Splichal like to think they are big-time criminals when they have no idea what big-time criminality actually is. However, regarding your first concern, I knew I had Splichal where I wanted him. I knew he would never pilfer again, but I wanted him to realize that there are consequences for his actions. I wanted him to know that we in the camp are more dangerous than the people he may sell his goods to. And I realized that there was another opportunity that I couldn't pass up."

"I don't understand," the corporal said, shaking his head. "What opportunity?"

"Remember back at the classroom when you asked me what we should do about Mueller's body?"

"You said that if we informed the Canadians, then we would automatically be suspects. They would take us in for questioning. And because of that, the rest of the camp could then assume that we were informers for the Canadians. I understand that, even though it's hard to think of Mueller still hanging there."

"But when I talked to Splichal and he mentioned he could get us anything, I realized that he has contacts with people on the outside. And to stop his pilfering, he would have to contact those people. So I decided to mention Mueller not just to frighten him but—"

Aachen cut in "—so he can tell someone about Mueller and the Canadians can learn about this from an anonymous tip instead of from us." The sergeant nodded slowly.

"But what if Splichal decides to tell somebody else about Mueller before he tells the Canadians?" Aachen asked.

"That information is too valuable for him to waste on another German. He'll need some currency in exchange for saying he has to cut back on the supplies he was shipping them."

Aachen went quiet for a moment. He looked about the camp, gazing into the distance of the dry Canadian prairie. A few puffs of cloud drifted over, causing shadows to race across the land.

"I'm sorry I doubted your actions, Sergeant," he said finally. "Once again, just like in North Africa, you were thinking several moves ahead of me."

"I was only thinking on my feet, just like I did in North Africa," Neumann said, touching the corporal lightly on the shoulder. "But you did what a good second-in-command should do, just like you did in North Africa: you questioned me to make sure I hadn't gone off the deep end."

"You've never gone off the deep end, Sergeant. It's one reason I'm still alive."

"You've forgotten the incident with the Tommies and their tanks. That was the craziest thing I've done any time in the two wars I fought. We were lucky to get out of that one."

"Not luck, experience. Only someone with your years in combat would have come up with that."

"Only someone with a few marbles knocked loose because of too much combat experience would have thought of that," the sergeant said tapping his head with a finger. "Don't forget, Aachen, you and I were very lucky to survive our battles in Africa. And you were lucky that you got wounded when you did in Stalingrad."

"Being wounded that way doesn't feel lucky. I almost lost the leg."

"But you didn't. Whatever shrapnel hit you missed vital arteries in your leg or the medic who treated you was better than average or the doctor happened to be sober at the time. Or maybe all of those things together. And, if you'd have gotten the same injury a couple of weeks later, they wouldn't have sent you home. They would have kept you there and the Ivans would have shot you in your hospital bed when they crossed the Volga and swarmed the 20th Infantry. Face it, Corporal Aachen, you and I are lucky to have survived so long."

The young corporal didn't say anything. He just reached into his pocket, pulled out a cigarette, and tried to light it. Due to the strong wind, his lighter kept blowing out, even when he tried to cover the flame with his hand.

Neumann reached out, grabbed the cigarette from Aachen's mouth, and put it in his own. A second later, he grabbed the lighter while Aachen looked on, wide-eyed with surprise. Turning his back from the wind and cupping his hand over the cigarette and the flame, Neumann lit the cigarette. He took a deep puff as he turned around, holding the lighter out for Aachen. The corporal didn't take the lighter, only stared at the sergeant.

"You said you weren't going to smoke until after your match," Neumann said after a moment.

Aachen sighed, shook his head, and snatched the lighter from the sergeant's hand.

"Okay, now that we've got that settled away, I need to ask you a question and I want you to answer with as much honesty as you can. Do you understand, Corporal Aachen?"

Aachen nodded. "Of course, Sergeant. As always." He tucked the lighter back into his pocket.

"I'm very serious here. I want your complete honesty. Don't hold back, don't worry about questioning my authority—I need you to be frank. Do I make myself clear?"

"Yes, Sergeant. Very clear."

"Even if something you say may look bad on another soldier, I want you to speak with complete candour, no matter how much loyalty you feel towards that soldier."

"Now you have me worried, Sergeant," Aachen said with a little smile.

"I'm not trying to be funny, Klaus. This is no laughing matter. This could be life and death, just like in North Africa."

Aachen nodded quickly. "Yes, of course, Sergeant, I apologize. I will speak with complete honesty."

"Good." Neumann looked about to see if there was anybody within earshot. There was a group of prisoners about twenty-five metres away watching another group play football, but that was about it. Satisfied all was safe, he turned back to the corporal, taking a puff from his smoke before he spoke.

"I am quite aware you took a number of classes taught by Captain Mueller."

"Yes. Mathematics and physics. I also took some sciences from Major Gunther as well."

"Yes but Gunther doesn't play in here because he's a grumpy old bastard like me. He's also still alive. Captain Mueller is a different story. As you heard from General Horcoff, the talk around camp is that Captain Mueller was a Bolshevik—"

"—He was not," Aachen said, cutting him off. "He was only trying to help younger soldiers like myself improve ourselves. Without Captain Mueller, I never would have passed the Abitur so that when I get home I can go—"

Neumann stopped Aachen's comments with a wave. "Yes,

yes, he was a good man, I understand all that. But talk is talk and if people like General Horcoff consider him to have Bolshevik leanings then that says something."

"That's quite unfair, isn't it?"

"This is war, Corporal; many things are unfair. But fairness or not, I myself have heard talk about Mueller's teachings, heard that along with his classes, he mentioned other things. Such as the state of Germany's war effort. Which is the main question I have to ask you: have you yourself heard Captain Mueller say such things in his classes?"

Aachen paused, looking uncomfortable. "I don't think he meant to criticize anyone, he just talked about possibilities."

"Possibilities of what?"

"Possibilities of…" Aachen trailed off, watching the group of prisoners play football in the distance. They were decent players, their passes crisp and with purpose. The defence was also very solid, every player marked, breaking up forward movement only to go back on the offence. After a moment, Aachen looked back at the sergeant. "His words were harmless. He only said what many of us were thinking."

"Harmless or not, what did he actually say? Remember I asked you to be completely honest with me and you promised you would be. This is very important, Klaus, not just in possibly determining what happened to Mueller, but in your future as well."

"I don't understand, Sergeant. Why would something Captain Mueller said in class have any bearing on my future? They were his words, not mine."

"True, but if Mueller said anything that could be perceived as traitorous, and you didn't report it, then you and anyone else in that class who also didn't report it could be seen as in collusion with his feelings."

"If I reported everything people said to me that could even be considered slightly traitorous, then we'd all be in big trouble."

"Typical grumbling is fine. The military expects its soldiers to grumble, but speaking out loud in a classroom in which you are teaching younger soldiers is something different. Especially now, after the invasion. Some people are very sensitive about certain things when there is a setback in war. Do you understand?"

"Yes, Sergeant. I do."

"So tell me, what did Captain Mueller say. Doesn't matter if you remember word for word, I just need the gist of his conversation."

Aachen again looked over to the game. He sighed and even though there was no one within earshot, he lowered his voice.

"Not long after the invasion, when we were feeling depressed that the Allies established a beachhead, Captain Mueller told us not to worry. He told us that this meant we would be going home in a year. That the Allies would progress through France and take back the rest of Europe, forcing the Führer to sue them for peace. Or they would continue across the Rhine and, in time, defeat us. Either way, that would mean the war would be over and we could go home."

"And did he repeat those statements again in later classes?"

Aachen rubbed his sweaty hands together and nodded. "A number of times. He also hoped that Germany would sue for peace before the Allies got too close but he said the Führer was too stubborn and could draw us into a deeper hell than the one we're in now."

"That's not good," Neumann said after a pause. "Not only did he voice the possibility that we would lose the war on a number of occasions, but he criticized the Führer. And he did so while acting as a mentor to a group of younger soldiers like yourself."

"I don't think he meant for us to deny our loyalty to Germany and the Führer, he was just expressing an opinion, trying to offer a positive viewpoint on the invasion. I'm pretty sure that most of us, even those in the battlefield, would prefer for this war to end and to go home to our loved ones."

"All soldiers wish war to end, but we don't speak out loud hoping for our side to lose. There's a difference."

After a moment Aachen nodded. "I didn't take his talk as treasonous."

"But others would. And you know the kind I'm talking about. And based on your view of his words, you did not report this to anyone."

"No, Sergeant. Only to you, right now."

"Good. Now I want you to remember that because it is possible that someone in your classroom did report Captain Mueller and that someone in this camp, someone with power and a connection to the command structure, determined that he was a traitor and doled out punishment. And if that happened, they may have also mentioned the names of the other soldiers in that class. And while the punishment for not reporting may be less, one can never know.

"So what I want from you—and this is a direct order from me, not a request—is to say, if anybody asks why you didn't report it, that you did report it, right after you heard it. And I want you to say that you reported it to me."

"But I didn't, Sergeant. I only just told you now."

"But they don't know that. And they never will because I've given you a direct order to say that you did report it. Furthermore, I want you to say that you individually told all your other classmates not to worry about reporting it because you would do so for them. That way, we're protecting not just you but your other classmates."

"What about the one who did report? He'll know I'm lying."

"Not if you say you knew he was going to report it so that's why you didn't talk to him. In this way, everyone's covered."

"Everyone except you, Sergeant. They are going to ask why you didn't report it."

"I'll just say I took the matter into consideration, but considering all the work I've had to do in the past couple weeks, I didn't have time to file an official report."

"You could be in trouble too. They could use the same traitor argument on you that you said they could use on me."

"True, but you aren't the great Sergeant August Neumann, a hero of the First World War."

Aachen laughed. "No, I'm not. Thank you, Sergeant, that's very decent of you. Not just because of me, but for all the other men in the class."

"Bah, you're only boys, despite the fact that you've been in battle for the past few years. You all survived this far—I would hate for something stupid like this to cause difficulties for you."

Neumann spat on the ground and threw his cigarette away. He hitched up his pants and rubbed the dust from his face.

"And now that we have that out of the way, I need you to do something else for me," Neumann said.

"Anything for you, Sergeant," Aachen said seriously.

"I need you to do your KP duty now."

"Why now? I always do it following the evening meal."

"Yeah, but, as you noted, Chef Splichal now knows that the Captain Mueller is dead so if you do your KP now—"

"—I can keep an eye on him so when he tells his informant, we will know when to expect a response from the Canadians," Aachen said, his eyes bright.

The sergeant gave the corporal an exasperated look. "You know Aachen, once in awhile it would be nice if you let me finish my orders before you jump and tell me what I'm thinking."

"Sorry, Sergeant," Aachen said, sheepishly dropping his head. "Please forgive my intrusion and tell me what you wish me to do."

"There's no point in my doing that now because you've already figured that out. So go. Go keep an eye on Splichal and try to notice when he passes on the information about Mueller." Neumann lit another cigarette.

"It will probably be a Canadian, won't it?"

"Of course it's a Canadian. Who else would it be?" the sergeant said, waving his hand in annoyance. "It's probably a civilian making the deliveries, taking his cut even before it's delivered.

No way would one of the Veterans Guards be involved in something like this. Those old bastards are too tough and honourable to be mixed up in this."

"Okay, I'll keep an eye out for the chef talking to a civilian."

"And don't let him see you hanging about. If he does, then he won't say anything and Mueller will be hanging there for days."

"I'll do my KP at one of the neighbouring messes," Aachen said with a snap of his fingers. "Probably Mess 2 because they deliver there before Splichal's mess. And when the deliveries come, I'll help out. And pretend to take a break and have a smoke at the back so I can watch for the chef."

"Good plan. But what if people ask why you are doing your KP now instead of at your regular time?"

"I'll just tell them I have to do some training tonight to get ready for the match," Aachen said with a shrug. "Everyone will believe that."

"Good plan. Okay, Aachen, off with you. Do your job and don't get seen. Be quiet like—"

"—like the time with the Tommies and their tanks." When he realized what he had done, once again, he stepped back and flushed. "Sorry, Sergeant."

The sergeant waved him away. "Just go, just go."

Aachen nodded, turned, and started to walk away. After a few steps, he turned back. "But what should I do once I see Splichal make contact with his informant?"

"Come tell me," the sergeant shouted back.

"Where will I find you?"

"I'll be at the Rhine Hall."

"What will you be doing there?" Aachen asked, eyes narrowing.

"Don't worry about it," the sergeant said waving his hand. "You have your orders."

"But Sergeant—"

"—You have your orders, Corporal Aachen. Go carry them out."

Aachen paused, but then stiffened and nodded. Without a word, he turned and walked away.

Sergeant Neumann watched him for a moment. Then he finished his cigarette, dropped it onto the ground, and pressed it into the dust with his boot. He turned and slowly headed north.

7.

Fifteen minutes later, Aachen was out behind Mess 2 sitting on a stool near a large stainless pot, peeling potatoes. The pot was massive, almost a metre high and a metre round, and when it was full of potatoes and water, it required two prisoners to carry it and lift it onto the stove. There were three other soldiers sitting on stools around the pot with Aachen, each one with three buckets of potatoes that they needed to peel.

Two of the soldiers Aachen knew from North Africa; both were corporals, serving in different squads than him, but in the same battalion, and both were from the same area, some village around the Ruhr Valley.

The one directly on Aachen's right was named Karl Wissman. The son of a coal miner, he was short and stocky, similar in stature to Aachen, but just a bit shorter and with less muscle. He was missing a few teeth and his nose bent to the side as if it had been broken when he was younger. Even though he only had a year or two on Aachen, he looked a decade older.

The other, Christian Tenfelde, had been an industrial worker, making appliances before joining to fight. He wore wire-rimmed glasses, but always seemed to be squinting when he looked at something. He had been skinny in Africa but now, like many of the prisoners, he had gained weight, developing a paunch that didn't sit well on his frame.

Wissman and Tenfelde talked constantly as they peeled potatoes, remembering skirmishes they had been in, women they had slept with, superiors they had hated, and good times they had enjoyed after battles—the typical stories that soldiers have talked about since the beginning of time. It was all small talk, though. Nothing about the war, or whether the invasion of France meant Germany was failing and would, in time, lose the war.

Aachen didn't join in much, only contributing when something came up that involved him, but he laughed at all the jokes the two Ruhr boys told.

The other soldier with them, a former butcher called Olster, had also been in North Africa but in a different division. He was older than the others and had been in Poland, France, Belgium, and many other battles—almost everywhere Germans had fought since the mid-1930s, except for the Eastern Front. He was a humourless sort, with thick arms, meaty hands, and a scowl that never left his face.

He glowered constantly at Aachen, and when Tenfelde laughed about a skirmish near Tunis which resulted in someone calling an air strike on a goat, Olster gave an indecipherable growl of contempt.

"What's wrong with you, Olster?" Wissman asked. Nobody called Olster by his first name because most people didn't know his first name. "You have a liking for goats?"

"Ha, everybody in the Fourth Division has a liking for goats," Tenfelde said, punching his friend on the shoulder. Wissman laughed.

Aachen smiled, but didn't laugh. He was trying to watch the ex-butcher closely, but discreetly.

"Bah, you morons talk too much," Olster said, waving an arm in their direction. "Always chatting like old women. Chat, chat, chat."

"I think he likes old women too, along with the goats," Wissman said. And the two Ruhr mates laughed aloud again.

"Shaddup," Olster said, but the two ignored him. "You think you are so funny, but you aren't. Nothing is funny about this stupid place and this stupid KP. Especially today with him here with us as if everything is fine." Olster nodded his head in Aachen's direction. The corporal noticed the contempt in Olster's voice but he ignored it.

"You just don't like Klaus because he beat you last week," Tenfelde said.

"He didn't beat me. I fell."

"Ha. You fell a lot of times, then," said Wissman, laughing. "Because when it was all over, Klaus had ten points and you had two."

"Little fucker got lucky. And he's a slippery bugger, moving all over the place. No respect for the traditions."

"Tradition didn't help you in the match did it, Olster?" Wissman said.

"He's gonna need all those traditions when he faces that U-boat monster, Neuer. He's bigger than me but he's not slow like me, Aachen. You try to run around him and he'll have you on your back."

Aachen peeled a potato and dropped it into the pot, a loud clang sounding as it hit the side. "I'll take your advice, Olster. You've faced Neuer before and I haven't, so any words of wisdom will be appreciated."

"Fuck you, Aachen. I know I'm supposed to be on your side because we're both in the Wehrmacht but I really hope the submariner breaks your back."

"Hey, come on," Wissman said. "You can't support the submariners in this, Olster, even though Klaus beat you. We infantry types have to stick together on the battlefield."

"We're not on the battlefield, you pissed up idiot. We're in a fucking prisoner-of-war camp peeling fucking potatoes. And when we get back home, it's not gonna be all roses and champagne. It's gonna be fucking hard because there won't be any fucking Americans, Tommies, or fucking French to shoot. And there'll be no fucking work for me cause there'll be no fucking meat left. And you know for sure there won't be any fucking potatoes."

"Jesus Christ, Olster, if you miss fucking killing things, you could always join the French Foreign Legion after the war and go kill the Indochinese," Wissman said. "Loads of Germans became legionnaires after the other war. Or joined when we weren't allowed a real army. An older cousin of mine did that. He wanted to be a soldier so much, he joined the Legion."

"Fuck legionnaires," Olster said. "Bunch of criminals and traitors if you ask me."

"I've talked to a couple legionnaires in the camp; they seem like decent fellows," Tenfelde said. "They mostly keep to themselves in that hut of theirs but they're decent enough."

"You step in that legionnaire hut of decent fellows, Tenfelde, and they'll slit your throat just for walking in that door."

"I don't think it would be that bad—" Tenfelde started but Olster cut him off.

"—Don't fucking tell me about legionnaires. When I was in Turkey, I had to fight fucking legionnaires. Even German legionnaires on the other side, shooting at us. Germans shooting at Germans. And what made it worse, we also had a group of German legionnaires on our side fighting against the German legionnaires on the other side. Every one of those fuckers should be lined up and shot."

Tenfelde and Wissman looked at each other and smiled. "Holy Jesus, this is the most I've heard this fucker ever say," said Tenfelde. "And we've been peeling potatoes for six months together."

"Yeah, come on, Olster, keep it coming," Wissman added. "Let it all out."

"Fuck off," Olster said, but he didn't stop talking. He pointed his vegetable peeler at Aachen. "Tell me something, if you can, you two. What the fuck is he doing with us, peeling potatoes? We've been doing this pissy job for so long, and it's always been us three. Why is he here doing this now? What's his game about?"

Wissman and Tenfelde looked at each other for a second and then at Aachen. "Holy fuck, Olster has a point. What the fuck are you doing here, Aachen?" asked Wissman.

"Yeah, normally you and Neumann are walking around, looking for troublemakers, that sort of shit," said Tenfelde. "You normally do your KP after the evening meal, don't ya?"

Aachen shrugged as if there was nothing wrong. "Olster said so himself. I have to face Neuer in a few days. And like he said, the submariner will be tough. I have to train at night more, so I decided to do my KP now."

Tenfelde shrugged, but Olster and Wissman shook their heads. "Fuck that. There's something else going on," Olster said. "You're here for a reason. And it better not be to watch out for us, because I've done nothing wrong. Kept myself clean, did my work, and didn't cause trouble. These two as well, although they won't stop talking."

Aachen didn't say anything for a bit. But with the three men staring at him with concern and distrust, he put down his peeler and leaned towards the pot. The other three leaned in with him. "Okay, I'll let you in on why I'm here. And you've got to promise that you won't tell anyone, okay? If Neumann finds out, he'll have my ass."

"Promise," said Wissman, holding his hand to his heart. Tenfelde shrugged and Olster grunted.

"Okay, you know Chef Splichal? Runs the kitchen next door?" Aachen said.

The two Ruhr men nodded, but Olster spat. "Fucking criminal. I know he's fucking pilfering from his kitchen, selling it in the camp for favours, booze and what not. Hangs out with Staff Sergeant Heidfield and a bunch of small-time ex-gangsters from Frankfurt, acting like tough guys because they can make booze and sell you extra supplies on the side. He asked me if I could get him some meat from our kitchen here. I told him to fuck off."

Aachen waved that away. "Ahh, we already know that. And take it from me, the sergeant dealt with that so there's no way Splichal will be continuing that business any longer."

"His partners won't like it," said Olster.

"Fuck his partners," Aachen said. "This is our camp, not theirs. No way me and the sergeant are going to let a bunch of small-timers steal from good soldiers like you."

"So then what? What else is up with Splichal?" Wissman asked.

"The sergeant thinks he's an informer for the Canadians."

Wissman and Tenfelde gasped, while Olster threw a potato to the ground in disgust.

"Fuck him. Fucker. I know what I said about the fucking legionnaires, but at least they have some sort of military honour. Nothing's worse than a fucking traitor. Drawn and quartered, like they used to do in the old days. Take out his fucking intestines and show it to him while he's still alive and then slowly hang him so he can feel the fucking pain for hours," Olster said, his face beet red.

"Well, we're not entirely sure about that so please keep your butcher fantasies to yourself, Olster. And if he is an informant, you better keep your hands off him and let us officials take care of it," said Aachen, sounding much like Sergeant Neumann.

"You better do a good job—no mamby-pamby isolation for him," Olster said with a sneer.

"You don't have to worry about that. I agree that there's nothing worse than an informant and so does the sergeant. You can be sure things will be handled in the proper manner," said Aachen.

"So you're watching him from here to see if he does something wrong?" Wissman asked, turning around to look at the back door of Mess 3.

"But you can't see him from here," said Tenfelde. "He's always inside his kitchen. How can you tell if he's an informant from here?"

Olster slapped Tenfelde on the back of his shoulder. "You idiot. There's no one in the kitchen for Splichal to inform to now. Everyone's a German. He's got to wait for a Canadian to come."

Wissman snapped his fingers. "The delivery! You're waiting for the Canadians and their daily delivery of food to the messes and then you'll see if Splichal makes contact with one of them."

"Jesus, it's like a spy novel, isn't it?" Tenfelde said. "We're standing here watching to see if the double agent makes contact with the person on the other side."

"What if he doesn't do it today?" Wissman asked. "Are you going to peel potatoes with us every day from now on? Because if you do, people are going to notice."

"Don't worry," Aachen said. "It will be today, you can be sure about that."

As soon as Aachen spoke, a klaxon sounded to the south. All the prisoners in the area looked up from their work, but when there was only one sound, they went back to whatever they were doing.

"The delivery, it's coming," said Tenfelde, a bit of excitement in his voice. "What do we do?"

"Shut up," Olster said, throwing a potato at Tenfelde. It bounced off his shoulder. He grimaced and rubbed the spot where the potato hit him. "Aachen is on a reconnaissance mission. He is, in a sense, sneaking into enemy territory to find information on a traitor. It is our job to cover him while he does so. But if we make too much noise or do anything that attracts the attention of the enemy, his mission is dead. Got that?"

Wissman and Tenfelde looked at each other and then back at Olster. They gave him a nod. Aachen also gave the ex-butcher a nod as thanks. And then the group went back to peeling potatoes, as if nothing had changed.

A few minutes later, the truck carrying the goods to be delivered made its way to the back of the messes. It was a large two-and-a-half ton truck, the kind used to ferry soldiers, but this one had the tarpaulin and the benches removed to allow the goods to be loaded. The entire back was filled with boxes and bags of varying types of food. The driver of the truck, a civilian, had the windows closed and did not look or make any connection with any of the prisoners.

Almost all the prisoners in the area watched the truck as it crawled to the first mess—this kind of movement was a form of entertainment. Yet no one approached it. An entire squad of

Canadian soldiers, twelve of them, walked beside the truck, the way guards walk beside a vehicle carrying VIPs during parades.

These guards were all old, the youngest probably just over forty, but they were large men, hard men. They walked with ease and confidence through the camp of 12,000 Germans, even though they carried no guns. Instead, each of them carried some kind of truncheon. Some of the truncheons were simple bats, either cricket or American baseball bats, but customized in some way with nails or barbed wire to create maximum damage. Some were police-type clubs that the Canadians tapped against the palms of their hands or twirled about using the strap wrapped around their wrists. The remaining few were army-issued batons from the Great War, heavy cudgels made of wood and iron, their heads either filled with lead or spotted with extruded knobs of steel. And as they walked along the truck, they did not watch the vehicle; they kept their gaze on the prisoners who were nearby.

Some of the prisoners shouted at the guards, insulting them, making lewd comments about their mothers, their wives, their daughters. Many of these insults were in English, but when they weren't, gestures with hands and hips translated them clearly. Still, the Canadians ignored them completely.

The four prisoners peeling potatoes watched the truck and the squad of Canadian guards. It stopped at the first mess and a group of kitchen helpers slowly came out, hands in the air, showing they were harmless. The Canadian squad commander, a hefty grey-haired man with a handlebar moustache, pointed his cudgel at the kitchen helpers indicating that they should stop. The cudgel was almost four feet long with a head about six inches in diameter wrapped by a two-inch-wide ring of worn metal. The weapon probably weighed almost ten kilograms, but the Veterans Guard brandished it like it was a small riding crop.

He didn't say a single word, in English or German, but he didn't have to. After several seconds of looking over the kitchen helpers, the commander slowly lowered his truncheon and nodded to the helpers. They immediately jumped into action and started unloading. The commander and some other Canadians held batons at the ready, pointing them in the direction of the helpers. The other ten scanned their areas, dutiful sentries on the watch.

"I don't know why we never rush them," Tenfelde said. "They are only twelve while we are thousands."

"Go ahead, you start," said Wissman. "They'll knock you down in an instant."

"And that's not some simple swagger stick that old soldier is carrying," Olster added. "That's a German trench club from the last war. He probably took it from some poor sap after gutting him with his bayonet. So if you want to join that poor sap in hell, you go ahead and take on that old fucker. He'll knock your fucking head off and then go home and have tea in your skull."

"Sure, they could cut some of us down, but we outnumber them more than a thousand to one. If we have a coordinated action, maybe with a few of the kitchen helpers, we could take these Canadians with only a bit of German blood lost."

"And what would happen then if we take them?" Olster demanded. "These aren't Italians, you know. These are the fucking Canadians. My brother faced a battalion of these fuckers in Dieppe."

"Ha, we beat them in Dieppe," Tenfelde said. "Stupid idiots."

"Yeah, we beat them, but my brother said those Canadians were the toughest motherfuckers he ever faced, even when losing. A perfect mix of the big Americans with the fucking stubborn toughness of the Tommies. And like the Ivans, they're cold fuckers. Probably starve us out if we tried anything like rushing the delivery truck and the squad, let us live in our own filth for a few weeks and then come in, take back the camp when we're weak from no food, and hang a hundred of us just because."

"And you've forgotten the towers, you idiot," Wissman said to Tenfelde. "No doubt there are two snipers or more in each one, aiming at us right now as the truck moves through, ready to blow our heads off as soon as we make any kind of move."

"Yeah, maybe one of them has your head in his sights right now, eh Tenfelde?" Olster said with a cruel laugh. "You blink or make any false move with your potato peeler and boom, your mama gets a telegram from the Führer."

Tenfelde looked around as if he was being watched, making the other two laugh. Aachen only smirked, watching as the delivery to Mess 1 was completed and the truck crawled to the next stop. A group of kitchen helpers came out, did the deal with the squad commander, and then started unloading.

Instead of watching the helpers, the squad commander stared at the potato peelers, his face impassive. The ex-butcher tried to stare back but the old Canadian guard didn't blink, and ever so slightly raised his truncheon. It wasn't much, but it was enough for Olster to get the message and look away. He turned and continued peeling. "Fucker," he muttered under his breath.

"Go ahead, Tenfelde," Wissman said, nudging his friend. "Make your move. That son of a bitch will cut you down in half a second, then go home and fuck his wife tonight as if nothing happened." He looked over at Olster. "After he has tea in your skull, of course."

Tenfelde ignored the ribbing and quietly peeled his potatoes. The squad commander only turned his gaze away from the group when the delivery for Mess 2 ended. Even so, as he walked away with the truck to the next stop, he turned back once, looking at Aachen. The corporal made brief eye contact then went back to peeling.

When the truck stopped at Mess 3, the group turned to watch, peeling potatoes slowly as a trio of kitchen helpers came out of the kitchen. They all leaned their heads up, looking for the chef, but Splichal didn't come. It was only the kitchen helpers, unloading the goods from the truck and carrying them into the kitchen, just like the other helpers did in the previous messes.

After several minutes, the delivery was done and the Canadian commander gave the signal for the truck to continue on its way.

"Guess you guys were wrong about Splichal, Aachen," Wissman said, back to peeling his potatoes. "Maybe we'll see you again tomorrow."

"You'd be welcome, too," added Tenfelde. "We can use a few new faces. I'm sick of staring at these two."

Aachen put his peeler down. He was ready to find the

sergeant to tell him the bad news. But suddenly there was a commotion from Mess 3. Splichal came running out, waving a piece of paper, and yelling at the truck.

In an instant, every one of the Canadian soldiers whirled towards the chef, lifting their batons up, ready to strike. A second later, half of them broke away, covering the area around them, looking for any other threats coming their way.

Splichal froze at this sight, his hands thrown in the air in appeasement. "Please, please," he shouted in English, waving the sheet of paper in his hand. "Don't hit me, don't hit me."

The Canadian commander broke from his stance a moment later, and with a jerk of his massive baton, bade Splichal to step forward. The chef did, taking each step slowly, shaking the paper in the air. The other Canadians kept their sticks ready for action.

"A mistake," he said in English, pointing at the paper. "There's been a mistake."

When Splichal got closer, the commander grabbed the paper from the chef's hand. He then brought up his club and pressed it into Splichal's chest, pushing the fat chef back. Splichal almost fell back on his ass, but he caught himself, waving his arms.

The Canadian squad commander looked at the paper, looked at Splichal, and looked at the sheet again, not once lowering his hefty club. Gathering his balance, Splichal tried to get closer, to point at the paper, but the old Canadian waved the club at him as if he was swinging at a pesky insect.

After a long minute, the commander dropped the club, gave Splichal back the paper, and then gestured the chef towards the driver. Splichal nodded, bowed his thanks, and slowly walked over to the driver.

Tenfelde whistled while Wissman nudged Aachen.

"Son of a bitch," Olster said. "He *is* a fucking informant. Fucker."

The chef tapped on the window and the driver rolled down the glass. Because of the distance, no one could hear what the two were saying, but they talked for a couple of minutes.

Olster was fuming, peeling potatoes with a vengeance. "Son of a bitch. He served with us North Africa and here he is, informing on us to the enemy. He's a fucking traitor and he's going to get what a traitor deserves." He threw a potato into the pot with disgust.

"Don't worry about that, Sergeant Olster. There is a process for how to deal with these things," said Aachen.

"Fuck the process. If you were so worried about process then why did you tell us he may be an informant, huh? I'm not the greatest wrestler out there, you showed me that last week, but I'm not an idiot. You told us about him for a reason—not because you wanted us to wait for the process, but because you wanted us to know and maybe do something about it. But don't you worry, Corporal Aachen, we'll make sure to keep him alive for your process although I don't think he'll be in good shape."

Aachen said nothing. He just stared at Olster for a second and then nodded. He turned his gaze to the chef who was now backing away from the driver, bowing to the commander, and moving to the back of the truck to get a package of something.

He picked it up and backed into the kitchen, bowing like

some kind of toady. After a moment the truck continued on to Mess 4.

Tenfelde whistled again while Wissman shook his head in disgust. Olster worked to finish his potatoes, the anger still flushing his face.

Aachen moved his bucket of potatoes next to Wissman's.

"Off already, Corporal? You're not done yet," Tenfelde said with a smile.

"Leave him be," Olster growled. "He's got to report his findings to his superior."

Aachen walked over to the ex-butcher and put his hand on the man's shoulder. "Do what you have to do, but leave some for us, okay?"

Olster nodded, then jerked his body to get away from Aachen's touch.

8.

While Corporal Aachen was peeling potatoes, Sergeant Neumann arrived at the Rhine Hall, one of the two recreation halls located in the camp. The buildings were identical in design and size, located about 100 metres north of the barracks area. They were just simple clapboard rectangles, sixty by fifteen metres, with a set of double doors and four high windows on each edge. There were also high windows, ten for every side wall and each about three metres long and one-and-a-half metres wide, situated two-and-a-half metres above the ground.

When Neumann walked up to the south door, he heard some shouting coming from the inside. He immediately realized it was coming from a group doing some close order drilling, so he decided to walk around the hall and enter through the north doors.

The path around the building was well-defined. Neumann

could see a large number of prisoners also walking along the well-trodden path just along the inside of the barbed wire fence. Since it was a good four-kilometre walk around the inside perimeter of the camp, many prisoners passed their days continually walking this route.

As Neumann arrived at the north end of the Rhine Hall, the sound of short order drilling faded and was replaced by music. Beethoven's *Symphony No. 3*. Neumann stood outside the door listening to the piece as it moved through the horn calls from the lively scherzo of the third movement.

He waited until the end of the movement and then entered the hall. As the door opened, the metal plating on the lower edge scraped against the wooden flooring, creating a loud screeching noise. The dissonant sound distracted some members of the orchestra and soon the whole piece fell apart.

Neumann was confronted with the scowling faces of the conductor and some other members of the full orchestra. "Sorry," he muttered.

The conductor, a former platoon commander with the unfortunate name of Liszt, looked back at his orchestra with anger. He gave his baton three hard taps on the podium."What is wrong with you fools? It was only a small noise, less than a cough at a concert hall, and you lose your place in the music!?" he shouted at them. "Pathetic! This kind of mistake is unworthy of musicians of your age and calibre. I've conducted small children as young as five, children whose parents have fed them sweets and chocolates before the performance, and they have had better concentration skills than you. If you can't keep going because of a simple noise, then you should leave and go walk the path with all the other good-for-nothing layabouts in this camp."

Liszt threw his baton into the orchestra, the wind instruments ducking as it flew past them, and waved his hands in the air. "Bah. Never mind, you useless children. Take a break," he shouted. The musicians smiled, nodded at each other. "Go smoke your cigarettes, but only for ten minutes and then we start again. And we better get this right with no lapses in concentration or I'll keep you playing until your lips and fingers start to bleed."

He roughly closed the arrangement on the podium and cradled his head in his hands for a few seconds. By this time, most of the musicians were standing up, stretching, pulling out their cigarettes, and heading to the door.

While Liszt was shouting at his charges, there was another man shouting in the recreational hall. But his words weren't angry, just the typical barking noises a parade leader makes during close order drill.

Neumann turned his back on the conductor and his orchestra, leaning against the edge of the stage to watch a group of about 250 prisoners clad in black naval uniforms march about the main area of the recreation hall. There was also a third group of prisoners in the hall, a group of about thirty gymnasts dressed in their white sporting outfits tumbling, flipping, and building human pyramids in the far southeast corner, but it was the precise movement of the prisoners in black that kept his attention. They moved seamlessly as one, reacting instantly to the commands made by their parade leader, a short, thin naval captain, also dressed in black and sporting a salt and pepper moustache with a goatee. He stood along the east wall of the building rocking side to side on his feet, as if he was on the deck of a ship, snapping out his commands cleanly and clearly, the way a parade marshal should.

Neumann watched the man for several minutes until the conductor gathered himself, stepped away from his podium, and jumped off the stage. He walked over and stood next to Neumann, watching the naval soldiers march about.

"Ahh, submariners," the conductor said with a tone of disdain in his voice. "Who does close order drill inside during the summer? Or, in fact, in the middle of a prisoner-of-war camp?"

"They're submariners. They spend most of their time stuck in a metal tube underneath the ocean. Not a lot of space to walk around down there," Neumann said. "So once they get up on solid ground with all this fresh air around, they have to move about."

"Then why can't they just walk like regular soldiers do? Why do they have to walk in formation all the time?"

"Different breed of soldier, these submariners. Tough, disciplined, have to know their place in the world since theirs is usually pretty small."

Liszt cleared his throat. "Ahh, they're just morons without an original thought in their head. No imagination, no spontaneity. Following orders is fine, but if you want to win the war, you have to allow people on the ground to think on their feet."

"They are never on the ground, that's the problem," Neumann said. "What about you, though? Yelling at your charges like that, controlling their playing. Is there any imagination and spontaneity in that?"

"Of course there is. My boys may have to follow the notes of the music and my conducting, but you of all people should know that there is more to it than that. Each musician has his own essence, his own temperament that he brings to his playing. A good conductor allows that originality in every musician to come through."

"I could hear that. The third was sounding very good." Neumann turned to face the conductor. "Sorry about the distraction though. They should fix these doors."

Liszt waved him away. "My boys shouldn't be bothered by a little noise like you. But I'll make them pay for their lack of concentration."

Neumann chuckled. "Hearing that makes me glad I didn't take you up on your offer to join your little musical group."

"Offer is always open, my friend. The violas are one of the weakest parts of the orchestra."

"Weak? You have Gottfried Pfeiffel in the first position. He used to play with the Philharmonic in Hamburg."

"Pfeiffel is a joy but he's got no backup. The second isn't too bad but the third and fourth are very weak amateurs. No skill, no timing. And obviously no original essence to bring forward. If I had you backing up Pfeiffel, we'd have one of the strongest string sections in the German empire. But you have your little police job and you must—how do the Amis say it in their movies—'walk your beat', and I have a weak viola section."

"Better than a foxhole in the desert."

"Sometimes yes, but when you hear those two play, sometimes not."

Neumann laughed. "The crosses we have to bear." He turned to watch the submariners drill.

"So what brings you here then, Sergeant Neumann?" asked Liszt. "You didn't just come here to rub my nose in the viola section, did you?"

"No, I actually didn't know you'd be here." He pointed at the rocking submariner commander. "I'm following a hunch."

"With him? Good luck. I might be an asshole on the podium but at least it's only on the podium. He's an asshole all the time. Strutting around with his medals like some kind of god."

"Well to his men, he is a bit of a god. Sinking 500,000 tonnes of enemy ships makes him almost as big as Baron von Richthofen in the naval world."

"Captain Hans Koenig would still be an asshole even if he was a barber or a policeman like you. Sinking those ships only helped enhance that part of his personality. In a way, he reminds me of you, though. Stubborn, set in his ways, sure of himself."

"You forgot asshole."

"You're only an asshole when times call for an asshole. You forget that I've seen you in action. You listen to your men when they've got something to say, take their opinions when you think they matter. And while I've seen you berate your men when they've done something stupid, you only do it because you worry about them losing their lives. I only do it when they fuck up the music. Koenig, he doesn't care about his men. He only cares about power."

"Well, let's see what happens when we meet." Neumann started to walk away, but Liszt grabbed his forearm, holding him back for a second.

"Approach from where he can see you coming. All that time in a steel tube playing cat and mouse makes submariners a jumpy, nervous lot."

"I'll be careful," Neumann said with a nod. And when the conductor let go of his arm, he resumed his walk. "Just watch me."

"Yes, I'll be watching," Liszt the conductor said. "And I'll be here if you need backup."

Neumann waved his right hand at the comment but didn't turn around. "I won't need backup."

Liszt chuckled. "But I'll be here anyway," he said to himself.

9.

Sergeant Neumann approached the submarine commander the way Liszt recommended, angling in from the side so that Koenig could see him approach from a good distance away. It was less of a precaution for Neumann and more of a pre-interrogation tactic: show the subject that someone is coming for them, but move towards them slowly so they won't be too startled.

Koenig saw Neumann approaching out of the corner of his eye. At once, he wrapped up the close order drill and brought the group of submariners to a full stop, standing strictly at attention in a complete square.

Koenig spun quickly, snapping his heels together.

"Sergeant Neumann," he barked, giving a quick nod.

Neumann returned the nod with a Wehrmacht salute. "Captain Koenig."

Koenig glanced at Neumann's salute, raised his eyebrows,

and then raised his right arm in the Nazi salute. "Heil Hitler," he barked.

"Heil Hitler," Neumann barked back, his right arm raised only slightly.

"A bit of a surprise to see you here, Sergeant Neumann," Koenig said, lowering his arm.

"Oh, wherever my work takes me is wherever I go."

"So your work takes you here. To me." Koenig's tone was formal and a bit dismissive, like an aristocrat talking down to one of his servants.

"Yes, to you I have come. Begging your pardon, Captain, but there has been an incident and I have come to you to see if you would answer a few of my questions."

"An incident. With one of my men, I hope not," he said, sending a glance to his group, all of whom were still frozen at attention.

"That has yet to be determined. However, if you please, Captain, my questions?"

"Yes, of course. If the Head of Civil Security has a few questions for me, it behooves me to answer them."

Neumann stepped away from the ranks of submariners in order to speak more privately. Koenig waited for a moment, and then followed him.

"Thank you, Captain, that is much appreciated," Neumann said in a much quieter voice. And though Koenig outranked him, Neumann's tone was insistent. The implication was clear: he was not officially under Koenig's command and wanted to ensure the captain understood that. But Neumann knew that one had to be subtle about such matters.

Neumann paused, looking Koenig in the eyes, and then moved back one step. "I am unfortunately the one to tell you the news that Captain Mueller is dead."

"Mueller?" said Koenig, taken aback only slightly. "The Communist? The one who teaches some of the more gullible and naive boys about the ways of Marx and Lenin?"

"Well, mostly I think it was mathematics and science."

"Yes, he did teach them that, but I've heard that was only a ruse and behind all that mathematics and science he was teaching them about the equality of men, which quite frankly is Communism propaganda."

"Be that as it may, he is dead."

"Hmm. Natural causes?"

"If it was natural causes, I would not be here talking to you. Based on my experience, Mueller was murdered."

Koenig blinked twice and then let out a quick exhalation. "That's very interesting."

Neumann paused and looked the captain. "Yes, it is very interesting," he said slowly. "But I find it even more so when that's your reaction. I thought the fact that a German soldier has been murdered would cause you to a react with shock, dismay, or maybe even outrage."

"Well, I've seen my share of death in this way, Sergeant Neumann—one more isn't going to shock me."

"Yes, maybe in battle, but we aren't in battle. We're almost as far away from the war as we can be. So the fact that one German soldier seems to have been murdered by another should be shocking."

"Are you sure it was another German who did this? Maybe the Canadians did it."

"I find that very hard to believe."

"Why?" Koenig said, stepping to the side and waving his hand. When he did, a submariner stepped out of formation and made his way towards the two. Neumann seemed unaware of the situation. "In my opinion, Mueller was a Bolshie and probably in league with the Canadians to convince some of our young soldiers that fighting for the Führer is a lost cause. But they had a falling out, or he refused to do their work anymore, so they killed him."

"That theory is hard to believe."

"So is your theory that a German soldier did it."

"Well if some German soldiers thought he was a Bolshevik and was teaching our boys propaganda, as you suggest," Neumann stepped again into Koenig's personal space, "then they would consider him a traitor and deal with him in the manner suitable for a traitor."

Koenig was unperturbed by Neumann's close proximity and in fact leaned closer, shifting his weight on his feet instead of stepping forward. "Are you intimating that me and my men were involved in Mueller's murder, Sergeant Neumann?" he asked.

"Intimate that you and your men are responsible for Mueller's murder? I would do nothing of the sort," Neumann said with a wry smile. "Since you and your men have a history of dealing with so-called traitors in your own way, I am asking you outright if you and your men had anything to do with Mueller's murder."

"Those men were traitors and as such deserved what they got."

"And who determined they were traitors? You?"

"Of course it was me, since I was the most senior officer in the camp at the time."

"Did you conduct a formal hearing on this? Did you hear evidence on what each condemned man's actual crime was or did you just go by the word of someone you liked? Or someone who said what you wanted to hear?"

"We're at war, Sergeant; there is no time to hold hearings. Command decisions have to be made and those in command have to make them. I determined that those men were traitors and that was that."

"There's a difference between making decisions under battle stress conditions and in a prisoner-of-war camp. You had plenty of time to hold justifiable hearings—you just decided not to."

"That's the problem with men like you and the men that run the camp now: too much reliance on military administration and protocol. It's blinded you and made your men soft. And you've forgotten that we're still at war and we still need to battle the enemy in and out of this camp."

"So am I your enemy, Captain Koenig?"

"Officially, since you are also a German soldier, you are not my enemy per say. But in war, the sea is always changing and a good commander must be prepared for these changes."

"Is that why you've asked one of your men to come up behind me?" Neumann glanced behind him at the submariner standing close by. "Am I about to be punished for some crime the same way you punished various men when you were in command— the way you punished Mueller perhaps?"

Koenig blinked twice in surprise at Neumann's awareness of what was happening behind his back, and took two steps back. But then he placed his hands behind back, leaning forward again on his toes. "You can think what you want, but in reality, Sergeant, you know nothing. You are completely oblivious to what is happening in this camp, completely unaware of the decadence and decay that's come over the men. Or maybe this is the status quo for you infantry types, living in squalor and filth. You don't find that kind of German or these conditions in a U-Boat. We believe in structure, respect for command, and honour."

"So did you respect the honour of the men you hanged without due process? When you hanged Mueller?"

"While some actions may not seem pleasant to others unused to such situations, they are necessary in order for us to succeed in war. That's what you people seem to forget by your lack of discipline. If the Führer saw you and the conditions you live in and by, he would be most displeased."

"You know, I really hate it when people assume to know what would displease the Führer. I would ask you to please stop using his name in vain."

"And what would the great Sergeant Neumann do to prevent me from continuing in such a way?"

"There are a wide variety of options available to me."

"Is that a threat, Sergeant? It sure sounded like one to me. And to me, making such threats to a higher ranking officer can be seen as an act of treason."

"So what is your judgment then, Captain Koenig? Am I to

be hanged like many others or will your henchman behind me think of a more unpleasant way?"

"Lieutenant Neuer could snap your neck, if I commanded him too. And then he would do the same to your assistant, Corporal Aachen, in their upcoming match."

"Personally, I think Corporal Aachen would have something to say about that," Neumann said, not breaking his gaze with the submarine captain. He did, however, raise his eyebrows. "Don't you, Corporal Aachen?" he said in a loud voice.

"It is good to see you, Sergeant Neumann," Aachen replied, walking towards the three men standing in the middle of the Rhine Hall. He was about fifteen metres away and moving quickly. "Although I was hoping for a more pleasant welcoming committee than what you are facing."

If Koenig was surprised to see Aachen, he did not show it. "As you have seen in his matches, Neuer is much faster than expected for a man of his size. He could snap your neck before your beloved Corporal Aachen arrives."

The sergeant raised his eyebrows again and then lifted up his left hand as a signal to stop Aachen. The corporal did stop, his hands clenched into fists by his side, ready to be used. "Is everything all right, Sergeant Neumann?"

"Everything is fine, Corporal Aachen. The captain and I were having a discussion on the speed of Lieutenant Neuer and the difference between the members of the Wehrmacht and members of the Navy."

"Ah yes, the age-old question," Aachen said.

"Please, Corporal Aachen, keep your comments to yourself

and let me finish this conversation so we can leave and get back to our regular rounds."

Neumann took a step towards the submarine captain. Koenig didn't move and the large lieutenant also took a step to follow Neumann. "Let's forget for a moment the threats made and the fact that if any move is made on me, there are a large number of Wehrmacht soldiers in these buildings, and many more on their way since one of the men in the orchestra already left to garner reinforcements, and that these soldiers, many of them veterans of battle, would take an unkind view of someone attacking me."

"I have 300 of the finest submariners in the Navy at my command. And I would easily pit them against any number of infantry soldiers you could throw at us," Koenig said through clenched teeth, using a tone of disdain when he said the word infantry. "And no matter what would happen to us, you, in the end, would be dead."

"I agree with you, Captain Koenig. You do have a fine group of men under your command. Strong, disciplined, and loyal. I commend them and their efforts in their fight for the Fatherland. They have had difficult tasks in facing the enemy, tasks I would not take on myself, so I honour them. I also honour and respect you. You are a great strategic officer, Captain Koenig. Your victories in battle and the total tonnage of ships you have sunk are to be celebrated by all loyal Germans."

As he spoke, Neumann reached into his pants pocket and pulled out an object which he concealed as best he could with his hand. Koenig didn't notice the movement because he was too close, but almost everyone else did. And when they saw what the sergeant was brandishing, they stiffened. Liszt sucked in a breath through his teeth. His first move was to back away, but then he stopped himself and started slowly walking to stand next to Aachen. The tumblers formed a line, ready to move.

"You think a few compliments can win me and Neuer over, Sergeant Neumann? In any battle between the infantry and men like mine, you would lose, which I assume you know," Koenig said, ignoring the movement around him. "And that is probably why you lost in North Africa, why you surrendered. It is Germans like you, soldiers of your ilk, who are the main reason that we are losing this war."

"Losing the war? Who said anything about losing the war? I should tell you that any German soldier, even one captured by the enemy, who promotes the idea that we are losing this war is committing a treasonous act, one that could be subject to a penalty of death. But I will let that comment slide due to the stress of the situation. And also because I just want to tell you one more thing."

"And what is that?" Koenig spat back.

"You will be dead if Neuer makes any move on me."

"Ha, I don't think so. Neuer is much faster than you think. He would snap your neck in—"

"—in a second, yes, yes, I heard you the first time. However, in that fraction of a second, I would shove my knife into your belly and gut you so that you would bleed out like a fucking pig." Neumann looked down at his right hand, revealing a homemade knife just inches from the submarine captain's belly.

When Koenig looked down and saw it, he stiffened, the

colour draining from his face. "Sergeant Neumann, that is totally unnecessary."

"Yes, it probably is. However, let me explain before I move away. I was honest in my comments about respecting and honouring you and your men. I know you submariners to be great soldiers, great strategists, who gave their all to fight for the Führer and the Fatherland. But fighting in a U-boat is different than fighting on land. For the most part, you submariners kill your enemy from a distance. You strike quickly and then dash away, and never see the faces of the men you have killed. We do that in the infantry sometimes as well. But for a lot of our battles, we see our enemies face-to-face. And we try to kill them any way we can because they are trying to do the same to us. There are times when we have to fight hand-to-hand, using whatever tools we have at our disposal. So a smart infantry man prepares himself for these kinds of situations, ensuring that he has many weapons at hand, because you never know what the battle brings up."

He held the knife up, waving it slowly in front of Koenig. The captain's eyes watched it warily. "I wasn't planning on using this knife. In fact, I was meaning to throw it away once I took it off that private from Berlin," Neumann continued. "But something made me keep it, something only another infantry man would understand. And like any good infantry man, I will use it if I have to, but I would not like to. Do you understand, Captain Koenig?"

Koenig nodded quickly and with that movement, the large lieutenant backed away.

"And in case you do not understand," Neumann said, putting

the knife back in his pocket and raising his voice to address the others in the hall, "in case no one else understands, Captain Koenig may be the highest ranking officer in this building, however, I do not report directly to him. I report directly to the commanders of this camp, who, in turn, report directly to the commanders in Germany and the Führer. So any threats or actions against me or my assistant Corporal Aachen, or anyone else I deputize to assist me, is an action against the command of this camp, the Leader, and the Fatherland itself. And thus, an act of treason."

Some of the submariners stiffened, but many sneered instead. Neumann walked up to Lieutenant Neuer, stood next to him, and spoke sharply. "Do you understand?"

The lieutenant snapped to attention and nodded.

Neumann shook his head and stood in front of Neuer. "I'm sorry, I did not hear that, Lieutenant Neuer. Do you understand?"

"Yes, Sergeant," Neuer barked.

"Again, Lieutenant. And louder please?"

"Yes, Sergeant!" Neuer shouted.

"And the rest of you. Do you understand?" Neumann shouted at them.

In a split second, all of the submariners snapped to attention, simultaneously clicking their heels and shouting, "Yes, Sergeant."

Neumann nodded and then tapped the lieutenant on the shoulder. "You are good soldier, Neuer. Loyal to your captain. I admire that."

Then he turned and walked over to Aachen, not looking back as Captain Koenig deflated and fell to the floor.

"Let's get the fuck out of here," Neumann said.

10.

Neumann and Aachen walked towards the south door of Rhine Hall passing the group of white-clad gymnasts. They were now standing in a group, like some kind of sporting street gang at the end of a match, hands clenched in fists, ready for a fight.

The eldest gymnast, a muscular ex-bombardier named Bruhl left the group and walked alongside the sergeant and corporal as they made their way towards the door. "Everything okay, Sergeant?"

"Everything's fine, Lieutenant Bruhl. The captain and I just had a few words."

"More than a few words. Seemed like the whole Submariner Corps was going to rain down on you. Even though I'm Luftwaffe, me and the boys would have been on your side. Fucking Koenig; when he was in charge of this camp, he ran it like his own personal fiefdom, using his fucking fanatical

U-boat crews and other diehards to push everyone around. He made us march like morons every day, in the rain and the cold, while he stayed warm and dry in his own cabin, being served by a bunch of cocksucking sycophants."

Neumann laughed and shook the bombardier's hand. "Glad you are still speaking your mind, Lieutenant. And though I knew your help wasn't needed, I'm glad to know I still had it."

"We Luftwaffe may be arrogant assholes, but the submariners are something else. They believe they are God's gift to the Fatherland."

"It's the claustrophobia," Neumann said. "Being stuck in a metal tube beneath the ocean is hard on the faculties."

"Ha. Try being stuck in a flying metal tube while being bombarded by flak with Spitfires and Hurricanes shooting holes in you. That is hard on the mental faculties, I tell you." The bombardier saluted casually, more like a greeting than a military address. "But never mind, glad you are okay, Sergeant. Take care of yourself. I have to go back and build a pyramid."

Bruhl turned and went back to his mat while Neumann and Aachen turned and went out the door. This time, there was a large number of prisoners gathered around the hall, milling about and anxiously glancing at the door, expecting something to happen. There was a collective sigh of relief when they saw the sergeant and the corporal step outside.

Neumann waved his hands in the air to get the prisoners' attention. "Everything is fine, gentlemen. Nothing to worry about and nothing to see, so please move on and go back to your regular duties."

"We don't have any regular duties," someone shouted from the crowd, eliciting a laugh.

"Then just disperse and find something else to do. There is no excitement here today."

The crowd muttered in disappointment and slowly began to disperse. Neumann and Aachen waited by the door as they did.

"That seemed to go well," Aachen said finally.

"Could have gone better," Neumann said with a shrug. "At least it didn't get worse."

"Yes, you only had to pull a knife on the former camp commander to stop one of his men from killing you. That wasn't too bad."

Neumann shrugged again, choosing to not respond to the sarcastic criticism of his underling.

"So, where did you get that knife?" Aachen asked.

"Took it off a radio operator from the 23rd Platoon. He fashioned it using one of the lathes in a workshop and was going to use it on some bunkmate he thought was cheating at cards. I convinced him that would be a bad idea and that if the Canadians caught him with the knife he would get at least two weeks in isolation."

"If the Canadians catch you with the knife, you'd still get the two weeks."

"The Canadians won't catch me with anything cause I'll probably just plant it on you," Neumann said.

"Glad to be of service then, Sergeant Neumann." He paused

for a second, then continued. "So, I'm assuming you accused Captain Koenig and some of his men of murdering Captain Mueller?"

"I didn't accuse him. I just asked him if they did it. I thought asking outright would the most efficient way to guage his reaction. Remember, it's how they used to operate when he was in charge of the camp, so I was wondering if they were doing it again. Especially since a lot of people thought Mueller was a communist."

"He wasn't a communist. He was only a teacher trying to help some of the younger soldiers."

Neumann looked at the corporal and sighed. "I know you thought highly of Mueller, but already a number of folks have expressed their opinions about his political leanings. And in a climate like this, sometimes someone's opinion about someone, even though it might not be based in fact, is enough. It's happened before and it will happen again."

"For Koenig to do such a thing, to kill Mueller for his so-called political leanings, means more than just what it looks like—it means that he is rebelling against the command of this camp."

"Not actually rebelling, but making a play for more power. Which is why he threatened me when I asked if he killed Mueller."

"But why would he do that? There is no way he would be allowed to run camp again."

"Well, there is a possibility that he sees the invasion of the continent and the despair it has caused many of the prisoners as an opportunity to push back against the present camp command. To show that whomever is in command of our camp is not as disciplined as they should be and that in order for us Germans to feel strong again, Koenig and his crew must take drastic measures. And the killing of Mueller is a message not just to the leadership of the camp and some who would support him, but to the overall population."

Aachen tucked his hands in his pants pockets and stiffened his body as the wind blew around him. "I really don't understand why people always seem to need to play these kinds of political machinations."

"That's because you have no desire for political power, Corporal Aachen. But you must realize that a crime like murder can involve many motives which may not be in your mind, but are in the mind of the person committing the crime. So while you don't have to understand them, you have to be aware of them. And you also have to realize that some of those ideas may just be distractions. There is a good possibility that Mueller was killed for a simpler reason."

"And that would be?"

"I have no idea," Neumann said with a shrug. "We are very early in our investigation. Mueller was just found this morning and it's not even lunch yet."

"So now what?"

Neumann finished his cigarette, put it out on the side of the building, and lit up another one. "I'm assuming your surveillance on Splichal was successful? That he did make contact with someone?"

"Yes, the civilian driver. He pretended something was missing from the manifest, but I'm sure that was the contact."

"You are probably right. No way he would come out for a small mistake like that. Anything else?"

"About the contact, not really. Although I did slip to a couple of prisoners that Splichal may be an informant for the Canadians even though you asked me not to. And when he made contact, they saw it was the truth."

"You slipped?"

"I guess I felt a bit angry when the chef bribed me then threatened me. No doubt he's done the same to other soldiers, probably with better success than with us. I didn't feel that he should be allowed to do such a thing without some form of punishment."

Neumann laughed deeply, slapping the flat of his hand against the wall of the Rhine Hall. "You claim you don't understand how and why the game works and you just made a fantastic play. I hope those boys aren't too rough on Splichal—we do need him as a cook."

"I told them to leave something for us to deal with."

"Well done, Corporal, well done." The sergeant leaned back against the wall, laughing and enjoying his cigarette.

Aachen looked about with a smile but still fidgeted slightly. After a moment, he spoke. "So is there something we should do now about Mueller?"

"Let me finish my cigarette first," Neumann said squinting at the sky. "And then let's go see what the doctor's been doing."

11.

Back at the classroom, Mueller was no longer hanging. His body was laid out on the teacher's desk, part of the rope still around his neck but cut in order to free him from the hook.

Despite being dead, Mueller did not look peaceful. His face was so contorted that he resembled a gargoyle: his eyes were wide with shock and his mouth was twisted with his tongue hanging out. A line of dried blood trailed from the same side of his mouth, across his chin, and down his neck. Mueller's shirt was also opened, revealing the front part of his torso. The skin was pale and hairless. There was not a single mark on it, save for some moles and old scars.

Standing over the body like a butler looking at a tea setting was Doctor Hermann Kleinjeld. The doctor was a tall, thin man with an aristocratic air about him. His cloak was always clean and his hair was shaved short above the ears. He resembled

Reichsführer-SS Heinrich Himmler with his wire-rimmed glasses that perched on his nose, but the good doctor was far less an intimidating and ominous figure.

Despite having to deal with a wide variety of ailments and injuries in the camp, from the basic cold and flu to sports and work injuries, from alcohol poisoning to damages caused by violent confrontations between bored camp members, he regarded almost everything with a uniformly somber, calm tone. Even as he leaned forward, probing Mueller's mouth with his long, elegant fingers, he seemed as if he was just window-shopping for a pair of cufflinks to wear that evening.

Also in the classroom with Doctor Kleinjeld was Corporal Knaup. Knaup was not calm and collected like the doctor. He sat in one of the classroom desks, his hands shaking as he nervously smoked. He stared in horror as Doctor Kleinjeld expertly prodded and poked at Mueller's dead body on the front desk.

Neumann entered the room and went immediately to talk to the doctor. It was Aachen who came up behind Knaup and set a gentle hand on his shoulder.

"Thank you very much for this, Aachen," he said with sarcasm. "I'm really glad to have been of assistance to you."

"Come on, Knaup, you've seen many dead bodies," Aachen replied. "What's another one?"

"Yeah, well, I was hoping never to see one again."

"War's not over yet."

Knaup grunted. "You didn't trust me enough to tell me what was really going on? You couldn't tell me that Mueller was dead?"

"We couldn't tell you that Mueller was dead because anybody could have heard, even through the walls of the barracks we were standing next to. And then this room would have been filled with curious prisoners and Doctor Kleinjeld wouldn't have been able to conduct his investigations in peace," said Aachen.

"You could have at least told me something," Knaup said, shaking his head slightly.

"Sergeant Neumann asked you to give a message to the doctor. And to help him," Aachen said. "He trusted you that much."

Knaup grunted, but did not reply. He turned to watch the doctor further inspect Mueller's body.

Neumann stood opposite the doctor with Mueller in between them on the desk.

"Sergeant Neumann, this—" he tapped Mueller's chest with a finger, "was a very unpleasant surprise. I liked Mueller. He was a good man, very helpful to the young lads. And to find him like this was … disagreeable."

"That's how I felt when Corporal Aachen and I came upon him this morning. I liked Captain Mueller as well."

"You obviously didn't like him enough to not leave him hanging, leave him for me and poor Knaup there to cut down."

"Knaup will be fine. He's been in the Wehrmacht for more than five years. He's seen much worse than this." Knaup shook his head, stood up, and left the room.

"Quite," the doctor said a moment later. "Still, I don't understand why you didn't cut Mueller down yourself."

"I wanted a professional to see him first."

"You are a professional yourself, Sergeant Neumann. Or, at least you were before this war began. You could have easily dealt with this scene before I got here."

"I meant a medical professional. I wanted someone who knew more about anatomy and injuries to look at Mueller before I stuck my nose in."

"Yes, well, you came to the right person. Although this is very unpleasant, as I said. Captain Mueller was a good man. Shame to see him die in such a manner."

Neumann put his hands on the desk, ensuring he wasn't touching the body and leaned slightly forward. "So, in what manner did he die?" he asked quietly.

Doctor Kleinjeld looked at him, raising his eyebrows. "Well it's not a way I would like to go." He took off his glasses and used them to point at Mueller's face. "Look at the bruising around his lip."

"Looks like someone hit him."

"Yes." Kleinjeld poked at Mueller's body in several places with his pen. "But why is there no bruising on his body? Almost every rib on this side of his body is broken and I'm pretty sure there's probably some internal damage as well. But there's not a mark on his body."

"That's unusual."

"Very. When someone is injured in this way, there is at least some bruising."

"Unless someone beat him in a manner that does not leave much bruising," said Neumann. "Before this war, I had a few colleagues who used rubber hosing or bags of rotted vegetables and fruit to punish certain people. Since they had no visible injuries, there wasn't any proof of police brutality."

"I hope you didn't stoop to such tactics, Sergeant."

"Waste of time and effort. There are better ways to deal with troublemakers than violence such as this."

"But you and I both know that Captain Mueller was not the kind of man one would classify as a troublemaker. He was an educated man from a good family."

"*I'm* an educated man from a good family," Neumann said, "but I've been called worse, especially by members of my own good family."

"You are certainly a different sort of fellow. No doubt the black sheep of your family," Kleinjeld said with a slight smile. "Still, Captain Mueller was a different sort of man than you." Kleinjeld tapped the chest of Mueller's body again. "He was refined, respected—not the sort of man who would become the head of a local police detachment, no offence."

"None taken. I understand. Mueller was cultured man. He would have made a terrible policeman."

"So we agree. Having two teeth knocked out is out of character for him."

"Two teeth knocked out?"

"Yes, two. Found one, he probably swallowed the other."

"So he was attacked?"

"Of course he was attacked. Despite his refined demeanor, I did hear that Mueller was an excellent strategist on the battlefield. That he was quite adept at destroying enemy tanks. So that tells me he was not the kind of person to back away from a fight, if someone forced him into it."

"So you're saying that he was in a fight."

"Not a fight, per se..." The doctor pointed at one of Mueller's hands. A couple of fingers were bent at odd angles and the knuckles were cut in various places. "These injuries show that he did try to protect himself. "

"Was he rendered unconscious?"

"Possibly. Broken ribs are extremely painful. He might have passed out, he might not have."

"And were these injuries bad enough to kill him?"

Dr. Kleinjeld pondered the question for a moment. "Not immediately. Possibly over time, but the cause of death here is obvious: asphyxiation."

"No broken neck?" Neumann asked.

Kleinjeld shook his head. "His neck is fine, save for some bruising and abrasions due to the rope and the weight of his body."

"So he choked to death. Because of the noose around his neck."

The doctor gave a small shrug. "Could be. But I also found this." Kleinjeld put his glasses back on his nose, grabbed his tweezers off the desk, and used them to pick up a small cloth, which was sitting next to Mueller's right hand. It was crumpled and torn, with small red stains on it.

"Where did you find that?" Neumann asked, squinting.

Using his other hand, the doctor pointed to Mueller's mouth. "In his throat."

"His throat?" Neumann hissed with surprise. "That was in his throat?"

The doctor nodded. "So it's possible that he asphyxiated because of it. Or because of the noose. Or both."

"You can't determine which?"

"Impossible. All I can do is look at what I saw—a dead man hanging from a hook with a rag in his throat—and determine that he probably died from asphyxiation. He could have had a heart attack as he was choking, though."

"You can't determine that?"

The doctor chuckled. "I'm a skilled doctor and despite being in a prisoner camp, our hospital is well-equipped and well-stocked. But I cannot, at the moment, determine with surety what exactly killed Captain Mueller. I'm pretty sure he did suffocate. But whether it was due to the noose, the cloth, or both, I cannot say."

"What if you did further study? If we took him back to the hospital?"

"We have fifty-eight patients at the moment in the hospital. We're in the midst of football season and with the heat, I'm expecting more. I think it would be best if we take Captain Mueller to the morgue."

Neumann nodded and stepped back from the table. He looked at Mueller for a few seconds and then grabbed Mueller's jacket and pulled it over his head. He stepped back, looking at the doctor.

"One more thing, Doctor Kleinjeld, if you may?" The doctor raised his eyebrows.

"Do you think Captain Mueller took his own life?"

Kleinjeld removed his glasses and rubbed the spot of his nose where they had sat. He paused for several seconds looking down at the body. He then put the glasses back on and rubbed his head.

"I'm not an expert in human psychology so I have no idea if Captain Mueller was hiding something, if he had some deep pain that he did not show the world. And, in my long medical experience, suicides can be very surprising, even to those who knew someone very well."

"In my experience as well. But take your best guess, Doctor."

Again, Kleinjeld paused to look at the body. After a moment, he sighed. "I doubt it. Mueller didn't seem like the kind of person to kill himself."

"If I had a mark for every time someone said that, I'd be a rich prisoner."

"The same for me. But the lack of bruising combined with the internal injuries, not to mention the cloth lodged in his throat … this situation is just too bizarre for suicide."

"Yes, it is clear that someone beat Captain Mueller. My guess is, beat him badly and then hanged him."

While Neumann was speaking, Dr. Kleinjeld rubbed his chin. "I don't like the thought of that, Sergeant," the doctor whispered after a moment. "It's very disconcerting."

"There are many men in this camp who have killed before," Neumann said with a shrug.

"Yes, but killed the enemy. And in battle, during war. We don't kill our own. We don't kill fellow Germans."

Neumann chuckled. "Come on, Doctor. You and I both know that there are plenty of men in this camp who would have no compunction killing a fellow German if they thought they had justifiable reasons. Hell, a lot of my neighbours back home, good Germans who lived in my village for generations, are no longer there. They've simply disappeared. Along with a lot of other Germans who didn't fit a certain mold."

Kleinjeld coughed with surprised. He turned red with embarrassment. "Yes, yes, that is neither here nor there" he said quickly, waving a hand. "But what justification would anyone have to kill Captain Mueller here?"

"I've heard he was a Bolshevik. And plenty of German communists have been killed in the past decade or so."

"Mueller was no Bolshevik," asserted Kleinjeld.

"You and I know that, but there are others who would think him one," said Neumann.

"And would those people kill him? Now? In this camp?" The doctor shook his head in disbelief.

Neumann shrugged. "I have no idea. And I'm not sure I want to find out either."

"So what should I do with Captain Mueller here?"

"What do you do with any dead body you find?"

"I note the time of death, find some way to take him back to the morgue, then notify camp command and the Canadians."

"The Canadians may already know about it. So I better go and leave you to deal with them when they arrive. Wouldn't be good if someone like me was here for that."

Neumann turned and started to walk away. But the doctor

cleared his throat to get Neumann's attention. "But what should I tell the Canadians if they ask me how he died?" the doctor asked.

Neumann turned. "They will ask you how he died. And so will everyone else."

"So what should I tell them?" the doctor asked.

"Tell them what you told me: you found him hanging and determined he suffocated."

"What if they ask the same questions you did about someone killing him?"

Neumann smiled. "None of the Canadians will ask you that. They'll assume that Captain Mueller was depressed because of the invasion of the continent and killed himself. "

"But what if a German asks me?"

Neumann pointed at the doctor. "Best if you act dumb. Insist that Mueller committed suicide."

"I'm not the kind of person who acts dumb, Sergeant."

"Doctor, if someone asks you those questions, they could just be curious. Or they may also know who the killer is, or they are the killer themselves. And if they believe that Mueller was a traitor, or at least accuse him of being one, it's not a big step for them to accuse you of the same thing, if you answer the wrong questions the wrong way."

Dr. Kleinjeld's eyes went wide with fear. Then he noticed a movement behind Neumann and his eyes went even wider. "Who is that?" he whispered, pointing at the door.

Neumann shrugged and slowly turned. "Probably Knaup…"

Neumann stopped speaking when he saw that the person the

doctor was pointing at was neither Knaup nor Aachen. Backing out of the doorway of the classroom opposite them was another German prisoner. He was an older soldier, at least a decade older than Aachen, lanky and unshaven. The prisoner froze, like he had been caught in a bright spotlight from one of the towers, but only for a second. He dashed down the hallway, heading towards the north entrance of the building.

Neumann gestured to Aachen who dashed out the door in pursuit. Neumann quickly followed, clambering to get around desks and chairs. He knocked over a couple, tripped on one of the table legs, and then tumbled to the ground. He jumped up almost instantly, kicked some more chairs out of the way, and rushed out of the classroom.

When he got to the hallway, Aachen had just reached the back door. Neumann raced down the hall after them.

12.

Once he stepped outside, Neumann saw the prisoner running away with Aachen right behind him. The prisoner moved from classroom to classroom, watching for any Canadian scouts who may be walking about, but also looking behind him to see where Aachen was.

Neumann went after them.

Even though the prisoner was faster than Aachen, he kept looking behind himself, and the corporal gained on him. Desperately, the prisoner entered a classroom building, opening the doors to the individual classes, interrupting the students as a distraction, and then dashing out the other side. But the corporal wasn't fooled; he simply waited outside for the prisoner to rush away, heading towards the lanes between the barracks.

Sergeant Neumann followed behind more slowly, leaving the pursuit up to Aachen.

The camp was still crowded and the fleeing prisoner tried to lose himself by weaving in and out of groups of other prisoners and backtracking through lanes. He slowed to a walk to avoid attracting attention. Aachen did the same. He walked in and out of groups, greeting various prisoners, and doing his best to blend in while still keeping an eye on his quarry.

Eventually, Aachen snuck into one of the barracks, and stood next to a window, keeping an eye on his prey. When the prisoner, still milling about with the others, his eyes darting side to side, seemed to relax, Aachen smiled. He waited for several seconds and when the prisoner took one last look about and started to move away, Aachen followed.

He stayed out of sight as the prisoner confidently walked along the lanes. When he came to his barracks, the most southerly building in the second row, he looked about one final time. Aachen ducked behind a corner, standing next to a group of prisoners smoking and playing cards. A few members of the group gave the corporal questioning looks but when he waved them off, they continued their game.

The prisoner entered and Aachen smiled again. He left the gamblers and walked towards the door. He grabbed the handle, but hesitated when he saw the insignia on the door.

He stood there for about half a minute, waiting for the sergeant to catch up with him. Neumann finally appeared, breathing a bit heavily. He looked at the door and sighed.

"He went in there?"

Aachen nodded.

"Damn. This only complicates things."

"I can go in after him, if you want," Aachen offered.

Neumann shook his head. "No. It's better if I go in. I have a bit more standing in this camp than you."

"I'll go with you, then."

"Thank you but no, Corporal. Best if I go in alone."

"I wouldn't advise that. The legionnaires are quite strict about their segregation. They will not be pleased that you are in their hut."

"I'm not pleased about going into their hut, but if I want to know why that soldier was there, I have to go in."

"Please reconsider, Sergeant. Let me go in with you."

"It's better if I go alone. Besides, if something happens and you get hurt, even slightly, you might have to forfeit your match."

"The match is of no real importance to me, Sergeant. I thought you knew that. I only do it because it keeps me fit and the men enjoy it, almost need it, especially since the war isn't going so well."

"Then all the better that you don't come in. The whole camp would be very disappointed not to see you take on Neuer. It's the highlight of the month."

"But what if something happens to you while you're in there?"

Neumann scratched his head and smiled. "I think I can take care of myself." He walked towards the door and grabbed the handle, but didn't open it. He looked back at Aachen.

"Don't wait for me, Corporal Aachen. Head back to the classroom and help Doctor Kleinjeld. He's going to need help to move the body."

"I'd rather stay here and wait for you, Sergeant."

"And I'd rather you go help the doctor ... and that's an order, Corporal, so get moving."

Aachen frowned. He opened his mouth to speak, but thought the better of it. Reluctantly, he began to move away, facing backwards for several steps, keeping his eye on the sergeant, before turning and walking away from the hut.

Neumann watched the corporal walk away, waiting until he turned the corner. After a second, he shook his head, opened the door, and stepped into the legionnaire hut.

The musky smell of hundreds of men living in close proximity to each other hit him as soon as he entered the building. Because he had come from the bright sun to a more dimly lit interior, he stopped for a several seconds as his eyes adjusted. In those seconds, two large prisoners stepped in front of him, blocking his way. Like the fleeing prisoner, they were older, perhaps in their thirties. They said nothing, just stared down at him with menace, their arms crossed in front of their chests. Neumann tried to move past them, excusing himself, but the two stayed with him, blocking his path. He moved to push between them, but they firmly pushed him back.

"Is there a problem, gentlemen? I would like to get through," Neumann said.

The two prisoners said nothing.

"As the Head of Civil Security of this camp, I must ask you to step aside."

"We don't accept your authority in this barracks," a voice said in the distance. "So it would be in your best interest to leave."

Neumann leaned to the side and peered around the two large

prisoners. In the shadows, a prisoner sat on the top berth of the closest bunk, his legs swinging below him. He was wearing the blue colours of the prisoner uniform, but it had been cut strangely, sewn into a robe like a Bedouin with a strip wrapped around his head like a keffiyeh. He also sported a full black beard and glasses and was knitting what looked to be a pair of socks.

"I was following a prisoner into the barracks and would like to have a word with him," Neumann said. "So it would be in *your* best interest to ask these fellows to let me pass."

"It would be in *your* best interest if you just turned around and left us alone," said the robed prisoner.

"You have me at a disadvantage. You seem to know me, but I do not know you."

The Bedouin sighed. He put his knitting down on his bunk and jumped to the floor. He adjusted his keffiyeh and walked over to tap one of the large prisoners on the shoulder. The giant moved aside, although he kept staring at Neumann.

"My name is Colonel Ehrhoff."

The sergeant snapped to attention and saluted.

"There is no need to salute me, Sergeant. Despite us both being Germans, you are Wehrmacht and I am Foreign Legion."

"Regardless, Colonel Ehrhoff, you are an officer and it's my duty to salute an officer, even one serving a different..." Neumann paused, trying to find the correct word for what he was about to say.

"The word you are looking for, Sergeant Neumann, is probably commander, although that would be incorrect, implying that we are in the same army, serving the same interests. We may not be enemies, but we are not on the same side."

"Still, you are an officer and since were not facing off in combat, I salute you the same way I would salute a German, a Canadian, even an American."

"Well, you have honour, I'll give you that. Which is one reason you haven't been tossed out of this hut the instant you walked in," said Ehrhoff. "I don't wish to see you come to harm. But if you insist on being persistent about your pursuit of our comrade, I will have no choice but to ask these fine gentlemen to remove you. And despite your size and probable strength, they will cause you harm."

"So you admit the man I was pursuing is a legionnaire."

"I admit nothing except that if you don't leave in the next several seconds, you will suffer many injuries."

Neumann looked at the two men, sizing them up. "Your men will suffer their own injuries if they choose to attack me, you can be sure of that."

"But your injuries will be worse."

"I doubt that."

Colonel Ehrhoff smiled without showing his teeth. "Hans, Philip, throw him out," he told the two men. The two legionnaires nodded as the colonel turned and walked back to his bunk.

The man on Neumann's left, the larger of the two called Hans, reached out to grab the sergeant's forearm, like a bouncer getting set to remove an unruly patron. Neumann batted the hand away and then slapped his palms against the man's chest, shoving him back the way one would push a barrel onto a cart. Surprised by Neumann's forceful attack, Hans stumbled backward several steps, losing his footing and falling against the edge of a bunk.

The other legionnaire, Philip, threw a right hook at Neumann's head. The sergeant leaned away, managing to dodge the bulk of the blow, but Philip's fist still glanced off his head just behind the ear, snapping his head to the side and causing his torso to twist away. Neumann kept his feet planted on the floor and like a sling-shot snapped back, torqueing his body quickly to deliver a powerful open-handed blow to Philip's solar plexus.

A rush of air blew out of Philip's mouth as the wind was knocked out of him. He fell against the wall and bounced forward. Neumann then delivered a hard slap to Philip's face, knocking him down to one knee. Philip gasped, trying to get his breath back.

By this time, Hans had scrambled to his feet and rushed towards Neumann, roaring like an animal. The sergeant had no time to move out of the way of this rushing train so he let his body go loose as Hans drove his shoulder and head into his stomach. As he flew backwards with the large legionnaire jammed into his torso, Neumann wrapped his left arm around Hans's head and jerked it over so it was nestled near his ribs. And when Neumann's back slammed against the wall, the sheets of clapboard cracking, so did the top of Hans's head.

The legionnaire went limp as they fell away from the wall. Neumann landed on the balls of his feet, still gripping Hans's head. With his right hand, he threw two uppercuts into the legionnaire's side.

Philip had regained his breath and jumped up, throwing a wild punch at Neumann and catching him on his left cheek. Blood sprayed from his mouth, splattering his face and Philip's hand. Neumann shook off the hit, released Hans from the head-lock, and pushed him aside with a quick jerk of his knee. Hans fell to the floor in a slump, spitting blood from his mouth and the top of his head bleeding from a large gash.

The sergeant brought his left arm up just in time to block Philip's follow-up right hook. He then grabbed Philip's shoulder and twisted, entangling the legionnaire's arm with his own. With his free right hand, he delivered two fast and hard punches to Philip's rib, the second one creating a cracking noise.

Philip screamed in pain, but still managed another attempt to throw a jab with his left hand. Neumann easily batted it away, slapping him across the face. Philip tried to raise his arm another time and again Neumann batted it away.

He pulled back his fist and made ready to punch the legionnaire in the face.

"Stop! Enough!" Colonel Ehrhoff shouted.

Neumann dropped his fist and then released Philip's arm. He pushed the legionnaire with the flat of his palm and Philip staggered back a step or two, hit the wall of the barracks, and then slid down to the floor in a seated position.

Neumann snapped to attention, his lip still trailing fresh blood, as Colonel Ehrhoff walked towards him. "I hope you're proud of yourself, Sergeant Neumann."

"Colonel Ehrhoff, I did not come here to get into a fight with you and your men," he said, holding his position and not making eye contact with the colonel. "I just wanted to talk with the man who recently walked in here. It's very important that I do so."

Ehrhoff sighed deeply. He looked at his two guards as they slowly struggled to their feet. "And the purpose of this conversation?" Ehrhoff asked.

"I'd rather not say."

"Sergeant, we are at an impasse and I am willing to be flexible. But only to a point."

Neumann looked at the two guards, then at the colonel. "If you wish, Colonel Ehrhoff, you could send another couple of your legionnaires to throw me out. And then we would be back in this position again. However, I would prefer if I could discuss this without any witnesses. Or more violence."

The colonel looked at the guards. The two battered men looked at Ehrhoff, but they seemed to be having trouble focusing. They attempted to stand at attention, but didn't have the coordination, leaning on each other like drunks after closing time. "Go get yourselves cleaned up. I'll talk to you later."

Philip helped his partner Hans and turned around. They staggered away.

"Okay, Neumann," Ehrhoff said once the injured guards had moved out of earshot. His arms crossed in front of him. "You have the floor."

"This morning, Corporal Aachen and I discovered the body of a Wehrmacht soldier."

"Whose body?" asked Ehrhoff, raising his eyebrows.

"A tank commander named Mueller. Captain Mueller."

Ehrhoff's eyes widened for a second. Then he blinked several times. "The teacher?" he said from behind his hand.

Neumann nodded.

"He was a good man," Ehrhoff said with a shake of his head. "How did he die?"

Neumann wiped the blood from his face with the back of his hand. But he said nothing.

"Speak up, Neumann, or I'll get more. And now that he's dead, it's not going to hurt him for you to tell me."

"You knew him? How is that possible?"

"It's a small camp," Ehrhoff said with a shrug.

"Yes, but he was like me: Wehrmacht. And you are Foreign Legion."

"Some of us did fight alongside you desert rats in Africa. Why do you think Rommel did so well? We were the ones who had the most experience fighting in sand and dust. Many legionnaires gave up the Legion when they transferred into the Wehrmacht."

"So is that how you knew Captain Mueller?"

Ehrhoff dismissed that conjecture with a quick wave of his hand and slight spitting from his lips. "I would have never given up the Legion," he said, insulted.

"But you are German. Didn't you want to serve your country and fight along your fellow countrymen?"

"I already did that in the First War, Sergeant, just as you did. However, once the war ended, I didn't like civilian life. Didn't like living in a country full of cowed people. I wanted to continue to fight. But we Germans weren't allowed to fight. So I did what many of us displaced veterans from the First War did: joined the French Foreign Legion. And not just Germans, either. There were English, American, Canadian fellows who were trying to kill me one year becoming my brother soldiers the next year."

"But why didn't you come back when Germany needed veteran soldiers again?"

"Joining the Legion isn't something one does on a lark, Sergeant Neumann. When you make a pledge to serve in the Legion, it's pretty much a lifetime commitment. You can do your five years and get out, but that's why the French give legionnaires citizenship after those five years, to further deepen that commitment. Most legionnaires don't go back to their regular lives or transfer to another army just because their home country needs them. Legion patria nostra is one of our most important mottos which means that the Legion is our new Fatherland."

"But you fought on behalf of Germany in the Wehrmacht?"

"Officially, we were fighting on behalf of Vichy France, alongside the Wehrmacht, even though we were wearing similar uniforms. That's how Rommel got us to fight for him."

"But that doesn't explain how you met Captain Mueller."

"We met on the transport over from Africa," he said with a Gallic shrug. "We weren't Foreign Legion or Wehrmacht in the hellish hold of that ship, we were only Germans working together, doing our best to survive. I could tell you more, Sergeant, but if your trip over was anything like ours, it's probably something you don't wish to remember. Just get on with it and tell me how Mueller died."

"He was hanged," Neumann said.

"By his own hand? That can't be possible."

Neumann shook his head.

"Murdered?" Ehrhoff said in a stage whisper a moment later.

"We are investigating a variety of possibilities and leads, which is why I need to talk to the legionnaire that fled into this barracks."

"There is no way Legionnaire Pohlmann is mixed up in any of this unpleasantness. He doesn't have it in him."

"He's a legionnaire. According to legend, you are some of the best fighters in the world."

"That's overstating things, Sergeant. We are men of war, but we are also men of honour. We do not murder."

"But many so-called honourable men have murdered. Why is Pohlmann any different?"

Ehrhoff laughed. "If you knew Pohlmann you would understand. He is a decent soldier, loyal to his comrades, holds his own in battle, but only fulfills his required duties, never exceeds expectations."

"Doesn't sound like he fits the legend of great fighters."

"As I said, the stories about legionnaires being great soldiers are overstated. We are only soldiers, just like you in the Wehrmacht. We might have more experience in battle than most, but we are just average soldiers. Pohlmann is simply a solid workhorse. Strong and durable, follows orders very well.

This got him into the Legion and allowed him to stay. But there's no way he would murder someone. He doesn't have it in him."

"I never claimed he was the murderer," Neumann said. "But he was seen leaving the building in which Mueller was found. I was pursuing him, hoping to talk to him, ask him why he was there."

"There are plenty of reasons. He could have been working there, he could have been studying."

"Then why did he run?"

"You are a very intimidating man, Sergeant Neumann. Don't you know that? Especially with your history. It's possible that Pohlmann was working in that building and came upon you and a dead body and got frightened."

"Yes, those are fine theories. But since there is a dead body involved, it would be best if I talked to him to see what his reasons were. If he is, as you say, not the kind of person who would murder and is not involved in this, then there should be no problem."

Ehrhoff rubbed his beard. After a moment, he nodded. "Okay, Sergeant Neumann. I will instruct Pohlmann to talk to you."

"With all due respect, Colonel, I would prefer to talk to Pohlmann now."

"Neumann, that's as far as I'm willing to compromise."

"But, sir…"

"However, I will ensure that Pohlmann will discuss the situation very soon. Hopefully tonight. Probably tomorrow."

"Tomorrow will be too late.

"That's it. Take it or leave it. As I said, we are not under your or anyone else's command in this camp. We may be Germans, but we serve a different command. And that will never change. No matter what they do to us."

Neumann looked closely at the colonel for a second. He tilted his head. "Did something happen, Colonel?"

"Besides one of my men getting beat up last night by a bunch of thugs on your payroll, then no, nothing happened."

"I don't have any thugs on a payroll. It's only me and Corporal Aachen. However, if you fill me in on this situation, I can do my best to investigate it."

"Don't waste your time because I know what will happen," Colonel Ehrhoff said. "You will say you will look into the matter, but in the end find nothing and we will be accused of anti-German sentiments."

"I will look into the matter. I take such actions very seriously."

"I'm sure you do, but there are some things you can't change, even at this point in the war."

"Regardless, we can't let anarchy reign in this camp. You have your pledge to the Legion, Colonel, and I have my pledge to the camp. My duty is to protect residents of this camp from harm, the same way I protected the people of my village before the war. And if someone harms one of these residents, it's up to me to bring justice to the situation. I don't care if you're Foreign Legion, Wehrmacht, Luftwaffe, or SS. It's my job to protect you."

"I can see why people look up to you, Sergeant Neumann. You have some very admirable qualities. You would make a great legionnaire."

"Thank you, Colonel, but at the moment, I have other responsibilities."

"Then maybe when the war ends and you find yourself unable to return to normal life in Germany, you should think about it."

Neumann looked at the colonel for a second, who smiled at him. "You don't have to say anything, Sergeant. I know the walls can hear things and report them to superiors. Even here it happens, so maybe it would just be best if you left. Someone will contact you when Pohlmann is ready to talk."

Neumann snapped to attention and saluted. "Thank you, sir."

The colonel hesitated and then saluted back. Without another word, Neumann turned and walked out of the legionnaire's barracks.

As he moved away from the building, he walked straight and proud, as if nothing was amiss, but as soon as he rounded the corner he found a quiet spot on the wall behind some bushes and sat down hard. He stayed there for more than ten minutes, groaning, catching his breath, and rubbing the side of his torso.

13.

When Neumann arrived at the classroom building where he had left Doctor Kleinjeld, Corporal Aachen, and the dead Captain Mueller, there was a crowd of about 300 prisoners gathered around the front door. A couple of Canadian scouts stood at the top of the stairs. The crowd was boisterous, hurling insults and obscenities at the Canadians, but not yet out of hand. However, the crowd was growing exponentially as more and more prisoners made their way towards the buildings.

Though the Canadians gave the appearance of being tough and in control, they eyed the crowd warily, stealing glances towards the gate into the camp, seemingly hopeful that reinforcements would soon come. But even if they did, there were over 12,000 German prisoners in the camp and only about 500 guards. If the crowd turned violent, shots could be fired, which no one really wanted.

Neumann pushed his way through the crowd. At first, the prisoners complained and rebelled against him, but when they realized who was pushing them aside, they backed away. Soon, the crowd parted enough for him to make his way to the front.

It was there that he ran into Corporal Aachen.

The young corporal's eyes went wide when he saw Neumann. He pulled him aside, near the corner of the building and away from the crowd.

"Sergeant! What happened?" he asked, his eyes darting back and forth as he looked at Neumann's injuries. "Are you okay? Are you hurt?"

Aachen reached a consoling hand, but Neumann gently batted it away. "I'm fine, Corporal Aachen. It's nothing for you to worry about."

"But your face, your lip—you're bleeding."

"Let's just say I ran into a couple of legionnaires that didn't like the questions I was asking and we had a spirited discussion."

"Looks like the discussion went into knock-out time. Are you sure you are okay?"

Neumann raised a hand. "I'm fine, Corporal. A little tender in spots, but fine. I appreciate your concern."

"If I may say so, Sergeant, you look like shit. Like you were run over by a tank."

"Two tanks, actually." Neumann smiled but then grimaced in pain, quickly touching his split lip.

"You got into a brawl with two legionnaires? I told you not to go in that hut alone."

"It wasn't a brawl, Corporal Aachen. It was a quick skirmish.

However, it is not the time and place to discuss such things. At the moment I think we should deal with this situation before it gets out of hand."

Aachen nodded and looked about, eyeing the crowd. "Quite right, Sergeant."

The throng of German prisoners had grown much larger and more belligerent. Several prisoners were throwing dirty pieces of laundry at the Canadians, but soon the projectiles of socks and underwear could become rocks.

Neumann walked up to the steps, looked at the Canadians who were visibly fearful, and stood on the first step. He held his hands in the air, causing a good part of the crowd to pay attention.

"Gentlemen, gentlemen!" he called out, attracting the attention of the rest of the prisoners. The angry clamour of the group died down somewhat. They looked on in expectation, interested to hear what the legendary Sergeant Neumann had to say to them.

"I know why you are all here and I'm here to confirm the rumours." He paused and the whole group hushed to hear. "Captain Mueller is dead."

The effect on the crowd was instantaneous. Men screamed and shouted, fists were raised, and a few people wailed in grief. Bits of paper, garbage, and fruit peels were thrown at the steps, hitting the sergeant, Corporal Aachen, and the two Canadian scouts, who raised their hands to protect themselves.

The sergeant moved up to a higher step, just below the Canadians and raised his arms again. He shouted again at the crowd, imploring them to stop, but to no avail. The crowd kept pelting them with refuse, building up their anger to the point of becoming riotous. Neumann attempted to calm and quiet the crowd from the steps for several more seconds, but frustrated by the lack of response, he stormed down the steps and waded into the crowd. He pushed against some of the prisoners, slapping a couple who were preparing to fling objects towards the front of the building. Corporal Aachen quickly followed after the sergeant, but did not strike anyone.

"What the hell is wrong with you?" Neumann shouted at them, his voice taking on the tone of a military training officer. "Are you German soldiers or are you football thugs?"

There was a soldier standing next to Neumann, an older soldier, over forty, thin and short, with a moustache, a balding scalp, and a pair of wire-rimmed glasses. In his hand, the prisoner held a rock the size of a field hockey ball. Neumann shook the soldier, knocking the rock out of his hand.

"Is this how you show that you are an honoured veteran of the First War, Sergeant Holm?" Neumann shouted. "Is this how you expect your men to act, like a bunch of hoodlums, drunk on a Saturday night, looking for windows to break or good girls to harass?"

Holm shook his head feverishly. He opened his mouth to speak, to defend his actions, but Neumann released him, shoving him aside. The sergeant whirled on the rest of the crowd, waving his hands. "Is this how proud German soldiers react? Is this how you were trained to be in a military camp? To act like buffoons, to act like morons?"

"But Captain Mueller is dead," shouted a soldier from the back. A series of mutterings in response rippled through the crowd.

"Yes, Captain Mueller is dead. That is true. And for those of us who knew him, it is very sad. He was a good man." Neumann raised his hand in the air, pointing in the direction of the voice that made the comment. "But Captain Mueller is not the first man, the first German, to die in this war, and he won't be the last. He is also not the first person to die in this camp. We had that young boy from Dortmund who drowned last summer, and the crazy Sudetenlander who froze to death trying to escape in January. And Major Frank, the Luftwaffe pilot who fell off the back of a farm truck less than a month ago. Not to mention those other unmentionable few who decided to take their own lives because they were too weak to spend several months in a prisoner-of-war camp. All of those men died and we never gathered like a unruly mob. Even with the suicides, we treated those men with honour, buried them like German soldiers. What makes the death of Captain Mueller so different from those?"

Holm, the older soldier that Neumann had jostled, stepped forward. "They said the Canadians killed Captain Mueller. That's why they're acting this way. With guards on the door and more Canadians inside the classroom."

Neumann laughed a hearty laugh. He reached out to put his hand on Holm's shoulder, but the smaller veteran flinched. Neumann paused to show that he meant no harm and then grabbed Holm's shoulder. "Who told you that?" he barked. "Who told you that the Canadians killed Mueller?"

"I don't know," Holm said with a shrug. "I heard someone from the mess talking about it."

"From the mess," Neumann said with a smile. "How long have you been in the Wehrmacht, Holm? 1915?"

"1914. I was in Mons when an English sniper almost took off my head," the old veteran said, pointing to his left ear, which was missing a chunk of its lobe. "I turned my head at the last second to respond to a command and he clipped my ear instead."

"So you've been in service longer than me," Neumann said. "So you know that rumours are rampant in the Wehrmacht. You've probably heard hundreds of things that some have said was the honest truth, especially talk in the mess."

"More than hundreds," Holm said.

"And this is just the same. Mueller was no more killed by the Canadians than he was killed by me. Or Corporal Aachen. Or even you."

"Then how did he die?" someone shouted from the back. "Who killed him, then?"

Neumann stepped away from Holm. He started walking towards the steps, talking loudly as he did. "At the moment, the only thing I can tell you is that he was found hanging in his classroom."

A shocked gasp rippled through the crowd. The mutterings that followed got louder until they reach the level of indignation they had been at when Neumann originally arrived.

"This is no way for us to behave," he said, waving his hands at them.

"But we want answers," someone shouted.

"Yeah, we want to know what happened," added another.

The crowd echoed these sentiments.

"We must be patient, we must wait. Because at the moment, even I don't know what happened. But I promise you, I will find answers for you."

Some members of the crowd nodded and murmured positively, but the majority of the men weren't appeased. They began jostling each other, and moved towards the sergeant aggressively.

Aachen stepped in front of the sergeant to protect him. He was supported by a few others. They pushed back and forth at each other like opposing teams in a rugby match.

Neumann put two fingers in his mouth and whistled. The sound got the attention of some and the jockeying between various soldiers stopped for a moment.

"So you want to behave like baboons, then," he shouted. "You want to forget your discipline, forget you are German soldiers and become anarchists." When Neumann pointed at them, they shrank back, fear in their eyes. "And is this how you wish to act in front of our enemy? Is this how we wish our captors to see us? Because if we continue in this matter, then they will look down on us as undisciplined soldiers, soldiers who deserved to be captured." He paused, turning away from the Canadians who had no idea what he was saying, and addressed the crowd.

"They will consider us Germans to be no different than the Italians. Is that what you want? For soldiers of the Fatherland to be looked on as Italians?"

There were a few mutterings of "No!" from part of the crowd.

But there were still some who didn't want to listen. They started to turn on one another again.

In that moment, Sergeant Holm, the old veteran, stepped away from the crowd, stood at attention, and started singing.

"Deutschland, Deutschland über alles,

Über alles in der Welt."

Holm's voice was a clear baritone and it caught the attention of those nearby him. They joined in, standing at attention, singing loud and clear:

"Wenn es stets zu Schutz und Trutze

Brüderlich zusammenhält.

Von der Maas bis an die Memel—"

More and more soldiers joined in and soon almost all, save for a very few, were singing loudly. Those who did not sing were given dirty looks and admonishing slaps on their shoulders and backs by those who did. And then every single German soldier within a hundred metres was singing:

"Von der Etsch bis an den Belt,

Deutschland, Deutschland über alles,

Über alles in der Welt!"

When they completed the entire song, the group cheered and then slowly began to disperse, much to the relief of the Canadians at the door.

Sergeant Neumann turned towards Sergeant Holm and gave him a salute. The veteran saluted back and then strolled away, whistling Deutschlandlied to himself. Neumann turned away from the dispersing crowd and started to climb the steps. Aachen was right behind. The two Canadian scouts moved together, blocking the door. "No entry," the one on the right said, waggling a finger.

"I'm the Head of Civil Security for the camp," Neumann said in English. "I should be in there."

"Nein," said the other one with a smirk. "Get lost, Kraut."

Neumann looked back at the crowd and then back at the Canadians. "I just saved your lives, gentlemen. Saved you from being torn apart by an angry group of my countrymen," he quietly said in English, pronouncing each word clearly. The Canadians showed surprise at that. "I think you should let me in as a way of thanking me. Because if you don't, then I'll just call the boys back and we'll leave them with you. Do you understand what I'm saying?"

The Canadians looked at each other. After a moment, one of them opened the door for the two Germans. "Be my guest, Kraut. No skin off my nose if you want to deal with Major MacKay. He's a big pain the ass."

14.

Neumann entered the room. Along with Doctor Kleinjeld and Corporal Knaup there were also three Canadians—two scouts, both corporals, and another one who was looking down at Mueller's body and had his back to the door. This Canadian's uniform was one of a guard—one of the many Canadians who normally stayed outside of the wire. He was smaller than the other Canadians and leaned to the right, as if favouring a sore leg.

Doctor Kleinjeld was the first one to notice Neumann and Aachen enter the room. His eyes opened wide. "Sergeant Neumann," he said in German with a tone of relief in his voice. "Thank God you've arrived."

The two Canadian scouts, on opposite sides of the doctor, looked up in surprise. They jerked, as if they should do something to protect themselves, but since they had no weapons, they were at a loss.

The other Canadian turned slowly. He was probably only in his mid-twenties but even so, he did not seemed intimidated by the fact that he could have been the son of every soldier in the room save for Aachen and Knaup. He was an officer, a Canadian major by his markings, and no doubt the Major MacKay the two Canadians by the door were talking about.

Neumann and Aachen snapped to attention once they saw the younger man's rank, offering a quick salute as they did. The major looked at them quizzically and then replied with his own salute. Neumann and Aachen dropped their hands, but stayed at attention.

Major MacKay took several halting steps towards Neumann, hands behind his back, like a general inspecting his troops. He jerked his chin in their direction. "Who are these men?" he asked quietly. "And why have they been allowed into this room?"

"That's Sergeant Neumann, Major," one of the scouts said.

"Ahhhh," MacKay said, narrowing his eyes, as if he was squinting to see Neumann better. He limped closer to the sergeant, but not too close. "So this is the famous Sergeant Neumann."

"I wouldn't call him famous," the scout said. "He's just the local copper."

"I thought you scouts were the local coppers," MacKay said without raising his voice.

"Well, we are. Just that Neumann here is the local German version."

"Gestapo then?"

All of the Germans flinched, but said nothing. MacKay

harrumphed slightly and then lurched a couple steps to the side, as if Neumann was some kind of artifact he was examining.

Before any of the Canadians could reply Neumann shook his head and answered in English. "No, sir, I am Wehrmacht."

"Didn't think so. You don't look the type. No matter what your PHERUDA says."

The two Canadian scouts gasped and looked at each other at the mention of that word. The Canadian major waved them away. "Relax, boys. I know these Germans are the enemy, but I think they're smart enough to know about PHERUDA and what it means."

He turned to look at Neumann. "Am I right, Sergeant? You know what PHERUDA means?"

Neumann nodded. "It's a means of classifying prisoners into black, grey, and white, depending on their support of National Socialism, amongst other things."

The major raised his eyebrows, but nodded. He gestured to the other Canadians. "See? He knows. They all know."

He ignored the attempts of rebuttal from the two scouts and focused on Neumann. "They have you classified as a black, Sergeant Neumann, although looking at you and hearing how you deal with your camp, I would put you down as a grey."

Neumann said nothing to that. The major, seemingly tired of standing on his leg, sat down at the desk. "However, I believe you are probably the most dangerous man in this camp."

One of the Canadian scouts chuckled at that, but cut himself off. Still, MacKay slowly turned to address him.

"You don't believe me, Corporal Pier?" he said glaring at

the scout who had snickered. "You don't believe that Sergeant Neumann is the most dangerous man in the camp?"

Pier froze, tightening to attention, and said nothing.

"Come on, Pier. Don't be afraid. Feel free to tell me your thoughts about Sergeant Neumann here."

Pier relaxed, but only slightly. "Well, sir, I think the sergeant's partner, the young fellow next to him, is probably more dangerous."

The major turned and looked at Corporal Aachen, sizing him up. "Ahh, yes. The young Corporal Aachen." Aachen blinked quickly when his name was mentioned, but since he couldn't speak or understand English, he said nothing. "The great grappler you boys have been betting all this money on. I can see why you would deem him dangerous. He looks very strong, built like a bull. Could probably snap me in half with one of his impressive arms. But it's very obvious that the corporal answers to his sergeant. So while he's very strong, Aachen is less dangerous than Neumann. Which is why I need to know why he was let into this room without a guard and without anyone asking me about it."

The major waved at Pier. "Please, Pier, could you go and ask Oliver and Michalchuk to come in and answer that question for me?"

"Now, sir?" Pier asked. "They're guarding the door."

"There's no need for that now. The prisoners have dispersed and with Sergeant Neumann and Corporal Aachen already inside, they don't seem to be doing a very good job."

Pier shrugged and walked out of the classroom. The major

kept looking at Neumann, tilting his head back and forth, but said nothing. None of the Germans said a thing; they just remained where they were. A few moments of awkward silence later, Pier came back. The two guards, Oliver and Michalchuk, followed behind. They entered the room, stood at attention next to Neumann and Aachen, and saluted.

The oldest one of the duo, the one who had let the two Germans pass, spoke. "You wished to speak to us, sir?"

"Yes. Corporal Oliver, I was going to ask you why you let these two men into this room."

"Well, sir, the Kraut sergeant here, he did a top-notch job of getting the Germans to disperse. Pretty much saved our butts. Yours as well. And since we know who he is, we figured that it would be no problem if he came in. We figured you could handle him, sir."

"Well, that's darn nice of you to think I could handle him, despite my injury. I appreciate the sentiment."

"Thank you, sir."

"You're welcome. But again, do you really know who this man is, Corporal Oliver?"

"Don't know his name for sure, Neumar or something like that. But I do know that the Krauts think of him as a sort of chief-of-police in the camp."

"His name is Sergeant August Neumann and he's a little more than that." MacKay pointed at Corporal Pier who had gone out to get the two men. "Corporal Pier can you whisper to Corporal Oliver what I said about Sergeant Neumann?"

Pier hesitated but MacKay gestured for him to continue.

When Pier whispered in the Oliver's ear, Oliver chuckled. He turned to Pier and mouthed "*Really?*" Pier nodded.

"Yes, I do think that Sergeant Neumann is the most dangerous person in this camp," said MacKay. "And it's the reason I'm very upset that you let him into this room without telling me and it's why I'm going to write you up for it."

"But sir—" Oliver said.

MacKay cut him off, rising quickly and steadily to his feet. "—No 'but sir', Corporal Oliver!" the major shouted angrily. He wobbled a bit as his leg gave way because of the sudden movement, but he kept his balance by pushing a finger against the top of the desk. "You allowed a dangerous enemy soldier into this room without telling me about it and without escorting him. That's a major dereliction of duty."

"But, sir, it was only the local German cop. We've seen him around. He doesn't talk to us, but we know who he is. He's not a threat."

MacKay sighed, a hand to his forehead.

He waved vaguely in Neumann's direction but didn't turn to look at the sergeant. "Please, Sergeant Neumann, could you inform my fellow Canadians of why I think you are the most dangerous man in the camp?"

Neumann blinked, like an innocent man being accused of a crime. "I have done nothing in this camp to warrant the description you are speaking of. I follow the rules and ensure that others do the same," he declared in English with an accent that was easy for the Canadians to understand.

"Yes, yes," MacKay said with a couple of quick nods. "I am

sure you are a model prisoner: you do your duty, you show up on time for the counts, you cause little or no trouble. However, I am talking about your life before the camps, prior to the moment you were captured."

"If you are talking about fighting in North Africa and other locations, I was only doing what every single soldier does out of duty for his country in the time of war. Nothing more, nothing less."

"Okay, then. Let's try a different tact," MacKay said, slowly walking a couple of steps toward Neumann. He waggled a finger at Neumann's chest. "I know you do not wear them in the camp, but I also know you are a well-decorated soldier. You have earned some of the highest honours that can be bestowed on someone of your rank."

"I have been decorated many times, yes, sir, that is true," Neumann said, clearing his throat.

"Could you explain the reason behind them?"

"There were many reasons for them."

"Yes, no doubt since you served in the Great War like these fine men I command. You have probably done many remarkable things that deserved medals and honours." MacKay raised an index finger and joggled it in the air. He smiled at Neumann, but did not show his teeth. "However you did fight in the battle which we here call the Somme, did you not?"

Neumann paused for a second and then nodded. MacKay smiled and turned to Corporal Oliver. "Just like you, Oliver. You fought in the Somme as well." Oliver said nothing but looked at Neumann with narrowed eyes. The major turned back to Neumann.

"And how many people did you kill in that battle, Neumann? How many Canadian and British lads died at your hands?"

Neumann shrugged. "I don't keep count of such things."

"Yes, but you received a medal for that and when they give medals, they usually offer a figure, a number of enemies killed in order to justify the awarding of the medal. It is said you killed 128 men in that battle, and at least a dozen in hand to hand combat."

Oliver's face became red as he stared at Neumann. For the first time since he entered the room, Neumann made eye contact with the major. The major glared back. "I make it a point to know the background of all the key members of the German command structure in this camp. Like you, Sergeant Neumann, and you, Corporal Aachen. Not only do I know that Corporal Aachen has the distinct honour of being the only survivor of Stalingrad in this camp, I also know that this is not the first time you have been a prisoner of war."

Neumann said nothing in response to this.

"Come on, Sergeant Neumann, you know what I am talking about," MacKay said, moving his arms out to the sides, palms up. "I wish to impress on my men that just because someone looks harmless, it doesn't mean they are. Quite honestly, Sergeant, this is my first posting since I was wounded in Dieppe and since that venture was such a failure, I wish to do a better job here and help those who serve under me become better soldiers. You command men—perhaps you could help me in this matter."

Neumann cleared his throat. He hesitated. Finally, in a low

voice, he said, "Yes, I was captured in the First War." After a moment of silence, he added, "But only for a short time."

"Yes, four days, was it?" MacKay said, pointing both index fingers in the air.

Neumann nodded his head.

"And why only four days, Sergeant? What happened?"

"I escaped," Neumann said after a pause.

"Of course you escaped, but could you be a bit more specific? It would very much help my men understand that they must not let down their guard at any time."

Neumann paused for several seconds. And then he took a breath. "It was war."

"Of course, of course. It was war," MacKay said. "I'm not holding a trial here, Sergeant. I'm just trying to make a point."

"Then make it," Neumann said quietly.

"Okay, Sergeant Neumann, I won't force you to talk. But I will tell the story." The major sat down at a desk. He turned his body to address the other Canadians. "You see, this Sergeant Neumann, as a younger version of himself, probably even younger than me, was captured by a squad of Brits. But instead of accepting his fate, he convinced an unsuspecting guard that he was sick. And when that guard came to help him, he killed that guard—strangled the life out of him with his bare hands. Then he stole that poor Tommy's knife, sliced a couple of throats, made his way from our side of the front to his own, and killed anyone who got in his way. Got a medal for it."

Every single Canadian soldier in the room looked at Neumann with a mix of awe and disgust.

"So you see, gentlemen, this man you allowed to enter this room without informing me and without escort is one of the most dangerous men in this camp." MacKay pointed at Corporal Pier. "Turn your back on this, man, Pier, and you may never see your lovely wife again."

"Corporal Jenson," he said, pointing at the Canadian scout who was standing next to Doctor Kleinjeld, "Sergeant Neumann would rather kill you than look at you."

"And you, Corporal Oliver," the major said, spitting the words as he spoke, "you managed to survive the previous war but twenty-something fucking years ago a good many others didn't because this German, the one you let in without notice and without an escort, decided that he didn't like being a prisoner. So he killed them. With his bare hands. Without a thought, without remorse. So now do you understand why I'm going to put you on report, Corporal Oliver?"

Oliver didn't back away. "I had no idea."

"Of course you didn't. That's why you shouldn't have let him in unescorted and without telling me. Do you understand?"

Oliver snapped to attention "Yes, sir. I am sorry for letting our guard down. It will never happen again."

MacKay took a deep breath and gathered himself. The tension in his body faded and his shoulders and head drooped as if deflating. He sat in that position for several seconds, as the rest of the men in the room stood in an awkward silence.

After a moment, he snapped to life again, raising his head and straightening his shoulders. He stood up and clapped once.

"Okay then. I guess we're done here," he said with enthusiasm. "Nothing for us to do now but finish up."

He slowly turned away from Oliver and limped across the room to the table that held Captain Mueller. "So, Doctor, you are quite sure of your assessment that this man, Captain Mueller, died of asphyxiation?"

Doctor Kleinjeld nodded. "That is my assessment, yes."

"And you found him hanging from a coat hook."

"Yes, in the corner over there," the doctor said.

"Were you by yourself or was there someone with you?"

"Corporal Knaup was with me." Kleinjeld said, pointing with his chin.

Knaup stiffened at the sound of his name, his eyes darting back and forth.

"Does the corporal speak English?"

The doctor shook his head and the major shrugged. He turned to look at Knaup.

"Corporal Knaup. Was Captain Mueller hanging from the coat hook when you came in with the doctor?" MacKay asked in German, much to the astonishment of almost everyone in the room. His use of the language wasn't perfect but it was clear enough.

Knaup's eyes flickered.

"Please, Corporal Knaup, the question. Could you answer?"

"Uh, yes, sir. When Doctor Kleinjeld and I came into the room, Captain Mueller was hanging from that coat hook." He pointed to the corner.

"You cut him down?" MacKay asked.

155

Knaup nodded quickly. "The doctor asked me to."

"And was he dead?"

Knaup did a double-take at the question. "Excuse me?" he said after a moment.

"Captain Mueller? He was dead when you cut him down?"

Knaup looked about at his German counterparts, looking for some kind of assurance or assistance.

"Please, Corporal Knaup. Was Captain Mueller dead when he was cut down?"

"Yes, of course he was dead. He was hanging from the coat hook in the corner. Why wouldn't he be dead? I don't understand."

The major didn't answer, only turned away from Knaup, indicating he was done with him. Knaup, with doubt and confusion on his face, looked to Neumann for answers. The sergeant shook his head at Knaup, giving a slight wave of his hand as a signal that he would deal with the situation later. Neumann then turned his attention to the major.

"So a man found hanging in a room, with indications that he died of asphyxiation. Sounds like suicide to me," MacKay said in English. All the other Canadians in the room nodded.

MacKay turned slowly because of his leg and pointed at Sergeant Neumann. "Is that your conclusion, Sergeant Neumann?" he asked in English. "That Captain Mueller killed himself?"

"It seems so," Neumann said.

"It seems so? That's the best you can do? It seems so?"

Neumann said nothing. The major looked at him closely, but the sergeant's face was a blank slate.

"Although I'm no expert, it seems to me that poor Captain Mueller decided to end his own life. For whatever reason."

MacKay pointed to Doctor Kleinjeld. "Okay, Doc, if you are finished, you can bring Captain Mueller to your morgue. We'll expect a report concerning his death from you and one of our own doctors may do an examination to confirm your diagnosis. If it's all kosher, then we'll leave it at that."

Doctor Kleinjeld and Corporal Knaup flinched at the Jewish term. MacKay gave a slight smile when he saw that. "And if it's not, chances are the Mounties will be called." The major looked at Sergeant Neumann as he made that statement. After a moment, he whirled his hand in the air, a signal to wrap things up.

"All right, men, let's leave our guests to deal with their friend. Doctor Kleinjeld, can you and the two corporals handle the transfer of Captain Mueller's body?"

The doctor nodded. "Yes. And if we need more help, Sergeant Neumann can pitch in."

"I don't think that will be possible," the major said shaking his head.

"Why not?" Doctor Kleinjeld was frowning.

MacKay gestured towards the two Canadian corporals at the door and then pointed at Neumann. "Because Sergeant Neumann will be coming with us."

15.

They put Neumann in a windowless room with a table and two chairs. A guard, not one of the scouts that had escorted him out of the camp, roughly pushed him down into the chair facing the door and pointed at him. "Stay put," the guard said. And then he left the room, locking the door behind. He didn't leave the area, though, his shadow visible underneath the door.

Neumann sat unmoving in the chair and waited for about fifteen minutes before footsteps could be heard outside the door. Voices whispered for several seconds until the shadow of the guard stepped aside and unlocked the door. The door swung open and in limped Major MacKay carrying a file. He was followed by the much larger and older guard, who wore the insignia of a sergeant. The sergeant was carrying a rifle, an Enfield with the wooden stock so polished it almost shone.

Neumann stood to attention and saluted the major. The quick

movement caused the guard to raise his rifle in alarm while MacKay only looked up. He glanced at Neumann standing at attention and then put his hand on the barrel of the Enfield, pushing it down.

"Stand down, Sergeant Murray. He's saluting me, not invading Poland," MacKay said with a quiet voice.

"You can't trust these Krauts, Major."

"Well I wish you were with me several moments ago. But my back's not facing him and you're armed and he's not. So I think we're okay."

"Just warning you, sir. You can't be too careful. I saw plenty of Huns like him in Belgium so I know what I'm talking about."

"Yes and I saw plenty of them in Dieppe last year so I know what I'm talking about as well. If you are going to hinder me in this investigation, you might as well leave."

Murray gave a distasteful look but said nothing. He lowered his gun and stepped aside. He stood in the corner near the door, at ease but intently looking at Neumann.

MacKay gestured with the file at the chair Neumann had been sitting in. "Please sit down, Sergeant Neumann. Hopefully this will only take a few moments."

Neumann only stared at the top of the door behind the Canadian officer. MacKay didn't seem to register this lack of movement. He set down and opened the file he had been carrying directly on the table. He pulled a small black notebook and pen from his pocket and set those down next to the file. After a moment, the major pushed up his glasses and sat back in his chair. There was a small look of surprise on his face when he realized that Neumann had not acquiesced to his request to sit.

"Please, Sergeant Neumann, there is no need for you to stand," he said, pointing at the chair. "Sit and make yourself comfortable."

Neumann did not move. The major looked at him for a moment, then removed his glasses and pointed them at the chair. "Come on, Sergeant, there is no need for these games."

After a moment, Neumann stepped in front of the chair and sat down. He did not lean back in it, but instead sat upright, like a musician responding to the rising baton of a conductor.

"Thank you. So much better, don't you think?" MacKay asked.

Neumann said nothing.

"So, Sergeant Neumann, even though we've already met, I haven't introduced myself. My name is Major MacKay and at the moment, I've been put in charge of the investigation into the death of your comrade, Captain Mueller. And it is my job to determine what role, if any, you played in Captain Mueller's death. Do you understand?"

MacKay gave Neumann an expectant look but got nothing in return. MacKay waved his right hand.

"You can answer or not, it's no matter to me. But it would make things go much more smoothly if you answer. I'm not asking for secret plans to Hitler's bunker or anything, I'm only asking if you understood why we're here. So if you do understand, then just give me a nod and I can move on. If you don't, then we'll just end things right here and Sergeant Murray will remove you from this room and place you in an isolation cell where you'll spend the next two weeks or so. Who knows, maybe in that time we'll have crossed the Rhine, overrun Berlin, and the war will be over. But even if that happens, I don't expect you'll be allowed to go home because then the RCMP will have this file instead of me and they'll probably charge you with murder. And with the war just ended, I don't think any Canadian jury will have any problem finding you, a German soldier, guilty."

Major MacKay leaned forward and rested his elbows on the table and then his chin on his palms. "Do you understand that?"

Neumann waited for a moment. Then he nodded, deciding to play along with this interrogation game for a bit. MacKay smiled and sat up straight. "Excellent. So do you also understand why we are here, why I must ask you questions about Captain Mueller?"

Again, a nod from Neumann.

"Very good, Sergeant. Two for two. Here's another one. Did you know Captain Mueller?"

Neumann nodded after a short pause.

"Good," said the major, picking up his notebook and pen and writing. "Let's try something verbal, okay? In what capacity did you know Captain Mueller?"

For the first time in the interview, Neumann looked directly at MacKay. "I do not understand what you mean by 'what capacity.'"

"Ah, he finally speaks," the major said, turning to look at the guard behind him. "See what a bit of determination can do, eh Murray?"

Murray grunted noncommittally.

MacKay turned back to Neumann. "I'm asking you if he was a friend of yours, if you served together in combat, stuff like that."

"Mueller was a tank commander, a captain. I am just a lowly sergeant in the infantry," Neumann said slowly, pretending he was trying to find the proper words in English, his responses prompting MacKay to scribble more in his notebook. "That should say enough about whether we were friends or not."

"So you did not serve in combat together while in Africa? You did not meet on the battlefield?"

Neumann shook his head. "Africa is a very big place. Millions of square kilometres. And there were millions of soldiers fighting on both sides."

"But you in the Afrika Korps were known for coordinating tanks with infantry. You did not meet Mueller then, during some coordinated battle?"

"No. I did not."

"But you did know him, did you not?"

"I knew him here in the camp. Probably in the same way you know your sergeant here and vice versa. That is all."

Sergeant Murray started to chuckle, but stopped himself. MacKay frowned. "But let's be truthful, shall we, Sergeant Neumann," MacKay said tapping his finger on the file. "While Sergeant Murray is a fine soldier who's served his country well, he is only one of several guards at this camp. You, however, are not an ordinary prisoner; you are part of the command structure, are you not?"

"I am the Head of Civil Security."

"And what exactly does the Head of Civil Security do in Camp 133?"

"As you already know, I am the person who is charged to keep the peace in the camp, to ensure that the prisoners act in a lawful manner, and to investigate situations when they do not."

"As you noticed in the classroom some time ago, some of our scouts say that means you are the local cop, the chief-of-police, so to speak."

"That is a good comparison, yes."

"But does your role go any deeper?"

"I don't understand."

"I mean is it your role to ensure that prisoners act in a lawful manner as outlined by your government—that they must act like good Nazis or be punished?"

"I do act according to German law and military law, but only in matters of civil security. It is not my job to control the political feelings of the prisoners."

"So you aren't Gestapo?"

"You already asked me that and I said I wasn't. I am Wehrmacht."

"Maybe you could educate me about it."

"I think you already know about that."

"If you please," said the major with a smile.

Neumann stared at MacKay. He shook his head in slight exasperation. "As you wish. Wehrmacht is the regular army. The Gestapo is the state police."

"So you serve the regular army, not the state."

"I serve the German commanders of this camp, many of whom are members of the regular army. Some are not."

"And those are?"

"Please, there is no point in me discussing the command of the camp with you because I know you already have that information, as well as the information about me and my role in this camp. And we have already discussed this."

"I'm just trying to point out that you are not just a member of the infantry, a lowly sergeant as you call yourself. You are the local cop in this camp. And as the local cop, you are probably more aware of your fellow prisoners' lives than let us say, I am aware of Sergeant Murray's life and vice versa."

Neumann nodded after a pause. "I'll grant you that."

"So I'm going to repeat my question from before: Did you know the late Captain Mueller?"

"Only slightly. We didn't mingle personally and I never took any of his classes."

"So he was a teacher?" MacKay asked, scribbling. "Interesting job for a tank commander."

"He was a professor before the war, mathematics and sciences. Since there was no longer any need for his skills as a tank commander in this camp, he decided to help the boys, give them something to do, maybe improve themselves during their incarceration."

"Sounds like a good man."

"He was a good man, at least from what I've heard."

"So why would he kill himself?"

Neumann shrugged. "Could be many reasons. But as I said,

I didn't know Captain Mueller very well, only by reputation. I wouldn't feel comfortable making guesses."

"Humour me," said the major with a smile. All he got back in response was a confused stare.

"I don't understand that expression, 'humour me.' Are you asking me to tell a joke about Captain Mueller? That would be distasteful."

"No, no," the major said, waving his hands. "I meant no disrespect. It's an expression and it means I'm asking you to offer some opinions about why someone like Captain Mueller would decide to hang himself."

Neumann looked at MacKay and sighed. He allowed his body to relax and leaned back into the chair. He leaned an elbow on the table and rested his head in that hand, rubbing his face for a moment. He looked at the sergeant and then back to MacKay. He shook his head and sighed again.

"Although I'm reluctant to discuss Captain Mueller personally, I can talk, at least vaguely, about possible explanations for why someone would take their own life in this camp."

"Sounds good to me. Let's start there," said the major.

"First of all, I do not wish for you to take this personally, both of you. As far as I and many other prisoners are concerned, we have been treated very well by you Canadians. You have provided us with adequate shelter, plenty of nourishment, and enough facilities, tools, and opportunities to keep us busy.

"That said, none of that can hide the fact that we live in a prison, that our lives are under the complete control of our captors. You tell us when to wake up, when to stand to be counted, when to eat, when to stand to be counted again, when to go to bed. You control what information you give us and force us to attend classes on democracy, as if we don't understand how the concept works."

"You are ruled by an authoritarian society headed by a man you all call the Führer, are you not? Our reeducation efforts are designed to open your eyes to other political opportunities and systems."

"You have forgotten that the Führer was lawfully elected by German citizens to be the political leader of our country in 1933 so we understand how to vote."

"Yes, but the Enabling Act of—"

Neumann cut the major off with a wave if his hand. "I really do not feel comfortable discussing the German political situation with those who are, at the moment, members of the army who are the enemies of my country. You have asked me about the possible reasons why someone in this camp would consider suicide and I would prefer to continue in that vein."

"Okay, certainly. Please go on."

"Being captured by the enemy in battle is very difficult to deal with. Defeat and surrender are difficult for soldiers."

"Defeat and surrender are a part of war," said the major.

"Yes, but defeat is very destructive to those on the losing side, and not just physically. Look at you, Major. I am quite sure that you are still recuperating from your defeat at Dieppe, especially considering the circumstances in which it occurred. No doubt your leg injury is the least of your anxiety."

MacKay flushed but Neumann either didn't notice or didn't

care; he turned his attention to Murray. "And it is extremely difficult when many of your countrymen are still fighting and you are prevented from doing so because of something out of your control, like how age is preventing a well-seasoned veteran like yourself, Sergeant, from serving on the battlefield."

"I serve where I am ordered to serve," Murray said grimly, his face unchanging. "That is all I can do."

"Still, I'm quite confident in saying that this is probably the last place you would like to be."

None of the Canadians said anything for several seconds.

Neumann sat up straight in his chair. "See what I mean? That kind of guilt or disappointment can be hard on a man, any man, no matter how strong they may look on the outside."

After a moment, MacKay spoke. "So, you are saying that this is what happened to Captain Mueller? He felt guilty about being captured and would rather be back on the battlefield?"

"Remember, I am not specifically talking about Captain Mueller. I am only discussing the circumstances in this camp. And you and I both know that there have been other prisoners who have taken their lives, some even leaving notes to explain their feelings—the feelings I have just talked about. And considering the recent invasion of the continent, I believe there will be a few more."

Sergeant Murray grunted. "Then good riddance."

The major turned towards the sergeant. "Please, Murray, keep your comments to yourself. You are not helping matters. If more of the men in the camp decide to kill themselves, it will not make our lives easier. It's better if we find some way to keep the men as happy as possible. Or at least, not suicidal. More deaths would not look good to command, if you get my meaning."

Murray shrugged, muttering to himself.

The major then turned towards Neumann. "So to prevent any such deaths, is there anything we can do to help you, Sergeant Neumann?"

Neumann looked at the major and blinked. "There is one thing you can do."

MacKay turned to look at Sergeant Murray who responded with a slight rise of his left eyebrow. The major turned back and leaned forward with anticipation. "And what is that, Sergeant Neumann?"

"Stop asking me questions," Neumann said, tiring of the game. "Send me back to my camp and let me do my fucking job."

The major shook his head and smiled. "Suit yourself, Sergeant Neumann, it makes no difference to me. As far as I'm concerned, I don't give a shit how this Mueller died. Don't care if you killed him, someone else did, or he killed himself. Maybe after the war someone might but now, he's just another dead Kraut. And the more dead Krauts we have in this war, the better."

MacKay gathered up his file. "Please note, Sergeant Murray, that I attempted to interrogate the prisoner about the situation and in the end, he refused to further answer my questions."

"Noted," said the Canadian sergeant.

"And lock him up," he said to Murray. The large Canadian sergeant nodded.

Within moments, Sergeant Murray was roughly shoving

Neumann into a three metre by three metre concrete cell. The large Canadian guard chuckled as he shut and locked the door.

For several seconds, Neumann stood in the middle of the room, staring at the wall across from the door. The only furniture was a small twin bed with a straw mattress covered by a rough wool blanket. A metal sink and toilet were bolted to the floor. Light slanted into the room from a small window near the top of the ceiling.

He thought about the situation regarding Mueller, but pushed it aside. It was obvious that someone in the camp had killed Mueller, but there was no real rush to figure out who it was. He had done enough for one day and nobody in the camp was really going anywhere.

Besides, for the first time in more than five years, he was alone. There was no one above him, no one on the ground next to him. He sat down on the bed, smiling, enjoying the solitude and silence. He sighed, then lay down on the bed, and fell asleep.

16.

After the Canadians took Sergeant Neumann away, Corporal Aachen helped Doctor Kleinjeld and Corporal Knaup take Mueller's body to the hospital. They fashioned a litter of sorts by removing the top of the teacher's desk. It was heavy work— the distance between the classroom and hospital was a couple hundred metres—and a good many of the prisoners crowded around as they made their way through the camp, coming up in groups or individually to see who was dead. Many already knew it was Mueller, but were curious to see the body for themselves.

Doctor Kleinjeld attempted to order the prisoners out of the way, to give them room to travel, but to no avail. Aachen wished Sergeant Neumann was there because he had the authority, not just in his position, but in his person, to clear the crowd. But Neumann was in the hands of the Canadians and Aachen had no idea when they would release him.

So it took almost half an hour before they managed to get the body into the hospital and over to the morgue. It was there that Doctor Kleinjeld was able to prevent those with a morbid sense of curiosity from following them.

When they finally transferred the body onto a table, Knaup stepped away and collapsed on a chair, puffing and covered in sweat. Kleinjeld attended to Knaup first, offering him a drink and then calling for an orderly to get the corporal to a bed where he could rest and get some fluids in him. "Don't let him get heatstroke, and make sure he's completely hydrated before you let him go," the doctor ordered. "Let him sleep if he wants. Don't push him."

The orderly, a slight private with a pencil-thin moustache, nodded and then led Knaup out of the room. Kleinjeld then turned to Aachen.

"How about you, Corporal? Are you feeling well?"

"I'll be fine," Aachen said. "It was difficult work, but my training has accustomed my body for such an effort."

"Of course, but make sure you drink some water and get something to eat before you leave. Some fruit will be good."

"I'll be fine," Aachen repeated.

The doctor nodded and the two of them stood in the room with Mueller's body on the table between them. They silently looked at each other for several seconds. After a few moments, Kleinjeld cleared his throat.

"You do not have to stay, Corporal. I appreciate your help transporting Captain Mueller over here, but you may go."

"With all due respect, Doctor, I believe it's important that I remain here as you conduct your autopsy on Captain Mueller. It's something Sergeant Neumann would have done and since he is … indisposed at the moment, it falls to me to carry out his duties."

Doctor Kleinjeld stepped around the table and touched the corporal gently on the forearm. "I'll be sure to mention your dedication to duty the next time I see Sergeant Neumann. But it's better if you go."

"I prefer to stay."

"Well, there really is no need for you to stay because I wasn't going to conduct the autopsy on Captain Mueller anyway."

"But the Canadians…"

"I already know how Captain Mueller died. And so do you, so there is no need for me to cut him open, remove his organs, weigh them—all that nasty business. Best to leave Mueller in peace, don't you think?"

"Are you sure that's best? Won't an autopsy better determine how and why the captain died?"

"Probably, but as I said, we both know how he died." The doctor stepped back and moved towards the door of the room. He turned to look at Aachen. "And so does Sergeant Neumann."

Aachen didn't move, choosing to stay next to the table and Mueller's body. "But you told the Canadians that Mueller killed himself. And a Canadian doctor may be called to conduct his own autopsy. Won't he be able to tell that Captain Mueller was beaten first?"

"Possibly, but I don't think they'll do one. An autopsy is a lot of work and since there is already a doctor who has done some kind of investigation, they'll probably take my word for it. And my word will say that Captain Mueller died of asphyxiation as a result of hanging. That will be enough, even for a Canadian doctor."

Aachen stood there for several seconds, confused over what to do next, staring down at the sheet covering Mueller.

Kleinjeld rescued him from his thoughts. "You are a very dutiful soldier, Corporal. I see why Sergeant Neumann always speaks highly of you."

Aachen waved the doctor's compliment away then shook his head and crossed the room in three strides to stand next to the doctor.

"You are correct, Doctor Kleinjeld. I cannot stay here; I must get back to work. That is what Sergeant Neumann would have done. And since he is not here, I must report what has happened to him to command so we can determine a course of action until he returns."

"Are you sure that is wise, Corporal?"

"And I will need your help, Doctor. I will need you to come with me."

"I have a lot of work to do here. This weather has resulted in many heatstroke and sport injuries."

"You must realize that since Sergeant Neumann is now with the Canadians, there are those who may look on him as an informant. And if it's just me that files a report saying that he went unwillingly with the Canadians, that informant stigma will likely remain because I am considered a biased party, only looking to protect my direct superior. However, if you, a respected and impartial member of the camp, comes with me and confirms that Sergeant Neumann was taken by the Canadians against his will, the thought that he is an informant will be diminished."

"No one will think ill of Sergeant Neumann. He is a great hero of the Fatherland. Nothing can diminish that. And no doubt the Canadians *have* reported that they have taken him into custody so there is no need for you to get involved."

"But there are those who may look upon this situation and become suspicious of the sergeant's actions."

"Then it would be best if we don't further attract their attention by doing what you suggest."

"I only wish to help the sergeant."

"I know that, Corporal, and I commend you for it. Again, I see why Sergeant Neumann has you as his assistant. But in my opinion it's best if we just let this stand as it is."

"I don't understand."

Doctor Kleinjeld looked around and then stepped forward so he was very close to Aachen. His voice dropped to a whisper as he spoke. "As you said, Corporal, there are those in this camp who will be suspicious that the Canadians have taken the sergeant. However, if you and I go traipsing into their offices to claim that there is nothing suspicious about the sergeant being taken by the Canadians, it will only make things worse."

"Why?"

"Because these are the kind of people who see suspicious things everywhere, especially in places where there aren't any," Kleinjeld said, lowering his voice further. "They won't see your report as a means to exonerate your sergeant, but as your attempt to protect him. And having me there to back you up will only exacerbate the situation further and draw further suspicion on the sergeant, as well as on me and you." The doctor stepped back. "You know I am right in this," he said after a pause.

"But I must do something," said Aachen.

"Well, there is nothing for you to do here. Nothing you can do for Captain Mueller and nothing you can do for the sergeant. I know it must be hard to accept that, but find something else to do to pass the time. Do some KP, train for your match, take a nap, anything, but don't try to help Sergeant Neumann. That will be a waste of time and only hurt him in the end."

Aachen sighed, then nodded. "Thank you, Doctor, for everything," he said with a salute. "I will leave you with your patients."

And before the doctor had a chance to reply, Aachen marched out of the morgue and the hospital. He grimaced as he stepped out into the harsh wind, but did his best to ignore it.

17.

Aachen was planning to take the doctor's advice, but only part of it. He planned to do some more KP and a bit of training, but first he had another duty to perform. He walked over to one of the buildings originally designed to be a classroom that housed the German administration. Located about fifty metres directly south of the hospital, the rooms were filled with desks where various officials oversaw the operation of the camp with typical German efficiency.

Every prisoner had a file and that file not only included all the typical military information—what unit all the prisoners had served, where they had served—but also where and when they had been captured, and which building and bunk they were now housed in.

Other officials oversaw the movement of supplies, be it food, medical, recreational, or otherwise. Every single detail needed to run a camp of this size was overseen from this building. There was even another building, slightly smaller than the main administration, where every single piece of mail, incoming or outgoing, was inspected to ensure the contents were proper— not just for military purposes, but for political and social ones as well. And any inappropriate or irregular comments were severely censored as well as noted and reported for possible discipline, depending on the type of transgression.

But the room Aachen was heading for was in the back of the main administration building tucked in the northeast corner, an area of the building that rarely got any direct sun. Aachen paused outside the room, took a deep breath, and then stepped in through the door.

There was a reception desk of sorts, a wooden table devoid of papers, save for the one single sheet on which the receptionist was writing. He was an officious-looking lieutenant, thin but not skinny, his hair slicked back, a pair of reading glasses perched on his nose. He sat erect in his chair, his posture perfect, and the only parts of his body that moved were his arm, hand, and wrist as he made notes on the sheet of paper. He wrote quickly, each pen stroke sharp and determined, like he was carving a piece of wood.

Instead of the typical prisoner outfit with the red circle on the back, the lieutenant wore a uniform similar to Aachen's. But Aachen knew that the lieutenant had never served in the Wehrmacht. He only wore the uniform because no prisoner was allowed to wear SS or Waffen SS uniforms or insignia.

Aachen did not move close to the desk, did not let his gaze

linger on the lieutenant or what he wrote, and instead stayed just inside the doorway, head erect, body somewhere between attention and at ease. He made no sound to draw attention to himself or to distract the SS officer from his task.

Even so, the lieutenant finished a line, flipped his sheet over, and set his pen parallel to the paper. He looked up, his expression empty as he gave Aachen a brief appraisal, quickly determining which card catalogue he belonged in.

"Corporal Aachen," he said in a quiet tone.

Aachen knew better than to expect anything else—a query on why he was there, and if he needed assistance. It was assumed that anyone entering this space had a definite reason to do so and had better get on with explaining what that reason was and not waste time.

He took two steps forward, snapped to attention, and saluted. The SS officer offered only a nod in response, not a salute, not even a "Heil Hitler."

"I'd like to report that Sergeant Neumann has been taken by the Canadians," Aachen barked.

The SS lieutenant blinked. "This occurred at what time?"

Aachen told him. And gave a quick description of what had occurred: Mueller's death, the arrival of the Canadians, and how they took away Sergeant Neumann. He said nothing of their discussions with General Horcoff or Captains Splichal and Koenig. The SS lieutenant took no notes of what Aachen said, again filing the information away in some type of mental card catalogue.

"We were aware of this situation, Corporal Aachen, but your report will be added to the information we presently have."

"Thank you, Lieutenant." Aachen said.

"Is there anything you wish to add?"

"No, Lieutenant. I just felt you should be aware of the situation."

"Yes. We…" the SS lieutenant paused for a second, searching for the proper word, "acknowledge that you have come here and given us this report."

"Thank you, Lieutenant."

"And you have nothing else to add?"

"No, Lieutenant."

The SS officer stared at Aachen for a couple of seconds, blinked once, then flipped over his sheet, grabbed his pen, and started writing again.

Aachen saluted—the gesture went unacknowledged—turned on one foot and made to step out of the room. However, the SS lieutenant called out "Corporal Aachen", stopping Aachen mid-step. He put his foot down, spun on the ball of that foot to face the desk, and saluted again.

"Lieutenant."

"Our reports state that you have taken a number of classes with Captain Mueller."

"Yes, Lieutenant, I studied mathematics and physics with Captain Mueller. For my Abitur."

"And did Captain Mueller discuss anything besides mathematics or physics in these classes?"

"No, Lieutenant."

"No political discussions, no references to the war or situations related to life in Germany or this camp."

"No, Lieutenant. The only real life references he discussed related to the mathematics and physics he was teaching us."

"Please explain."

"Since Captain Mueller was a tank commander, I recall he did discuss the calculations involved in determining the parabolas for firing the main guns and how those numbers would change during the movement of the tank."

"He made no comment about the necessity of these kinds of attacks or criticize them in any way?"

"No, Lieutenant. He only focused on the numbers."

"He made no political remarks at all. No criticism of the war effort, of the leadership of this camp, or of Germany as a whole."

Aachen remembered that Sergeant Neumann told him if he was asked this question, he should say he reported the matters to Neumann. But he decided that the sergeant could be in enough trouble already. "No, Lieutenant."

"You are absolutely sure."

"Yes, Lieutenant. I would report such remarks to you."

"You mean would have reported such remarks?"

Aachen paused, but only for a second. "Yes, Lieutenant."

The SS officer went on as if not hearing what Aachen had said. "Because such comments would be considered traitorous. Furthermore, if someone hears such remarks and fails to report them, as you well know, Corporal Aachen, then their lack of action is just as traitorous as those who speak those words."

Aachen said nothing in response; he only stared at the wall several feet behind the SS officer.

"You do understand what I am talking about, Corporal Aachen?"

"Yes, Lieutenant."

"So there is nothing you wish to add to your report that you have just submitted to me?"

"No, Lieutenant."

The SS officer stared at Aachen for a while longer. Finally, he put his head down and started to write on his sheet again. He said nothing to indicate dismissal but Aachen didn't need him to. He saluted, and again there was nothing in return from the lieutenant, then turned on his heel and walked out of the office.

Aachen strolled out of the building as if nothing was wrong, the speed of his footsteps never wavering. It was only when he got outside that he took a breath.

18.

Aachen strode quickly away from the administration building, across the camp, through a series of barracks, and into
the kitchen for another round of KP. For about an hour or so
he chopped a variety of root vegetables to be used for a stew
planned for that night's dinner. Even though other prisoners
whispered about him as he chopped, no one approached him
or talked to him directly. Everyone kept their distance like
he was some kind of pariah or a person with an infectious
disease.

It was the same at the workshop building, which had been
turned into an athletic training centre. Even though the place
was filled with the prisoners who regularly trained there, including many he had wrestled with in the camp as well as in Africa,
no one offered to spot him as he did his routine of weightlifting.
No one even offered to throw a medicine ball back and forth

with him. He resigned himself to bouncing the medicine ball off a wall.

He also completed half a round of his regular isometric exercises: a series of squats, dead leg lifts, and chin ups. Then he ran two laps along the perimeter path, which was approximately six kilometres. The path, as well worn as a Roman road, ran alongside the inner perimeter fence.

For the most part, the prisoners walked along the path in a counter-clockwise direction. Aachen ran in the opposite direction so they could see him coming and not be surprised if he ran up behind them. Even months from battle, several prisoners were jittery about sudden noises and movement. Everyone was used to him running around the camp on a regular basis, though, and for the most part, unless they didn't see him, they stepped out of the way to let him pass. Sometimes they would shout out to him, cheers or jeers depending on what company or service they were in, but this time, no one said a thing. They stepped out of his way, but did not meet his eye. It was as if he did not exist, like an old Jew in the street that no one had the heart or inclination to beat. Better to just ignore him until the SS took him away or he died.

So Aachen ran in peace, comfortable with the silence, doing his best to ignore the wind. He had completed two-thirds of his second lap when a football bounced in front of him. He stopped quickly and allowed the ball to go by. It hit one of the fence posts and bounced back, stopping in front of him.

"Can you kick that back?" a voice shouted out to him. Aachen looked over and walking towards him was Staff Sergeant Nico Heidfield, former leader of Hut 14.

Heidfield wore a pair of pilot sunglasses, making him look even more like a movie star. "Please, Corporal Aachen," he said with a smile. "The ball."

Aachen kicked the ball hard towards the staff sergeant. Heidfield caught it expertly, but instead of going back to his game, he continued towards Aachen. As he did, he tucked the ball under one arm, pulling a pack of cigarettes out of his shirt pocket with the other. By the time he reached Aachen, the cigarette was lit.

He held it out to Aachen, but the corporal shook his head. Heidfield shrugged, put the cigarette in his mouth, and took a drag.

"Hell of a day, isn't it, Aachen?" Heidfield said nonchalantly. "Shame about what happened to Neumann. Even more of a shame about what happened to Mueller. I liked him; he was a good man. A bit stodgy at times, but he knew his stuff and liked to help the boys out, which in my book is a good thing, don't you think?"

Aachen nodded and then pointed at the ball. "I think your teammates are looking for something." He gestured with his head at a group of prisoners who were standing in the middle of the field, waiting in clusters of four and five.

Heidfield looked at the ball as if he had forgotten it existed. "Right. Hold on." He turned and smoothly dropped-kicked the ball. It flew in a perfect high arc, bouncing once and then landing right next to a group of players. One of them stepped forward and stopped the ball with his chest, kicking it over to his teammate. The game continued on.

Heidfield watched for a second and then turned back to Aachen.

"Are you okay, Corporal? All this business with Neumann and Mueller not getting you down? Not going to be a problem with your match, is it?"

Aachen waved his hand. "I'm glad my well-being is at the front and centre of your concern, Sergeant. I appreciate that."

"Well, you have been successful on the mat. I would hate to have something ruin any chance for future success."

"I appreciate the sentiment although I'm guessing it's not just my success you are anxious about."

"Your success is good for my success—it's a connection we both have."

Aachen nodded. "Thank you for your concern, Sergeant, but if you don't mind, I have a run to finish. And I'd like to get it done before my mess shift starts."

"Yes, yes, of course. I just wanted to make sure you were okay."

Aachen turned to walk away but Heidfield called out to him.

"But one more thing, if you don't mind, Corporal? What did really happen to Captain Mueller? I've heard some conflicting reports so I was hoping you could set me straight."

"Captain Mueller is dead. Is that straight enough?"

"But how? Did he kill himself or was he murdered? Who found the body in the first place?"

"I'm sorry, but I can't provide you with any information about the investigation except to say Captain Mueller is dead."

"So there is an investigation. That tells me you think he was murdered."

"I don't think about anything, Sergeant Heidfield. I'm only a corporal and I only follow orders."

"But you must know something. Surely something must have come up since the Canadians took your sergeant away from you and locked him up. And since he is gone, you must be continuing the investigation in his place."

"Like I said, Sergeant, I'm only a corporal. I make no decisions except for when it's time for me to train and run. Which I would like to return to before my mess starts."

"Come on, Aachen. Why can't you tell me something? People are asking and I'm wondering if there is any way I can profit from this information. It won't do any harm to tell me something, especially if I can share whatever I get with you." Heidfield smiled behind his sunglasses. "If you want, I can order you to tell me to make you feel better."

"Ahh, now I understand. You wish to make money from the good captain's death."

Heidfield shrugged. "Many people have profited from many deaths these past few years, so why shouldn't I have a tiny piece of that pie. And I could use someone like you once the war is over. Not just someone strong but someone smart. My places of business after the war are going to need some security."

"Your places of business? How can you have places of business when you're stuck in a prisoner-of-war camp."

"I have my ways. But listen, Corporal Aachen, I'll take care of the business and financial side of things. I learned it at the feet of my father and he always told me to look to the future, to see where things are going when others don't. He saw the rise of the Führer and invested wisely. He also told me to stay away from the fighting, to attach myself to some administrative position. But I was young. I wanted to fight like my friends for the Fatherland. Although I was smart enough to join the Afrika Corps instead of go to Russia. Even a boy like me knew to stay out of that insanity. Only stupid soldiers and criminals ended up there."

"So I'm either stupid or a criminal."

"We're all stupid when we're young. Thinking in the now, not looking to the future."

"In my future I would finish my training for my match and have a shower. Maybe have something to eat."

"See? Only looking at the short term. Your match, your shower, food for the night. You're a smart man, Corporal Aachen, and I know you can do better."

"Thank you for your compliment, but please, I must go back."

Heidfield put his arm around Aachen like an old friend. "Bear with me for another moment, Corporal. The time you lose here could pay off in the end." He gently steered Aachen around and started them walking slowly around the path. "Look at these men, Aachen. For the most part they are all good Germans—some smart, some not, some strong, some not. But most of them fought well for the Fatherland. They had their reasons, like you and me, and they did their best in difficult situations. But in the end they got captured and sent here: a great place with good food and plenty of classes to take and games to play to pass the time. And sure, it can be boring but no one is trying to kill us, which is very good in my mind. Unfortunately, for the most part, most of the men here are wasting their time. They are missing a fantastic opportunity this camp can offer."

"Men like me, I assume?"

"No, no. Of course not, Aachen. Look at you and look at these men. Most of them are content to walk in circles, in the same direction, day in, day out. Some of them have been doing this every day for months, for years. They do nothing else except sleep, eat, and walk. You, at the very least, go the other way. And you run. That alone makes you a different sort."

"I only do that so I don't surprise these others with my running. It's nothing special."

"It shows how smart you are. You've looked at the situation from many angles and picked one that not only works for you, but also works for your fellow comrades. It's the same strategy you've used with Sergeant Neumann—attaching yourself to him. That was brilliant thinking."

"I did not attach myself to Sergeant Neumann," Aachen said with irritation. "He was my squad commander and I just decided to continue in that capacity here."

"Again, that shows how smart you are. Most men have forgotten what squad they fought with and let themselves settle into the boring life of the camp because it was the easy thing to do. And not only are you Neumann's adjutant, you've taken courses in order to pass your Abitur, which you did, I hear. This shows that you are looking to the future."

"You are assuming that I have put much thought into these things," Aachen said. "That every action I have undertaken is some conspiratorial attempt to improve my life. The reality is I've just done these things because they felt like the correct things to do."

"And that shows you have an instinctive desire to do things which are good for you. As I said, you see many angles before you act, and my goal here is to show you that there are many other angles out there that you haven't seen and to help you look for them."

"Could your discussion on angles wait until I finish my training? Geometry always made me sleepy."

Heidfield ignored him. "Well your training is part of one of the angles I wish to talk about." Heidfield stopped and removed his arm from Aachen's shoulders. He stepped in front of the corporal, standing only a metre away from him. "Please tell me Corporal Aachen, why do you train? Why do you put yourself through this difficult and time-consuming regime?"

"First, it makes me feel better. But second, if I wish to defeat my opponent in the match, then I must train hard. Lieutenant Neuer is a difficult opponent and no doubt he is training as well."

"But why do you need to defeat him?"

"I guess I don't need to defeat him. I would just like to."

"Why? Is there a trophy? Will you get a medal from the Führer? Is there prize money involved?"

"Of course not," Aachen said, now fully annoyed. "I don't wrestle for those things. I wrestle for the competition. For the honour of winning, I suppose."

"Honour is overrated. You know that. We were both in North Africa. You were in Stalingrad for God's sake. I bet you didn't see much honour on that battlefield."

Aachen took a step back from Staff Sergeant Heidfield. "I'm sorry, but is there a point to this discussion?"

"Of course, there is always a point in my conversations." He reached out and gently tapped Aachen on the chest with his finger. "What will happen if you lose the match against Neuer?"

"If I lose," Aachen said, blinking several times, "I guess I'll feel disappointed. But it's only a match—the disappointment wouldn't last."

"Ah, the disappointment wouldn't last," Heidfield said, raising his finger into the air. "And would your fellow soldiers be angry at you if you lost? Would they disrespect you?"

"A few, might," he said with a shrug. "But I believe most would understand as long as I put up a good fight."

"As long as you put up a good fight. Very good, Corporal Aachen." He tapped him again on the chest. "And what if I told you that there would be more potential for your future if you lost?"

Aachen straightened, a look of repulsion coming over his face. "I beg your pardon?"

"Oh, don't be surprised, Corporal Aachen. You know a large number of the men in this camp bet on these matches. They bet on everything in this camp. How long the count will take, how did Mueller die, there's even a poll on for when an escape will occur. It helps pass the time. And of course someone has to organize these things."

"As well as take a percentage."

"It takes a lot of work to deal with these things so those who do should be compensated. This happens with all gambling. Even the splendid casino in Monte Carlo operates in this way."

"So you are asking me to lose the match against Neuer. On purpose."

"I'm asking you to think more about your future, Corporal Aachen. You've done reasonably well working with Sergeant Neumann, passing your Abitur, but once the war is over, what will that give you? Neumann will go home and become the local copper in his village again. You can't go with him. As for university, most places of learning have been turned into rubble. No one will be getting an advanced education in Germany for a long time, I can promise you that. And young strong men like you will probably be conscripted into moving rubble or rebuilding things. So despite your efforts here, you'll just be another grunt moving rocks. But unlike you, I have made plans to ensure that doesn't happen to me. I—"

"—Yes, your nightclub, you have talked about it."

"The nightclub is only a minor part. Through this camp, I have made connections that I never would have made in Germany. I've connected with people who have other and even better connections than I do. My plans are much bigger than a simple nightclub. And I'm inviting you to be part of those plans. I need someone like you after the war—a good security man who is not only strong, but smart. That's a rare combination, you know."

"And all I have to do is lose my match against Neuer? That's it?"

"That's the first step in showing your commitment to my

plans. I would also ask you to pass on any information that could be useful to me. So I can adjust my planning."

"Such as?"

"Well, this morning you and Sergeant Neumann paid a visit to Chef Splichal about the pilfering of supplies in his mess."

"You wish for me to inform you when we are going to deal with people like Splichal?"

"No. Nothing of the sort. Splichal got out of hand and deserves what he gets. But if someone had known that Splichal was stealing so much, someone would have clamped down on it earlier so as not to attract attention."

"Ah, I see what you are getting at. It makes a lot of sense."

"It does, doesn't it," Heidfield said with a smile. "It's all about thinking and anticipating the future and adjusting to it so you can succeed."

Aachen paused and returned the smile. "Okay, Sergeant Heidfield. I understand and thank you for thinking of me. So let me start by telling you one thing and you can do with it what you want. At the same time, it will give you your answer to the request for me to lose my match against Neuer."

"Excellent, Corporal Aachen. I knew you were smart." Heidfield leaned in close after Aachen bade him to do so.

"Okay, Sergeant. You first asked me about Captain Mueller. So let me start there. I did file a report about the situation today, with everything that happened with Captain Mueller and Sergeant Neumann. Not much of a report, just a simple verbal description of what happened. All of which you probably know, given your sources."

Aachen tapped the sergeant gently on the chest, the same way Heidfield had tapped him earlier. "I gave that report to a lieutenant in the administration," he said, continuing to smile. "Although I'm not sure if you've met him. He's a quiet sort of fellow for a Waffen SS and he is very good at his job."

At the mention of this, Heidfield's smile vanished and he stepped back.

"I'll bet if you go and ask him," Aachen added, "he'd be keen on talking to you."

"That's not funny, Aachen. Not funny at all. I'm only trying—"

"—in fact, I'll do you one better since you're so inquisitive and so interested in my well-being and future. Next time I see this lieutenant, I'll mention your name and I'm one hundred percent certain he'll be keen on talking to you. Probably for a very long time."

Heidfield backed up quickly, hands in front of him. "Okay, okay, Aachen. I get your point. You don't have to be so malicious about it. I was just hoping to invite you into our plans."

"And I'll be sure to tell him that as well. No doubt he'd be very interested in your *operation*, so to speak."

Heidfield's face went white. He backed away farther. "No, no, no. That's not necessary. I mean, just forget I brought it up, there's no need to say anything. Just forget we even had this talk, okay, Aachen? There's no need to bring the blackshirts into this, okay?"

Aachen turned and started to walk away. In a few steps, his walk turned into a run. He ignored the shouts from Heidfield, picked up speed, and didn't even notice the wind. He also didn't notice that by the time he felt like stopping his run, he had done an extra lap of the camp.

For the rest of the night, he was left alone again. Even during supper in the crowded mess, he was on his own—a single prisoner at a table designed for six men, with his own bowl of food, the same stew that he had cut potatoes for, his own loaf of freshly baked bread, his own bowl of strawberries—enough food for six men. There was even one pint of beer for each prisoner, although Aachen was only given one, instead of six for his table.

He ate one quarter of the stew and bread, silently passing the rest on to a table of grateful prisoners, a number of whom had served in the same company in North Africa. Still, they only acknowledged their thanks with short, quick nods that were designed to be seen only by those close by.

Aachen kept all the strawberries, eating some of them at the table and taking the rest to his bunk. Taking food out of the mess was strictly forbidden, but no one prevented him from leaving with the strawberries. And as he walked the short path from the mess to his barracks, eating the strawberries like some kind of decadent Prussian aristocrat, not a single soldier came up to him to share in the booty.

The camp of 12,000 captured German soldiers surrounded by barbed wire and enemy soldiers with orders to shoot to kill was essentially a small town. And everyone in a small town knows when it is best to leave someone alone and how to treat someone who has become a pariah, even if that person had been a friend, someone trusted just months ago. So the prisoners left Aachen alone for most of the day. Until a group of them came to find him in the shower.

19.

Even though Aachen had already taken a shower after his run, he decided to take another one later in the evening. Even with all the windows open in his barracks, the heat was stifling. For some reason or another, the wind that blew during the day seemed to stop at night so no air moved. With over 500 men housed in the building, the place was a furnace.

The heat had been no different in North Africa: dry, stifling, relentless. However, the exhaustion from trying to stay alive, the falling artillery shells exploding, the strafing runs from enemy planes all made it much easier to sleep in the desert. It was worse at Stalingrad when the enemy deemed it necessary to also attack at night.

But in the Canadian prairie, thousands of kilometres from the battlefields of North Africa and Stalingrad, there was little for the men to do. Sure, they were no longer being shot, bombed, and strafed so they could relax, but for some, this only made sleep more difficult, especially in the heat.

When Aachen climbed down from his bunk, slid on the slippers that he bought from one of the camp's leather-making shops, and padded to the showers, he was not the only one who was restless.

At least one-fifth of the men in his barracks were awake. It was probably the same in all the other barracks. There were men reading, writing, sewing, knitting, polishing, grooming, staring off into space—all the things bored soldiers did to pass the time at night. There were scattered groups of three to six men playing cards, tossing dice, or sharing food or drink. Some men stood alone by open windows, smoking or just looking at the stars. There were also others gathered around open doors of the barracks, like friends at a pub, some inside, others out, smoking and joking among themselves. Technically, the ones standing just outside the doors were breaking the rules—no prisoner was allowed out of their barracks after 9 pm—but the Canadians were fine with some prisoners having a smoke just outside the doors at night. Better that than in their bunks where they could fall asleep and burn down the clapboard building and all the men in it in less than thirty seconds.

Aachen knew that somewhere in the camp, maybe even below his own barracks, there were soldiers digging tunnels to escape. Some of these tunnels were sanctioned by the camp's Escape Committee, the group that planned, coordinated, and approved escape attempts. Of course, because they were several thousands of miles away from the Atlantic, no one expected a German prisoner to make it all the way home following an escape. The point of escapes was to force the Canadians to waste resources that could be used in Europe or Canada.

Even the latrine area wasn't empty. The bathrooms were communal with no walls or dividers, and all the spaces—the toilets, the sinks, the showers—were filled with soldiers. In the actual latrine area, in which twelve toilets were lined up along the wall, sat four soldiers doing their business. They sat as far away from one another as possible, each of them doing their best to ignore the others, all of them reading something in order to feel as if they were alone.

In the washing area, in which metal sinks were also lined up along the walls, one soldier, an older sergeant by the name of Olson, was using a desk from one of the classrooms to set up a makeshift barbershop. He was using a straight razor, classified as an illegal weapon within the wire, to remove the lather from the neck of another soldier. The man in the chair was a large burly man, his face unrecognizable because of the shaving cream and the face cloth over his eyes.

A few seconds later, the barber finished his razor pass and looked up. He gave Aachen a friendly wave with his blade. "Corporal, hope you don't mind if I set up shop over here. I won't cause any trouble, you know." Olson spoke through the cigarette in his mouth. "I'll even give you the next one, no charge. It will cool you down. Make you feel so much better."

Aachen waved back but did not move closer. "You know we have an actual barber shop in Workshop 9, Sergeant Olson. You could easily set up shop over there, and make a better wage than here in the bathroom."

Olson waved his razor angrily. "Bah, those pretentious ass-holes told me since I didn't go to barber college and don't have any real papers from the Fatherland that I couldn't join their precious group. Even though my father was a barber and before that my grandfather and his grandfathers, one of whom, can't remember which one, gave the Kaiser a shave during a town visit. And those bastards call me unqualified." Olson shook his head. "So, I'm relegated to setting up in the barracks at night. Tonight it's in your barracks."

Olson expertly shaved a section of the seated man's neck, wiping the foam off on his apron and moved to do another pass. He looked up at Aachen. "You sure you don't want one? A shave? Or maybe a cut? I could trim you up well so you look good for your next match, no charge as I said."

Aachen waved a refusal. "Thank you, Sergeant, but no. I see you are a bit busy so maybe another time. I will just take a shower." Aachen turned and walked to the shower area.

"Another time," Olson shouted at him. "Same deal, no charge for you, Corporal Aachen."

Aachen offered a wave over his shoulder and entered the showering area. Like every other space in the bathroom, the shower room was communal. It was a large area, about 1000 square metres, separated by dividing seven-foot-high walls of concrete—walls not tall enough to touch the ceiling. Every metre or so, two pipes, one for hot, the other for cold, extended out from the concrete and converged into one which ran upward about another metre so that it extended above and then out from the wall, ending in a shower head about ten centimetres across.

Like every other space in the building, in every single building in the camp, the floor was concrete. But these floors were sloped slightly towards strategically placed drains. Long wooden pallets about a metre wide were in rows in the floor for the prisoners to stand on while they showered in an effort to prevent the spread of diseases of the foot. Even so, Aachen never removed his slippers from his feet when he showered and replaced his slippers every couple of months. The private that made his slippers had been a cobbler in his previous life and softened the leather on the bottom of the soles so Aachen could wear them in the shower and not slip on the wet floors.

Aachen slid off his boxer shorts and hung them on one of the hooks that was spaced between the water pipes just off to the side of a shower head.

He turned on the water, first the cold to cool off his over-heated body, and slowly adding hot until the temperature was almost exactly at body temperature. Having any kind of shower, especially one with seemingly unlimited hot water, was a luxury for any soldier. It was also a luxury for civilians, at least those in Europe where the war had created shortages of gas and coal which were used to heat simple things like water.

Aachen lingered in this water for at least five minutes. He used to feel guilty about such things when he first arrived in the camp and would restrict himself, taking only cold showers and eating only minimal amounts of food. He'd felt disloyal, not only to Germany but to his family, if he reveled in such things. But then he realized that his mother would have insisted that he not suffer on her account, that she would want him to come back home strong and alive, no matter what she had gone through. So he put the guilt behind him and determined that if he was still going to be a strong and contributing member of German society after he was released, he would have to take advantage of all the things the Canadians were giving him. Especially if he were to be called on to fight after his release, following the defeat of the Allies. Despite the recent invasion of the continent in France, Aachen still felt victory was possible and that there would come a time when he would have to fight for his country again.

He finished his shower, shook the water from his hair, and grabbed his shorts from the hook. He did not put them on because he was planning to walk back to his bunk naked and let the heat of the prairie night air dry his body.

But when he turned away from the shower, a fist came flying towards his face. He managed to turn his head so the blow was only a glancing one, but a second later, another fist connected with his stomach. He had tensed his body for this hit, his muscles preventing the air from being knocked out of him, but it still knocked him slightly off balance, causing him to fall back a few steps. His footwear, designed to prevent him from slipping, although probably not in this scenario, helped Aachen keep his balance.

He brought his fists up, quickly made note of the number of men around him—seven, though none identifiable because even though they were stripped to the waist, they were all wearing handkerchiefs on their faces—and started swinging.

Aachen's punches were calculated short jabs, designed to hit back while keeping his arms in a defensive position. Both of his initial punches connected, two of his assailants grunting in pain after each hit, and he managed to block several punches with his forearms.

Not to be thwarted that easily, the group expertly encircled Aachen, their attacks coordinated in order to take advantage of their numbers and any short openings he offered them. Aachen fought back as best he could, getting some good hits in with his fists as well as with his feet, his elbows, and once his forehead. Yet for each one, he got two or three in return.

They worked his body over, punches first coming in a flurry, but then targeted to specific areas like his ribs, kidneys, biceps, thighs, and lower back. His assailants were like a well-organized enemy mortar platoon. Their first shots seemed random, but were actually a means of determining their angles of attack. And once they got a bead on where Aachen was, they just kept pounding him, throwing mortar after mortar. These men were experts in this, well-versed in the kind of violence that causes as much damage with as little effort as possible.

Aachen decided that enough was enough. The only way he could survive this without too much serious injury was to collapse on the ground and fold himself into a ball. He tucked his head tightly into his arms, hoping his assailants would tire of their attack and only work him over to the point where he was near death rather than past it. When he did fall, he landed on a small object that dug into his skin. When he shifted slightly, the object fell between the slates of wood.

They kicked at his back, legs, and arms, the blows hard

and painful, but unable to connect with his head. After a few moments of this, they stopped the attack. Aachen did not relax and did not unroll from his protective ball in case their pause was a ploy to put him at ease so they could attack again.

But there was no more attack. Instead there was a shuffling of feet and a rustling, as if someone was pulling something out of a bag.

"Get him up," said a voice Aachen didn't recognize. Hands roughly grabbed at him. Though he struggled to maintain his position, there were too many of them and he was too weakened from the beating to resist for long. Still, it took four men to pull him to his feet and to hold him upright, his arms held out from him, like he was placed on a cross, his head and body open to anything they might do. Though his head was spinning with pain, he managed to note many distinguishing marks on the bodies of these men: scars, birthmarks, and a few tattoos in telling places. He also noticed that only one person seemed to have not taken part in the beating—which meant he was the one in command of this group.

The leader stepped forward and looked at Aachen. He too was masked and stripped to the waist. And though his body looked plump in places, Aachen could see that there was hard muscle underneath the fat.

"I'm sorry we had to meet like this, Corporal Aachen. I have heard much about you and your skills on the mat. And I see that these stories about your strengths and abilities have not been exaggerated. You put up a good fight, a strong fight, one of the best. A much better fight than the French, even better than the

Poles. You acted more like that British battalion who stopped our advance at Dunkirk, tough and hardened bastards, getting their potshots in, keeping us at bay. Although in the end, they all ran away and we took over the continent."

"But then they came back and invaded the continent with over a million men, and with more on the way," Aachen said, spitting blood out of his mouth and onto the floor. "So I'd be careful who you compare me to because you never know what will happen."

"You should be careful of the things you say, Corporal Aachen. Some could consider your words traitorous."

"I'm only stating the facts. The Allies came back and invaded Normandy after we defeated them at Dunkirk. Everyone knows that."

"Bah, things would have been different in Dunkirk if they hadn't issued the Halt Order. We would have captured all those Brits and the course of the war would have been very different. I'm quite sure we wouldn't be in this godforsaken camp talking about the invasion while you get the shit beat out of you, eh Aachen?"

Aachen chuckled, a sound that caught his assailants by surprise. "Criticizing the man who gave the Halt Order, the Führer, is also traitorous, don't you think, Sergeant Konrad?"

The leader of the group froze, and as he turned his head back and forth, Aachen could tell there was confusion and surprise at the mention of his name. "How did you…? Who told…" Konrad stammered.

"It's easy. Neumann and I heard talk of a new sergeant transferred from Medicine Hat, someone who, for some reason or another, became the new leader of Hut 14. You were called fat and ugly, a hairy obnoxious hobgoblin in a German uniform, which I first thought was unfair, but it seems they were very accurate in their description."

The men holding Aachen looked at each other. Without warning, Konrad punched Aachen in the face, the blow splitting his cheek as well as a couple of knuckles on Konrad's hand. The sergeant jumped back slightly, waving his hand in pain. Aachen's head snapped back, a flash of light exploding in his vision. He faded out for a second or two, then came back, his vision blurred.

By this time, Konrad had reached into a bag and pulled out a length of rope about three metres long. He waved it around at Aachen and then wrapped the rope around the corporal's neck, twisting it into a knot. Konrad yanked on the rope, pulling Aachen forward and his arms free from the hold of the other prisoners. His breath cut off. Aachen gasped for air and clutched at the rope, trying to wrench it off, or at least slip a couple of fingers between the rope and his neck.

It was to no avail. Konrad stepped to the side and swung part of the rope over and around one of the pipes, giving him a fulcrum of sorts. He hauled on it, the fibres digging into Aachen's neck, rubbing harsh burns into his skin.

Aachen struggled as he was lifted off the ground, clawing at the rope and kicking his feet. He made a bit of progress but the lack of oxygen depleted his strength. Quickly his struggles became weaker and weaker and Konrad's grip on the rope more insistent.

Aachen's vision blurred again as he slowly started to fade out of consciousness. Just before blacking out, Aachen heard screaming, a high-pitched wail of a sound, the sound, he thought, of death coming to take him away in its clutches.

However, the sound caused the rope to slacken and Aachen's feet to touch the ground. It was only a brief second, but that touch relaxed the pressure on his throat, giving Aachen a moment to suck in a short gasp of oxygen. And even that little bit gave him strength.

He reached his arms up and grabbed onto the pipes, pulling his body up as if he was doing a chin-up as part of his daily training regime. That movement slackened the rope farther, giving him more opportunity to breathe.

In that moment, he realized that the screaming wasn't just in his head. It was outside, in the camp. And it wasn't screaming, it was a siren, a wailing like an air-raid siren from back home. Since the Canadians were not subject to bombing, the siren could only mean one thing: it was an alarm to announce to all in the camp, especially the guards who were asleep in their own barracks, that there was an escape in progress.

The noise distracted Konrad and his henchmen, allowing Aachen to grab one of the water taps and turn on the cold water. The chilly blast caught the others by surprise, forcing them to jump back, while invigorating Aachen slightly. He pulled himself up higher and then swung his legs towards the sergeant. His feet connected with Konrad's chest, knocking him back and forcing him to release his grip on the rope.

Aachen dropped to the floor with a hard thud, his teeth

slamming together and part of his tongue, caught between them, slicing off. He ignored the pain and the iron taste of blood, jerking the rope off his neck. He sucked in as much oxygen as he could in his first breath.

An instant later, he struggled to his hands and knees. If he got to a more public location in the barracks, he knew he would be safe. Several of his assailants tried to grab at him, but he swung his hands at their feet, knocking a few of them off balance and into each other. The wet floor didn't help them either. Once he got free of their circle, he jumped to his feet, and started to run, his shower slippers allowing him to grip the wet floor and stagger away. His attackers, meanwhile, struggled to gain traction, some of them falling to the ground.

"Let him go," Konrad shouted. "We have to get out of here. If the Canadians find us out of our hut during the count, there will be hell to pay."

"He got the message," one of the others added.

When Aachen heard that, he stopped running and walked naked into the bunk area. Every single prisoner was wide awake because of the escape alarm and in the commotion no one really paid him much attention. When he finally got back to his bunk, he collapsed in it. Knowing he was safe, at least for tonight, he let the darkness take him.

20.

Aachen only got out of his bed over the next three days to piss and shit. His piss was bloody for the first day but cleared after the second. Once, he pressed his hands against his body, checking to see if there was anything broken. Nothing was. Corporal Knaup, who bunked several feet away, brought Aachen food and drink. He also covered for him during the count, telling the Canadians Aachen had relapsed into some kind of disease he had caught in North Africa. Knaup didn't specify the disease only to say it could be contagious to those who hadn't been exposed to it. A scout came the first day to double-check but didn't approach Aachen's bed. He seemed satisfied with the story and the Canadians left Aachen alone.

On the third day Knaup tried to get Aachen to leave his bunk and told him not to feel sorry for himself, but Aachen waved him away.

"Thanks for the food, Knaup, but leave me be. I need to sleep."

Knaup tried to argue further but Aachen snapped at him. "I said leave me be!" A wave of pain rolled through his body when he shouted and he fell back in his bed, groaning.

Knaup sat on the bunk across from him. "I should get the doctor. He'll help."

"Please, Knaup. No doctor. Not now. Just let me sleep and I'll be fine."

Knaup nodded and stood up. "Okay, I'll let you sleep. But if you don't get up tomorrow morning, I'm bringing Doctor Kleinjeld."

Aachen shut his eyes. He could feel Knaup still standing over him, watching him. So he pretended to fall asleep. And soon he stopped pretending.

When he awoke the next morning he felt a bit better apart from sensing that Knaup was hovering over him.

"Please, Knaup. I'm fine."

"You look like shit," Sergeant Neumann said.

Surprised, Aachen opened his eyes, a headache throbbing behind them. He moved to sit up but groaned with pain. There were yellow, black, and purple bruises all over his back, sides, and chest, as well as a rash of rope-burn around his neck and spots of dried blood on his face.

He stared at the sergeant. "I thought you were with the Canadians."

"They let me go this morning since I had nothing to offer them."

"But they put you isolation, didn't they?"

"Only for a few nights. They wanted to make a point about me not having enough information about Mueller."

"How did you sleep? Good?"

Neumann smiled. "It was glorious. The Canadians may think isolation is some kind of punishment but having my own room and my own bed to myself for the first time since I was born it seems gave me some of the greatest nights I've had in a long time. Even better than that night in Berlin before I shipped out to North Africa."

"You don't say."

"I'm telling you, boy. A night that would make your innocent mind shocked beyond all comprehension. Still, it was nothing compared to the sensational nights I had sleeping alone in the Canadians' cooler. Even with all the alarms going off the first night, it was still wonderful. If I die tomorrow, I'll be happy."

"I'm glad you had a good time off. My past few nights have not been so … entertaining."

"I can see that," Neumann said with a nod. "You better get cleaned up before this count. They're not going to buy you being too contagious for much longer. Especially due to the escape."

"Who made the run?" Aachen asked.

"I'll tell you later, but first let's get you cleaned up and dressed."

Neumann leaned forward, grabbed Aachen around the shoulders, and pulled him up to a sitting position. The corporal groaned in pain, but managed to get up. A few seconds later, the sergeant pulled him to his feet.

Aachen wavered for a moment, almost passing out, but the

sergeant hung onto him. "You're not going to throw up, are you?" Neumann asked.

"I should be fine, just get me under a shower."

"Right," Neumann said. Slowly, he guided Aachen to the latrine area. There weren't many prisoners around at the moment—most of them were at mess. The few that were left behind didn't dare say anything in front of Neumann about Aachen's condition.

"So what the hell happened to you?" Neumann asked as Aachen started to undress. The corporal moved his limbs and body gingerly, wincing in pain as he did so. While he removed the rest of his clothing, he told the sergeant about the attack in the shower and how they tried to hang him.

The sergeant whistled. "You get any looks at the men while you were fighting back?"

Aachen shook his head. "They masked their faces."

"What about their voices? You recognize any of them that way?"

"They only spoke with their fists. Except for their commander, that is. Big bastard though. Kind of like you, except meaner," Aachen said.

"I can be mean, you know."

"Not this kind of mean. This guy was a total assface. He acted like I was some kind of mouse and he was a cat who had brought me home to play with."

"But the mouse fought back, I'll bet."

"I got a few hits in. And I managed to get his name," Aachen said with a small smile forming on his face. "A

Sergeant Konrad. He's the one who replaced Heidfield as hut leader."

Neumann whistled. "Are you sure about that? We've never met this Konrad fellow."

"I made an assumption and called him Konrad," Aachen said with a shrug. "It was obvious by his reaction that I was on the mark. He didn't like that and gave me this." Aachen pointed to his split cheek.

"You didn't happen to notice anything else about them?"

"A few also had tattoos," Aachen added.

Neumann's eyes went wide. "What kind of tattoos?"

"Mostly they were SS tattoos, the blood type under the arm," Aachen said.

"That's not good," Neumann shook his head. "And some had other types of tattoos?"

Aachen nodded but waved the sergeant away when he pushed for more answers. "Please, Sergeant. Let me take a shower. I'll answer more of your questions later."

"Okay, Aachen, get yourself cleaned up. At least get the dried blood off your face. You look terrible."

Once Neumann got Aachen settled in a shower, he went back to get the corporal's uniform. By the time he had returned, Aachen was getting up from his knees, shoving one of the wooden pallets back against the wall.

"You lose something, Aachen?"

"Not me, someone else." Aachen said, opening his hand to show the sergeant the object he picked up off the shower room floor. "I believe one of them dropped it when they were beating me."

Neumann leaned closer to look at it. It was an oval piece of gold about two centimetres in width and resembling a laurel wreath. At the top of the badge was an eagle standing atop a swastika. Below the swastika was a cast of a submarine that lay across the length of the oval.

"Whoever dropped this might as well have been wearing a sign," Neumann said. He paused and then looked keenly at the corporal. "This is the other tattoo you were talking about. A sailor tattoo."

Aachen nodded.

"You know who this person is."

Aachen nodded again. "Sergeant Konrad I can understand because of the type of person he is," Aachen said. "But I did not expect it from this person. I thought he was honourable, and…" Aachen trailed off, the anger welling in his voice and face.

"Excellent. Anger and revenge are useful ways of dealing with this. Use them when you need them," Neumann said, his eyes staring straightforward. "But at the moment, let's just focus on what's going on here." Neumann stepped back after finishing the buttons on Aachen's shirt. The corporal looked exhausted and the bruise on his face would be questioned by the Canadians if they saw it. He could say he got it in a sparring match that got out of hand, and if he wrapped a handkerchief around his neck, the way many of the tank crews from North Africa did, he could hide the rope burn without looking out of place.

"Did you learn anything else while I was gone?" Neumann asked.

Aachen walked over to the sinks and then drank by cupping water in one hand. "Doctor Kleinjeld is afraid."

"Afraid? Why would you say that?"

Aachen told the sergeant about his conversation with the doctor and how Kleinjeld refused to go with him to confirm Aachen's report.

"So the man has a healthy respect of the Gestapo—nothing wrong with that."

"True, but I think there might be something else. I don't know, he just seemed a little too frightened for my taste."

"Okay, maybe you have something there. We'll file it away. Anything else?"

Aachen told Neumann about how Sergeant Heidfield just happened to run into him on the track and how he started asking about Mueller.

"Why would he care about Mueller?"

"He said he could profit from the information, although I can't figure out how that could happen."

"People will buy schnapps from Heidfield, as well as information for gambling, but I don't see why they would buy information about Mueller. It makes no sense."

"That's what I thought. That's why I told you."

"Good catch, Aachen. We'll keep that information on file as well, and a little closer to the surface than the Kleinjeld information. Heidfield may be friendly and a good supporter of the men in many ways, but he always seems to be out for himself and can't be completely trusted."

Neumann rubbed his hands together. "Okay, Klaus, I think

we're ready for this morning's count. If the Canadians ask about your face—"

"—I'll tell them it happened in a sparring match that got out of hand."

"Excellent. And good work on the doctor and Heidfield. Whether they have anything to do with Mueller's death is to be determined yet."

"So we are still investigating what happened to Captain Mueller?"

"Of course. That hasn't changed. In fact, the case has expanded into new territory."

"New territory? I don't understand. Where has the case expanded?"

"Ahh, you were mostly unconscious for the last couple of days and you have no idea what has happened."

"I do know that someone escaped. The alarm distracted my attackers, which is why I was able to get away."

"But you have no idea who escaped, do you?"

Aachen shook his head. And when Sergeant Neumann told him, Aachen almost passed out.

"Holy shit," was all he could say.

21.

Even though it was several days after the escape, there were more Canadian guards than normal during the count and they weren't in a happy mood. They kept the prisoners in formation for much longer than usual, double-, triple-, and quadruple-checking to ensure that no other prisoners had escaped. It didn't help matters that in every hut there was a group established whose job it was to harry the Canadians as they counted.

These prisoners had a variety of strategies to annoy the Canadians. They gave incorrect names when asked, pretended they couldn't speak English, and moved around in their lines, appearing at another location in the group after they were already counted. And since the Canadians were already frustrated because of the escape, these prisoners put a little more into their efforts.

So when a guard walked past Aachen during the count, he

gave a hard stare at the injury on the corporal's face, the spot where he was struck by the hangman's fist.

"What the hell happened to you?" the Canadian asked, looking at his clipboard. "Says here you were sick the last few days, but looks like it was something else." This guard was smaller than most, only an inch or two taller than Aachen. He also seemed older, somewhere in his mid-fifties rather than mid-forties, which was the average age for a Veterans Guard. Still, the Canadian looked tough, his nose bent at several angles as if it had been broken many times. One of his eyes seemed to be made of glass, his hands had scars all over the knuckles and backs, and both his ears looked like tiny pieces of cauliflower.

Aachen looked confused for a moment, and then looked at Neumann. The sergeant leaned over to speak for him.

"My colleague was training and got injured when one of sparring matches got out of hand," Neumann said in English.

"He looks like he got the shit beat out of him, if you ask me," the guard said, checking off his count on his clipboard. "What kind of match was he training for?"

"My colleague is a wrestler. He has an upcoming match in the next few days. Very important, but then the training got out of hand."

"Yeah, you said that." The Canadian leaned left and right to look at Aachen's ears. They too were like cauliflowers, but not as pronounced as the older guard's. "Okay, you're a wrestler all right, I can tell by the ears, but that's not a wrestling injury by a long shot. Don't bullshit a bullshitter. What really happened to him?"

"Well, when I mean the sparring match got out of hand, I

mean my colleague was training with someone he had beaten earlier and this person was still angry about that. So during the training, he struck my colleague here. No harm done, though."

"Looks like plenty of harm done to me. You sure you don't want to file some kind of complaint?"

"No, no," said Neumann. "No complaint is necessary. We wish to file nothing."

"Gonna handle it yourself?"

Neumann and Aachen said nothing, so after a moment, the Canadian shook his head. "Okay, if you're not going to file a complaint, I can do nothing for you. However, I would recommend he get that checked out."

"Yes sir, we are going to the doctor's right after the count. Thank you for your concern."

"Fuck off with the niceties, Fritz, I work for a living," the Canadian said sharply. Then he tapped his clipboard on Aachen's chest and lowered his voice. "And if you are going to handle it yourselves, don't go overboard. Just give him back what he gave you and leave it at that, you hear me? And next time, don't have someone lie about you being sick or I'll stick all of you in the cooler for two weeks."

Neumann nodded. Aachen as well. Even though he didn't understand English, he got the gist of what was said and knew a nod was expected. The Canadian continued on with his count. By the time the prisoner tally ended for Neumann and Aachen's hut, they were an hour late for their time at breakfast. And though they could still get fed, Neumann suggested they skip it. Considering the identity of the prisoner who had escaped that night, Aachen was highly inclined to agree.

Aachen made to move towards the legionnaire hut because he assumed that's where the sergeant wanted to go but Neumann held him. Instead, they made their way out of the barracks towards the fence and the path that encircled the interior perimeter of the camp.

"Is this really necessary, Sergeant?" Aachen asked.

"I just want to see," replied Neumann.

"The Canadians will have the holes in the wire repaired already."

"I am quite aware of that but I just want to see where he escaped."

Aachen sighed but walked beside the sergeant as they made their way around the track. It was a bright, beautiful day, the sun shining in a sky of blue that stretched on seemingly forever. Light clouds drifted here and there and even the wind decided to take a break today. Yet, due to the escape four nights ago, most of the German prisoners remained inside after their counts, in or near their bunks, at the mess, or in workshops and classrooms. There were only a few who walked about as well as a couple of groups playing a game of football at one of the makeshift fields.

Most of the people outside were Canadians. Patrols on the outside of the wire had doubled and the scouts roaming around the camp now patrolled in groups of two or three, rather than by themselves. Germans who were found outside were questioned repeatedly, sometimes in a belligerent manner. The escape had angered the Canadians and pissed off Canadians were very unpleasant folks to deal with.

Neumann and Aachen were stopped by guards a number of times, questioned, and then released when they explained that they were only out walking the trail for exercise. Deliberately, they did not stop, nor even slow their pace at the point where the wire had been cut. They did however turn and look at the scene. As Aachen guessed, the fence had been repaired with new wire. There was a small group of Canadian guards gathered on the outside of the fence by the repair. They glowered at Neumann and Aachen as the two passed by.

About twenty metres from where the hole had been cut in the fence, the sergeant made a small hum in his throat.

"You noticed something, Sergeant?" Aachen asked.

"I'm not sure. Obviously this was the location of the escape but something about it bothers me," said Neumann.

"The escapee?"

"Yes, that bothers me, of course. But there's something else. Something about the landscape around where he escaped."

"It's nothing but an empty, open field. A seemingly endless open field."

"That's the problem. There's really nothing out there in that field, absolutely nothing. So why haven't they caught him already? It's been three days; he should have been found by now. They should have found him a couple of hours after the sun rose the day after he escaped. His trail would have been plain to see. And there really is nowhere to hide," said Neumann, stroking his chin.

Aachen nodded. "He must have gotten far in that short time and then headed for more suitable hiding ground."

"But there really isn't anything in the way of suitable hiding ground. That's why they built the camp where it is. And if he headed into the town, someone would have spotted him immediately and reported him."

"Need I remind you that other soldiers have snuck into town before, Sergeant? And they weren't reported."

"But those soldiers worked outside the camp and just snuck away from their work farms to go see a movie as a lark. They didn't really escape and there wasn't an alarm that woke the entire area. If any one of us was seen in town, even one of the outside workers, we would have been reported. As I said, by all accounts he should have been caught by now."

"Unless someone helped him," Aachen said. "And is still helping him."

"That exact thought crossed my mind," the sergeant said. "Too many questions, too many coincidences. Time to get some answers."

22.

Neumann and Aachen both made their way to the hut where the legionnaires bunked and pushed their way in. Instead of the usual two legionnaire guards at the door, there were four including the two Neumann had dealt with before.

The sergeant held a hand up at the men as they approached. "Gentlemen, you know why I'm here and instead of acting all provocative and protective, just find Colonel Ehrhoff and tell him I wish to talk to him," he said. "We don't want any repeats of what happened last time, do we? That was an unpleasant experience for some of you and with Corporal Aachen by my side, I'm pretty sure the repeat experience would be even more unpleasant."

Hans, one of the men Neumann had bested the other time he was here, gritted his teeth and clenched his fists, moving to step forward. But Philip, who also had been in on the fight, placed his hand on the chest of his partner, holding him back.

"Go find the colonel. Tell him who is here," Philip told Hans.

Hans looked at his partner for a second, shook his head, and grunted.

"Go," Philip said, this time in French. "And go fast before I beat you."

Hans paused, spat in the direction of Neumann and Aachen, and then stormed away. A few minutes later, Colonel Ehrhoff, dressed in the same Bedouin style as before, walked into the room. The guards parted to let him by.

"Sergeant Neumann. Why am I not surprised to see you? Although I heard that you were being held by the Canadians."

"They let me go after a couple of nights. They wanted to make a point to me about something, but I wasn't sure what it was. All I know is that the first good sleep I've had in a very, very long time was interrupted by one of your men escaping the camp in the middle of the night."

"Yes, Legionnaire Pohlmann."

"Who just happens to be the very man I chased in here four days ago. The very man who ran from the scene where Captain Mueller was found. The very man you agreed to let me talk to. And now he's escaped. I find that highly coincidental."

Ehrhoff sighed. "Yes, that is troubling isn't it? Not just for you but for us as well."

"Then, hopefully, we can talk about it."

Ehrhoff rubbed his face and then nodded. "Of course, Sergeant Neumann, we should talk about it. But not here. I know a better and more pleasant place where we can speak in private."

"As long as that private place doesn't involve a quiet, yet hard discussion with your men here."

Ehrhoff laughed and shook his head. "You are one of a kind, Sergeant Neumann. Before I met you, I thought I would hate you, considering your position in the camp. But in reality, you seem to be an honourable man. As I said before, I am sure you would have made a great legionnaire."

"Again, I'll take that as a compliment, but it doesn't answer my question."

Ehrhoff stepped forward and put his arm around Neumann like an old friend. "One thing I learned during my time in the Legion, more so than during the First War, was the concept of honour. And not just from my fellow legionnaires. The Bedouins, you know, have great honour. They live and breathe it every day, a code of honour so deep and complicated, entrenched in their community for thousands of years, that it is difficult for an outsider like me to even begin to comprehend the intricacies. One day, you do something considered to be an act of great integrity, and then the next day, the same act is an insult. It's very complicated, and has much to do with who you are dealing with, the time of day it is, the weather at the time, the season perhaps, even the location you are in. I still cannot comprehend most of it."

"Yes, that is very interesting," Neumann said, his voice dry. "But you still haven't answered my question."

"I am, Sergeant Neumann, in my own way." If Ehrhoff was annoyed with Neumann's sarcasm, he didn't show it. "You see, there is one aspect of Bedouin honour that is not open to interpretation. It is sacrosanct to them and even to an outsider meeting them for the first time it is obvious. To the Bedouin, there is no greater person in the world than a guest. If they invite someone into their tent or oasis as a guest, that guest and his compatriots are the most important persons in that tent. Nothing comes before a guest. A Bedouin would give their own lives to protect a guest in their tent, even if that guest is an enemy."

"That's a nice sociological lesson, but what does that have to do with this situation?"

"As you can tell by my dress, many of us in the Legion, especially those of us serving in Africa, like to emulate the Bedouins. So please, Sergeant Neumann, I invite you and young Corporal Aachen into my tent as my guest. We will drink tea, eat some good food, and talk."

"I could do without that food and drink and more with that talk."

"Of course, based on what happened four nights ago, we have much to talk about."

23.

The legionnaire hut was no different than any other hut in the camp. Soldiers sat on their bunks alone or in groups doing things that soldiers do in a military camp when they have nothing to do. They read, they slept, they smoked, they wrote, either letters home or in a journal, they tended to their uniforms, and they played various games, some for money. In short, they were all bored out of their minds and the appearance of two non-legionnaires, especially ones as well-known as Neumann and Aachen, passing through their hut was the high point of their day. Even though Ehrhoff called Neumann and Aachen guests of his metaphorical tent, it was obvious from the dark looks they got from many of legionnaires that they were not welcome.

That lack of welcome was also evidenced by the fact that as they followed Colonel Ehrhoff, they were closely flanked by Hans, Philip, and two other guards.

The one difference Neumann and Aachen both noticed about the legionnaire hut was how orderly and clean it was. There was an effort by the camp command to ensure that the Germans kept their living areas clean and tidy, as if they were in a military base in the Reich. But standards were more lax in the camp as prisoners resigned themselves to never seeing battle again.

The legionnaires didn't seem to have that resignation; they were still in military mode despite being held prisoner. Every bunk was made, every soldier's area pristine and ready for inspection. It seemed that they were ready to fight at any time. And that was probably true. After this war was over, it was highly probable that almost all of these soldiers wouldn't go home to their families like everyone else in the camp; as legionnaires, they would fight somewhere else.

At the end of the line of bunks, Neumann and Aachen spotted something that made them stop. Several of the bunks had been removed and in their place someone had set up a tent of sorts. It was made from what looked to be a series of sheets and blankets, the linens the Canadians gave each prisoners for their beds, sewn together to make a single huge piece of fabric. It hung like an Arabian tent from hooks in the ceiling and walls, draping onto floor.

Ehrhoff reached the entrance of the tent and then turned to Neumann and Aachen. The two stared at the tent, their faces incredulous with surprise. Ehrhoff saw their looks and smiled.

"Wonderful, isn't it? And I'll bet when I invited you to be a guest of my tent, you weren't expecting an actual tent."

Ehrhoff pulled the flap to open the entrance and waved at the two men to enter. "Please, as I said, be my guest."

Neumann looked at Aachen, shrugged, and entered the tent. Aachen went after him, followed by Ehrhoff and then his group of four guards.

The floor of the tent was covered by a carpet made out of blankets sewn together. A series of bunk mattresses and pillows were placed in a circle to make a seating area and in the middle of this seating area were two round tables, one with plates of cheeses, breads, and dried fruits, the other with an electric kettle, a teapot, and several cups that had been taken from one of the messes.

Ehrhoff moved to take the seat directly across from the entrance and gestured for Neumann and Aachen to sit near him, just off to the side. Again, Neumann shrugged and took a seat.

Since the other legionnaires chose to stand in strategic positions around the tent, Aachen opted to stand as well, behind Sergeant Neumann. If Ehrhoff found this unusual, he didn't give any indication.

He poured some hot water from the kettle into the teapot, waited a few moments, and then held the teapot and a cup towards Sergeant Neumann.

"Tea, Sergeant? It's not the best, but since the Canadians are descended from the English, it's not bad."

Neumann waved a hand to refuse. "I'm fine, thank you."

"Then some cheese or bread perhaps. You arrived here very shortly after the count, indicating that you haven't had breakfast, so please help yourself."

"No, nothing for me."

"Perhaps Corporal Aachen?"

"Aachen is fine. Thank you, Colonel."

"Please, Sergeant, indulge me. Have something to eat. Drink some tea. It's considered quite traditional in the Bedouin culture for guests to partake in tea and something to eat and then slowly ease into conversation."

"But I am not a Bedouin. And with all due respect, Colonel Ehrhoff, neither are you. We're Germans, Germans who may serve in completely different battalions with completely different traditions, possibly even values, but we're still Germans nonetheless. And all these trappings that you have and these so-called Bedouin customs you seem to have a deep affection for will not change that. So as a German who has little time on his hands and many things do today, I most respectfully request that we get on with this shit as quickly as possible."

Ehrhoff frowned. "You disappoint me, Sergeant Neumann," he said pouring himself a cup of tea. "I thought you would be a man of culture and appreciate some of the ceremony in a life such as this."

"I'm sorry if you thought so, Colonel Ehrhoff, but as another sergeant told me today, a Canadian one at that, 'Fuck off with the niceties, Fritz, I work for a living.'"

"These Canadians are so young as a country, they lack any culture to speak off," said Ehrhoff.

"They may lack culture but I faced many Canadians in the First World War and for a country so young they're fucking tough bastards. I guess you have to be tough bastards to live in a country like this with a land that seems to never end. And based on what I saw in North Africa, I'm betting your precious Bedouins are also tough bastards. So am I, as a matter of fact. You, too, Colonel, so, with all due respect, can we just cut all this bullshit and talk about Pohlmann?"

The legionnaire guards did not try to disguise the sour looks on their faces at this remark, but Ehrhoff showed no outward emotion towards them. He just drank his tea and chewed on his bread. After the colonel swallowed, he gestured to Neumann, the way a lord would gesture to a steward who wanted to discuss some monotonous detail.

"As you wish, Sergeant Neumann. Get on with it. Ask your questions, but be advised before you start that I may not answer all of them."

"I hope you'll do your best, sir."

"Please just proceed."

"There are plenty of questions, but it all pretty much comes down to one: Why did Pohlmann escape?"

Ehrhoff drank more tea and shrugged. "I have no idea. There are many reasons for people to escape from here, you know that."

"But not all those people were seen running from the scene with Captain Mueller and then asked to speak to me about it. You did ask him to speak to me, did you not, Colonel?"

"Of course I did. I found Pohlmann later that day, told him about your request, and told him to satisfy that request."

"You told him or ordered him?"

"Since I'm a colonel and he's a corporal, anything I tell him to do is an order."

"But was that obvious to him?"

"I have no idea what a soldier like Pohlmann thinks but in the Legion, when a superior officer tells you to do something, it's always an order, never a request. At no time does a Legion officer have to say 'that's an order' to a subordinate because it's always an order."

"So Pohlmann knew he had no choice but to talk to me? Knew he would be disobeying orders if he did not?"

"And he knew that we take a dim view on disobedience in the Legion."

"What about desertion? What's the Legion view on desertion?"

"Same as most military during a time of war. Death, usually being shot on the spot."

"So in the view of the Legion, has Pohlmann deserted?"

"At the moment, we have no idea. Pohlmann's act could be seen by some as taking initiative and causing difficulty for the enemy. If he is returned, we will probably call a tribunal of sorts and determine the matter."

"So was Pohlmann acting on his own initiative or was this part of a plan to disrupt the Canadians?"

"As you may know, Sergeant Neumann, we legionnaires do have our own escape committee but we usually work in conjunction with the overall camp escape committee, coordinating actions so we don't end up at cross purposes. It would be embarrassing for both sides if we started a tunnel without informing the camp committee and then ran into one of their tunnels while digging our own."

"So was your committee aware of Pohlmann's escape? Was it part of the committee's plan?"

"It was not," Ehrhoff said after a pause. "Pohlmann escaped of his own volition."

"And don't you find that highly coincidental that he did so not long after you ordered him to talk to me about the Mueller situation?"

"No doubt he was afraid of you. Like I've said before, you are a very formidable man, Sergeant Neumann, not just in size, but in presence. Also the way you handled Hans and Philip four days ago was most impressive, considering your age. Word about that scuffle has spread throughout our hut, much to the chagrin of Hans and Philip. The word is that you are not a man to be trifled with, and that you get your own way, no matter the obstacles in front of you. It's quite plain that Pohlmann was afraid of you."

"Afraid that I would accuse him of murdering Captain Mueller?"

"Pohlmann did not murder Captain Mueller. He does not have it in him."

"You've said that before, Colonel. Many people have said that about many murderers before and have been completely mistaken."

"I am not mistaken about Pohlmann."

"Tell me why."

"I would rather not."

"Please, Colonel Ehrhoff. Why are you not mistaken about Pohlmann? Why is he not a murderer?"

Ehrhoff sighed and poured himself more tea. As he did, he

gestured for Neumann to lean closer. "Because Pohlmann is a coward."

"Cowardice is not a good defence for murderers. Cowards are sometimes the best murderers because they are unable to face up to situations and instead kill to protect themselves."

"Maybe I misspoke, then. Pohlmann's very good at following orders, able to keep up in training, but in battle he only does enough to not be considered a shirker. He was always the last one to come out from cover and when he was put on point, he always had some type of injury."

"That's not a coward," said Neumann. "That's a smart man."

"Quite, but his lack of warrior spirit was why he was put into administration, pushing paper, filing files—important duties no doubt, but less so than fighting on the battlefield."

"Based on that, it doesn't seem like Pohlmann is the kind of soldier who would take it upon himself to escape from this camp in order to disrupt the Canadians. It looks like he did so because of something else. Because of fear."

"You wanted to talk to him and as I said, I'm pretty sure that would make him fearful."

"But, as you said, he's not the kind of person who does well on the battlefield. The way Captain Mueller was killed … it would take someone who is used to that kind of violence, used to seeing it and committing it. And in any case," Neumann looked at Aachen who was staring at the wall ahead of him, trying not to look too interested in the conversation the way a good adjutant should, "an attempt at murder, similar to the way Mueller was killed, was made a few nights ago, and there is no way Pohlmann could have been involved because it seems he was escaping at the time.

"So even if he was afraid of me, there is probably no doubt that I would find him innocent of the crime, given what you have told me. So what else is Pohlmann afraid of?"

Ehrhoff shrugged.

"Come on, Colonel Ehrhoff. You seem to understand your men, care about them in many ways, even those you call cowards like Pohlmann. Surely you might have some idea."

"I care about my men, Sergeant Neumann, because when you become a legionnaire, you pledge to give your life to the Legion and your fellow legionnaires. La mort qui nous oublie si peu. Nous, la Légion. But in this time, during this war, it's been difficult to know where our loyalties as legionnaires stand. To the allies, we are Germans, no matter whose army we serve. And when Rommel came to North Africa, he asked many of us to fight for him, saying that since Germany ruled France through Vichy, we were in fact part of his army. And many of us did join him because we were able to fight for both our loyalties. Many of our Legion commanders said it was our duty to do so. On the other hand, there were those who said we should fight for the Free French, and help to overthrow the oppressive Nazi government. Hence, in several battles of this war, you had legionnaires fighting against legionnaires. But in the end, once this war is over, we will all fight for the Legion again, because in the end, the Legion is our lives. This is just a temporary moment."

Ehrhoff sighed and drank some tea before continuing. "But it is still confusing," he said, his voice softening. "There are those legionnaires who don't understand this lifelong pledge and wish to integrate fully into the German military and forget about the Legion, to pretend that since they fought for Germany in German uniforms, their time in the Legion is done."

"What will happen to them?"

"If they haven't completed their tour of duty in the Legion, they are deserters."

"Like Pohlmann."

"We haven't decided on Pohlmann. If he returns, we'll make that decision."

"So if escape could brand him a deserter," Neumann clarified, "he must have had a good reason to escape."

"Like I said, he was probably afraid of you."

"Yes, he probably was, but in the end, I wouldn't have found him guilty of murder. So he would have been let go. There is something else he was afraid of, possibly someone else."

"Maybe he witnessed who killed Mueller?" offered Ehrhoff.

Neumann raised his eyebrows. "A fascinating possibility, but there might be something else. Please, Colonel Ehrhoff, despite my earlier impatience, I appreciate your assistance in this. But I have one more question: what did Pohlmann do in North Africa?"

"He was involved in troop movements, keeping track of the Legion liaison group. The group's job was to determine which legionnaires were serving with the Germans where and when so that their time with the Germans would count as time served and to ensure that they would get paid or honoured by the Legion in case they were killed, wounded, or captured."

"So Pohlmann would know who all the legionnaires were who served in the Wehrmacht, even those who did not wish to be legionnaires again."

Ehrhoff nodded.

Neumann quickly stood up to attention and saluted Ehrhoff. He then offered his thanks and left the tent, quickly followed by Aachen and the group of guards. Ehrhoff stayed in his tent and drank his tea.

24.

Neumann and Aachen left the legionnaire hut and headed east. As per usual Neumann led the way. The two weaved their way between the barracks. When they came around the corner of one, they ran into a group of Canadian gophers. This squad of Veterans Guards were given the duty of searching for tunnels in the camp. If they found any, they were also tasked with searching these tunnels for any prisoner or contraband as well as destroying the tunnels once their searches were completed.

This group of gophers numbered four and it seemed they had found a tunnel underneath one of the barracks. One of the Canadians grabbed a flashlight from a pack and looked to be heading into what appeared to be a narrow hole. They all turned to look at Neumann and Aachen as they came around the corner.

The two Germans continued on their way, ignoring the

Canadians. The gophers watched them for a moment and then turned back to their work once they realized Neumann and Aachen had nothing to do with the tunnel.

Neumann and Aachen doubled-back, heading away from the gophers before turning back in a northwesterly direction.

They found General Horcoff in his garden. They followed the same procedure of getting his attention and greeting him, a cough followed by salutes.

Horcoff wiped his spade on his pant leg and gave the sergeant the kind of greeting an aristocrat would give to a favoured servant; he grabbed him by the shoulders and gave him a friendly shake.

"Sergeant Neumann, my good man. It's good to see you again. The Canadians treated you well?"

"They did, sir. They gave me my own place to sleep in for a few days. Very quiet, very soothing."

"I hope you are joking, Sergeant. I don't think isolation would be very pleasant."

"For a long period of time, I agree it wouldn't be, but for the time I was there, it was actually quite pleasant. I had the whole place to myself. No one to give me orders, no Corporal Aachen to follow me around and ask me questions."

"Don't be so cocky, Sergeant Neumann," Horcoff said with a smile and waggling a finger. "Without order there is only chaos. And without Corporal Aachen, I'm quite sure you would be lost." Horcoff looked at Aachen and when he saw the large bruise and cut on his face, he frowned.

"Looks like Aachen was a little lost without you, Sergeant. If he was a normal soldier I would give him a dressing down for brawling but Aachen isn't the brawling type. What the hell happened to you, Corporal?"

Aachen tried to find the words to explain what had happened to him but couldn't. He stammered for a moment until Neumann came to his rescue.

"The night the Canadians took me in their custody, Corporal Aachen was set up in the shower by a gang of masked thugs. They beat him and then tried to hang him."

"What!? That's preposterous! I find that hard to believe. Aachen is one of the toughest men I know. No ordinary gang of thugs could take him on. Am I right, Aachen?"

Aachen flushed, but he remained silent.

"They weren't your ordinary gang of thugs, General Horcoff," Neumann said, trying to prevent the general from directly interacting with Aachen. "Corporal Aachen said they were experts. They wore him down over time and almost had him hanged and dead. Fortunately, he kept his cool, found a brief moment to act, and did so, breaking free of the noose."

"Of course he did. I told you no one gets the better of Aachen."

"But of course he did get a bit lucky. If it wasn't for the alarm that night, they would have succeeded in hanging him."

"Good for him," Horcoff said, turning to face Aachen. "Good for you, Aachen. I would hate to have to write a letter to your mother explaining how you died if these cowards got the better of you. Cowards, that's what they are. Wearing masks! I dare say, what kind of German soldier wears a mask?"

Horcoff thought of something and tapped his spade against

his leg. "Well maybe they were not Germans. Maybe they were Canadians who decided to take some revenge on you by targeting your corporal here."

"While I'd like to believe most Germans are honourable men, the Canadians didn't attack Aachen. That's not really their style is it?"

"Well it's not really the German style either, is it, Sergeant? Despite what some may think, I believe we have fought this war in a honourable fashion."

"I wish I had your confidence in the Fatherland, General Horcoff, but to be honest, there are some Germans who do not behave honourably. And based on what Corporal Aachen told me, the people who attacked him, at least some of them, are easily identified as Germans."

"How do you mean? You said Aachen told you they were wearing masks didn't you?" He turned to Aachen. "They were wearing masks, is that correct, Corporal?" the general demanded. "Didn't you say that they were wearing masks?"

Aachen nodded.

"So how could you tell they were Germans?"

Aachen said nothing, but Neumann spoke. "They did speak German, General."

"Many Canadians can speak German. I've talked to some of them myself. Excellent German, too. Sometimes even better than the German I hear in certain parts of the camp. So how they spoke tells us nothing. And I hope that's not the only evidence you're basing your assumption on, Corporal Aachen. I mean, I'm terribly sorry about what happened to you, but you can't just make false accusations about these attackers being German just because of the language they speak, you have to have more to go on—"

"—they had tattoos, General!" Aachen barked in frustration. "They had goddamn tattoos."

The general froze in surprise, not just at the tone of Aachen's speech, but at the words he said. Horcoff looked at Aachen for a second, then turned to Neumann. Sighing, he dropped his spade on the ground. He looked about for it for several seconds, found it, but decided to leave it there. "You are sure about this?" he asked in a quiet voice.

"Very sure."

"I mean Corporal Aachen, Sergeant. I know you are trying to protect your subordinate but I need to know from him if this is true."

"It is true, General," Aachen said. "I could recite to you the blood types I saw on the arms of these men. I also noted many scars and birthmarks on the bodies because while they were masked, they had stripped to the waist. We may have identified one as a submariner although Sergeant Neumann is quite sure there is no direct action from them as a group. Possibly a rogue sailor."

"This is good information that you can use for your investigation," Horcoff said. "And am I right in assuming that you consider these thugs to be the same ones that killed Captain Mueller?"

"Mueller was beaten and hanged, the same way Aachen was," Neumann said. "Quite simply, Mueller did not fight back as strongly as the young corporal here, hence the fact that he is dead and Aachen is not. Aachen was also lucky the alarm went off to distract them."

"There you go. But considering what you said about these men's tattoos, dealing with this will prove to be very delicate," Horcoff said. He started picking the heads off some of the flowers of his plants, slowly, one at time. "Very delicate indeed."

"And more suited to the work of a general than a lowly sergeant. Your hand would be more delicate in these matters, sir."

"Yes, I believe you are correct on this," Horcoff said, still picking the flowers and tossing them aside. "However, even with my delicate hand it's not going to be easy. Things are changing in this camp, especially since the invasion. Certain people are concerned with a so-called lack of discipline in the camp and diminished enthusiasm towards the German war effort, given our recent setbacks. There's been talk of clamping down on traitors, which is probably why Captain Mueller was killed. Because of his Bolshevik leanings, he was probably set upon and used as an example to others who may have been speaking out against the war effort."

"That is a good theory, General, one that could stand if we find the people who did this." Neumann stepped back, touched some of the plants in the garden and then brought his hand to his face to smell the aroma. "But that doesn't explain the legionnaire and his involvement."

Horcoff was so taken aback by that statement that he accidentally crushed one of the plants he was delicately trying to remove the flower from. He pulled the plant out of his hand and tossed it on the ground. He blinked several times, confusion on his face. "Legionnaires? What do the legionnaires have to do with this? Despite their mixed loyalties, they don't seem like the kind to beat and hang men. Besides, these men who attacked Aachen had SS tattoos. There is no way the SS would let in anyone who had the slightest connection to the Legion."

"That's where it gets confusing, General," said Neumann. "As you know, there was an escape a few nights ago. And the man who escaped was a legionnaire, which is nothing in and of itself except that while Aachen, myself, and Dr. Kleinjeld were in the classroom with Mueller's body trying to conduct a forensic investigation, we stumbled upon this soldier, who proceeded to flee. We chased him down, following him to the legionnaire hut where he disappeared. Fortunately, after a bit of a tussle, I managed to have a conversation with a Colonel Ehrhoff who—"

"—Ehrhoff? You talked to Colonel Ehrhoff? How is that possible?" the general said with surprise.

Neumann paused and gave the general a quizzical look. Horcoff's face was white, his eyes wide. "Are you okay, General? You look like you've overexerted yourself? Or maybe you've seen a ghost? Are you sure you don't want to sit down? Maybe some water. Aachen get the general some water."

Corporal Aachen turned to find some water but the general called him back. "No, no, I'm fine," the general said, shaking his head and gaining some of his composure. "Are you sure you said it was Colonel Ehrhoff? The legionnaire you talked to?"

"Yes, that was the name he gave me. Strange man."

"What did he look like?"

Neumann described the man, and soon the general nodded. His mind seemed to be somewhere else. "Yes, that's him," he said in an offhand way.

"Do you know the man, General?" Neumann asked.

"Vaguely, only vaguely," Horcoff said with a wave. "I knew of him in North Africa. He was the commander of a battalion of infantry and tanks and a number of times we had to coordinate our actions. Good commander—he knew how to move easily through the desert, which is one reason why Rommel used the German legionnaires. They knew the terrain, knew the people, and more importantly, knew how to survive in that climate. Although I had heard he was killed in action in Wadi Akarit, which is why I reacted the way I did."

"Well, I'm glad to be the bearer of good news, General. You should visit him," suggested Neumann.

"No reason for that. I didn't know him well enough and old commanders don't like to talk about the battles they've lost. Too maudlin for my liking. I'd rather just stay with my garden. But this legionnaire you were chasing, did you catch him?"

"No sir, we did not. And that's why I mentioned it. The man we were chasing was the same man who escaped, which I find a little too coincidental for my liking, especially since I had arranged with Colonel Ehrhoff to interview this man."

"He probably thought you were going to accuse him of murdering Captain Mueller and decided to flee."

"Possibly, but I specifically told Colonel Ehrhoff that I only wanted to question him, and that I wouldn't really look at him as a suspect until I had a chance to talk to him."

General Horcoff placed a hand on Neumann's shoulder and gave him a couple of friendly slaps. "Listen, Sergeant Neumann, I think you're reading too much into this legionnaire thing. Obviously, the man thought you were going to accuse him, thought he would be used as some type of scapegoat, thought he would be charged and then found guilty of Mueller's death, which would not be quite as impossible as it seems, given the situation facing the camp at this time."

"I would never do such a thing, General. It is my job to look at all the facts and determine the truth. I have never in my life brought someone to trial if I didn't have all the evidence pointing at that person."

"That's because you're an honourable man, Sergeant," said the general. "But you yourself said there are some in this camp who aren't so honourable, the kind who would wear masks to attack someone like Corporal Aachen and use this poor legionnaire as a whipping boy. So I would forget this legionnaire if I were you."

"I would like to interview this man when the Canadians bring him back."

"Yes, yes, talk to this man if you must," the general said, somewhat impatiently. "However, if he is caught, there's a good chance they may not bring him back here, especially if he gets far enough away; they may just transfer him to the closest camp to where he is captured. And if they do bring him back, he'll be in isolation for a long time. Either way, it's a dead end, Sergeant, so I would highly suggest that you focus your efforts on the people who attacked Corporal Aachen. Based on what you said about the attack, it sounds very similar to what happened to

Captain Mueller. However, that may become a dead end as well, considering who was involved in this. So like I said before, you will have to tread carefully in this. And, like with this legionnaire, you may have to discontinue your investigation for your own good."

25.

Neumann led Aachen back to the barracks. Along the way, he found Corporal Knaup as well as seven other Wehrmacht soldiers from their company back in North Africa and bade them to come with him.

Most of them were big men, soldiers who had fought hard in the desert. And since they all knew the sergeant from North Africa, they immediately dropped what they were doing and followed.

He took them into their hut, gathering them into a circle by his bunk. "Gentlemen, thanks for coming when I asked. I know it's been awhile since we've had any kind of assignment so I appreciate your attention. I need you all to get your dress uniforms from your bunk. Clean them up, polish your buttons, shine your boots. You have one hour."

The men looked at each other, confused. "I said you have one hour," Neumann barked. "Go."

The men scrambled away. All except Aachen who sat on his bunk. "Where are we going, Sergeant Neumann?"

"You are going nowhere, Corporal Aachen."

"I insist, Sergeant. You haven't undertaken a mission without me backing you up. I'm not going to let that start now."

"You are part of this mission, Corporal, just not this section. I need you to wait for me in a detention room. Have it ready for an interrogation."

Aachen shook his head. "They aren't going to like it, you know that."

"That's why I'm bringing a group of well-dressed Wehrmacht soldiers to help me. I'm going to make an impression." Neumann pulled out his duffel bag and started to dig through it for his dress uniform, medals, and boots. When he found the items he needed, he threw them on the bed next to Aachen.

"You're going to start another war, you know that," Aachen said, sitting up to get out of the way of the gear flying his way.

"Actually, I'm just doing the job I was assigned to do." Neumann pulled out a pair of boots, tossed one boot on the bed and then dug into the other one.

"They won't see it that way," Aachen said.

A second later Neumann pulled out a sock, reached into it, and pulled out an impressive medal collection. He casually tossed it onto the bed. "Listen, Aachen, I appreciate your concern but have faith that I know what I'm doing."

"But Sergeant—"

"—Enough," Neumann shouted cutting Aachen off. "If I stand here arguing all day with you, I won't have time to be ready. Remember I only gave those men an hour. So just go get a detention room for me and prepare it for an interview."

Aachen picked up one of the boots from the bed and started to look around for a rag. "I'll help you, Sergeant."

"There's no need for that, Aachen. I can dress myself in my pretty uniform. I've been a soldier long before you were born."

Aachen found a rag and spat on the sergeant's boot. He started rubbing. "True. But you were always slow, Sergeant. If I don't help you, you'll never be ready in time."

Neumann opened his mouth with a retort, but held it back. He let Aachen spit-shine the boots while he polished his medals.

Less than an hour later, Neumann was ready and dressed in his uniform. Aachen offered the sergeant his hat. Neumann took it, tucked it under his arm, and stood up straight. "How do I look?"

Aachen reached over and adjusted the Cross around Neumann's neck. Then he stood back and nodded. "Excellent, Sergeant," he said with a salute. "I barely recognize you. You almost look like someone I should follow into battle."

"Enough with the smart talk, Aachen," the sergeant growled. "Just go set up for the interrogation. If all goes well, we should be there in about twenty minutes."

"And if all doesn't go well?"

"When have my plans ever not gone well?"

"Your plans are always well-thought-out but the enemy never seems to take that into consideration."

"We are not dealing with the enemy here, Aachen. You know that?"

248

"Even so, be ready to improvise, Sergeant."

"Your input has been noted. Now go. Get the room ready for me."

Aachen again saluted, smiled at the sergeant, and walked out of the hut.

Not long after, all the other men had arrived. Neumann smiled when he saw them. They were dressed wonderfully, like real soldiers. He nodded at each one of them when they came into the area. He then asked them to line up in formation near the bunks.

"Thank you all for coming when I asked. And thank you for being so effecient. It is a great honour to see you dressed in this way."

The men beamed, pushing their chests out farther as they stood at attention.

"I have an important reason for asking you to do this. I have to question a person about a matter that has occurred in this camp. Unfortunately, there is the possibility that this person will not come quietly—or his superiors will not allow him to come with me. But do not be mistaken, I am not using you gentlemen as a show of strength, but as a show of respect. The people that this man serves are good German soldiers, honourable German soldiers, and should be treated as such. Like you, they have done a great service to the Fatherland in some very trying conditions that even I myself would find horrendous. So that is why I am approaching them in this way: to show respect.

"And I expect all of you to show the same respect. To honour these men as fellow Germans, fellow comrades in battle. And hopefully, through this show of respect, they may see to our request. Do you understand me?"

The soldiers snapped their heels together as one. They also spoke as one, shouting "Yes, Sergeant" in clear, strong voices.

"Good. Now we are going to make our way across the camp in two lines of two. Of course, our dress and demeanour will attract much attention."

"No shit," said one. A couple of the men chuckled at that, but then they quickly caught themselves and snapped back to attention.

"No, no. That is true. We are going to be as obvious as Frenchmen firing back. So once we step outside and start moving, I want you to act like you are on parade. In fact, imagine you are on parade for the Führer. Somewhere out there the Führer is watching and if you make just one simple misstep or glance slightly left or right, he will see you and you will have brought disgrace on yourself and your family. Do you understand?"

"Yes, Sergeant," the men barked at once.

"I asked you if you understood," the sergeant yelled in the voice he used to shout at recruits.

"Yes, Sergeant!" the men shouted again, their voices ringing off the rafters.

Neumann walked up the line, inspecting the men, adjusting certain things about them: a medal here, a belt there. When he came to Corporal Knaup, he stopped. He eyeballed the corporal, but Knaup did not budge, did not follow the sergeant or react to his gaze. Neumann placed a hand on Knaup's shoulder and squeezed it. "Good man, Knaup. You've done some great work for me recently. And along with this, I won't forget it."

Knaup blushed but still didn't break. Neumann nodded and then stepped back. "Okay, let's go." He led them out into the camp.

26.

The appearance of Wehrmacht soldiers marching in dress uniforms led by Sergeant Neumann, who had all his medals on
his chest, shining in the Canadian sunlight, attracted the attention of the other prisoners almost immediately.

They acted like children seeing a circus coming to town.
They chased after the group, calling out to them and trying
to block their way, more and more of them attracted by the
commotion.

To their credit, none of the soldiers Neumann selected broke
ranks. They walked true and tall, never wavering from their
march behind the sergeant as they made their way through the
barracks, past the mess halls, through the next section of barracks,
and then north past the classrooms and workshops. Near the end
of the march, as the men made their way to Recreational Hall 2, the
calls from the other prisoners lessened. They continued to follow

but they did so silently, showing respect for how the men looked and marched.

By the time they reached the Rhine Hall, almost one-sixth of the camp had gathered, with more on the way. A couple of Canadian scouts noticed the situation but only hovered around the edges as there was little they could do to break up the crowd. Neumann halted at the door and the soldiers halted with him. He nodded at Knaup who stepped out of line and opened the door. The sergeant walked in and the group of eight followed. Some prisoners tried to come with them, but Knaup stopped them with an upraised hand. It seemed that the dress uniform had some kind of hold over the men and they stepped back. Knaup stepped into the hall, shut the door behind him, and took his place in line.

Like the last time Neumann was in this building, there were three groups inside: the tumblers, the orchestra, and the marching submariners. The tumblers' pyramid building scheme collapsed at the sight of the Wehrmacht soldiers in dress uniforms. Once they recovered, one of the tumblers remarked, "This will be good." A few others saw the possibility of something bad and fled the building.

Since the orchestra was on the other side of the hall, it took several more seconds before someone there became aware. There was a loud squawk from a saxophonist, which threw off the entire piece and drew the ire of the conductor. But when a viola player stood up and silently pointed, Liszt turned and saw Neumann and his group.

"Holy shit," he said. "Rehearsal is over. Save yourself if you wish." Then he gathered up his score and dashed out of the other side of the building. He was followed by a number of the musicians, but like the tumblers, a few remained behind to watch. Or to participate in whatever happened next.

What happened next was that Sergeant Neumann marched his group up to the submariners who were again conducting some close-order drill. The presence of the Wehrmacht squad distracted a few and they stumbled. Captain Koenig barked angrily at his men, trying to get them into formation until he heard the sound of marching footsteps. He slowly turned, his face full of incredulity as he watched Neumann and his men approach him.

They marched with precision, every footstep sounding like one. Three metres away, Neumann stopped, turned to face Captain Koenig, and stamped his right foot on the floor. He barked out an order and the men turned to face the same way in two single-file lines. Another bark and the men in the front separated allowing the back line to move forward and merge with the front.

When they were done, Neumann took a few steps forward, and stopped in front of Captain Koenig who was still staring, his eyes wide. Neumann stomped his right foot again and stood at perfect attention. His right arm snapped out into a perfect forty-five degree angle, palm facing the ground.

"Heil Hitler," he shouted. There was no disrespect in his voice, no irony in his salute.

A half second later, the rest of the Wehrmacht soldiers repeated the gesture. "Heil Hitler," they shouted as one.

Koenig froze for a second, stunned by this spectacle. And then quickly, he replied, his salute not as crisp or as loud.

Neumann and his men stood at attention, waiting for Koenig to realize that he had to speak.

"What is the meaning of this, Sergeant Neumann?" he finally asked, icily. "Is this meant to mock me and my men?"

"No, sir. The furthest thing from my mind is to mock you. My men are here to show respect because I have a request to ask of you, Captain."

"A request? You have got to be joking, Sergeant. I'll have your stripes for this, no matter how many shining medals you may have."

"This is no joke, sir. I wish to talk to one of your men about an incident the other night."

"This is not about that Bolshevik, Mueller, is it, Sergeant? Like I told you four days ago when you felt it necessary to draw a weapon on me, my men had nothing to do with Mueller, despite his leftist leanings. We are civilized and honourable men, we who serve in the submariner corp. That cannot be said about you, despite your fancy dress."

Neumann ignored the jibe. "No, Captain, this is about another incident that occurred the night of the escape. One of my men was beaten by a group—"

"—and every time this happens you must lay blame on us submariners? I will not stand for this, Sergeant Neumann. I don't care what you did in the last war or how many medals you have. You have gone too far with this kind of harassment."

"I'm sorry, sir, but I am not laying blame on your men as a

whole. I just wish to speak to one who may have information about this incident."

"And why would one of my men have this information?"

"Because we have evidence that he was there."

"Evidence? Something you cooked up?"

"No sir, the victim identified him through various markings on his body including a tattoo and some scars."

"Really. And what kind of tattoos and scars?"

Neumann told him.

"Your plan is too obvious. Of course your victim has identified Lieutenant Neuer who has those same markings. And of course it is he who is facing your own Corporal Aachen in a match. So you wish to detain Neuer in order to prevent his victory over Aachen. I tell you, this will not work. I will not only report this matter, but I will ensure that Neuer defeats Corporal Aachen in the most terrible way possible."

"It was Corporal Aachen who was beaten. Although he claims he has recovered from his injuries, I do not think he will be able to continue with the match."

Koenig pondered for a moment. "Injured or not, he will either have to fight or forfeit. I will not allow you to postpone the match by detaining Lieutenant Neuer. It is a most devious plan, Neumann, but it will not work. You Wehrmacht scum will have to accept the loss. Lieutenant Neuer will not go with you."

"Then maybe you can return him his war badge. He seems to have dropped it. Corporal Aachen managed to pick it up after he was beaten."

Neumann held out the badge that Aachen found on the shower floor.

Koenig blanched at the sight of the badge and brought his hand to his mouth. He stared at the badge, saying nothing.

"Captain Koenig, I do not wish to bring disgrace to you or your men. I have great respect for the service you have done for the Fatherland and apologize for any untoward and unprofessional actions I have done in the past. I have come with my men, dressed as we are, to show you the respect and honour you and your men deserve. However, I have evidence that one of your men may have been involved in the incident with Corporal Aachen—"

"—Lieutenant Neuer!" Koenig shrieked in anger. "Front and centre!"

Neuer jumped out of the line and quickly moved to the front. He snapped to attention behind the captain. "Yes, Captain."

Koenig whirled on the lieutenant, glancing up and down at his uniform. "Sergeant Neumann said you were involved in the beating of Corporal Aachen a few nights ago, is that true?"

"No, sir. That is not true. They are only—"

"—Silence!" Koenig shouted. "One of the assailants had similar scars and tattoos that you have. How do you explain that?"

"Corporal Aachen and I have wrestled before. He would be quite aware of my tattoos."

"True. But tell me, Lieutenant Neuer, where is your war badge? The one I gave you personally for completing your second war patrol? I don't see it on your uniform. And as you know, during our training, I require all to wear their badges."

Neuer blinked several times, his face turned red. "I'm sorry, sir, I must have left it back at the barracks."

"Ah, a common mistake. One I will overlook this time as long as you can go get it."

"You wish me to get it now, sir?"

"That is correct. I wish for you to get it now."

Neuer didn't move for several seconds.

"Is there a problem, Lieutenant? You haven't left yet to fetch your war badge."

"But sir, I just … uh, I mean, it's just not the—"

Koenig's right hand flew up and struck Neuer across the face. Neuer's head snapped back, though he did not lose his balance. Koenig's hand came back the other way and he slapped the lieutenant on the other side of his face with the back of his hand. This time Neuer stumbled as blood flew out of his mouth.

"You are a disgrace, Lieutenant. You have brought dishonour to me. You have brought dishonour to your crew, your fellow sailors, and to all those who have served and died aboard the U-boats. You have brought dishonour to the Reich and the Führer." Koenig struck him again. "You have no right to be called a submariner and if I never see your face again, I would not miss it."

Koenig whirled around and faced the sergeant. He gave him the Heil Hitler salute which Neumann returned. Koenig took a handkerchief out of his pocket and wrapped it around his hand as a bandage for his split knuckles.

"Get this filth out of my sight, please, Sergeant. As quickly as possible."

27.

Neumann and his men quickly escorted Neuer out of the recreational hall and marched him to one of the nearby classrooms where Aachen had set up a space for interrogation.

The march, though, was not without its difficulties. Word had gotten around camp that the sergeant had captured someone, someone who may have killed Captain Mueller, so there was a mob outside the hall.

More Canadian scouts had gathered and made a move to push into the crowd. But the prisoners pushed them back. "This is German business, not yours," one prisoner shouted in English. More shoving ensued so the Canadians backed away. As soon as they did this, the prisoners again turned their attention to Neumann's escort and the Canadians made no more efforts to break things up; the crowd was just too big for them to deal with. A good number of the prisoners were just curious to know what was going on, others had heard rumours that Mueller had been killed by someone and were angry about that.

For the Canadians, as long as the mob stayed focused on matters within the camp and did not make any move towards the fence or any of the scouts, they seemed content to follow the crowd from a distance. A couple of the scouts, though, headed towards the gate, presumably to get direction on how to deal with this situation.

The prisoners allowed Neumann and his group to pass, but some jeered at Neuer, thinking he was responsible for Mueller's murder. And though Neumann's group was stolid in their movements, they marched at a much quicker pace than they had going to the hall.

Neuer tried to ignore the crowd but the fear on his face was obvious. Seeing his nervousness and certain of his guilt, many of the prisoners jeered even louder, picking up on the rumours.

Finally they arrived at the classroom building. As soon as they entered, they immediately locked the door and then collectively breathed a sigh of relief—including Sergeant Neumann. Corporal Knaup sat Neuer into a chair and the submariner collapsed, dropping his head into his hands.

Aachen glanced at him for a second and then peeked out of one of the windows. "Things aren't pretty out there, Sergeant. It's best if we stay in here until they settle down."

"Or toss that fucker out and let the mob have their way with him," said one of the escorts, a corporal named Seidenberg who had served in the same platoon as Neumann and Aachen. "Safer for us, too, because they're not going to let us leave."

Neuer looked up. His face was white. "You can't send me out there, Sergeant Neumann. They'll tear me apart."

"You should have thought of that before you killed Mueller, you motherfucker," Seidenberg yelled. "If the sergeant wasn't here, I'd kill you myself. Leave you hanging from the rafters in this room the way you left him hanging."

"But I didn't kill Mueller," Neuer pleaded. "I swear, I didn't kill him."

Neumann pushed the escort back. "That's enough, Seidenberg. Vigilante justice is what got us into this problem in the first place. I won't have it anymore. You agreed that you would show honour and respect."

"Honour and respect to those who deserve it. Not to this piece of shit. I'm sorry, Sergeant. I was glad to help in the beginning, but this is the end. That mob is going to knock you down to get at him. And they aren't going to be nice about it. The boys are out for blood."

Neumann paused for a moment and then turned to look at all the men in the room. Neuer wasn't the only one who was looking panicked; most of the other soldiers were looking the same way.

"What are we going to do, Sergeant?" Corporal Knaup asked. "We'll follow you wherever you tell us, but we'd rather not take on a suicide mission this late in the game."

"Don't worry, Knaup, I don't go on suicide missions," Neumann said clapping Knaup on the shoulder. "And I don't send any of my men on them either, am I right, Aachen?"

Knaup shrugged. "We're going to have to figure something

out soon because those boys aren't going to be content to stay out there for long. After awhile, a bunch of them will burst in and I doubt we'll be able to hold them back."

Neumann then turned to Neuer. The submariner's eyes were wide with fear. Beads of sweat started to form on his forehead. "Well, looks like we're stuck here. So what do you say, Neuer? Do you want to confess now or should I just leave you to the mob?"

"You can't leave me, Sergeant. You wouldn't. You're an honourable man. You wouldn't leave me to a pack of hounds like that, would you?"

Neumann shrugged. "Much as I hate vigilante justice, if I had to choose between my life, the lives of my men here, and yours, the choice is pretty easy. I have honour, but only to a point."

"But I didn't kill Mueller. I had nothing to do with that," Neuer said, the fear rising in his voice. "You have to believe me, Sergeant. I had nothing to do with the murder of the captain, nothing at all."

"Sorry, Neuer, but I hear that all the time. The fact is that the evidence is incontrovertible. You were involved in the beating and attempted hanging of Corporal Aachen. All we have to do is gather more evidence to tie you to the death of Captain Mueller."

"I had no reason to kill Captain Mueller. No reason at all."

"But he was a communist, your commander said so."

"I don't give a shit about anybody's politics, Sergeant. That was all Captain Koenig's beef. I'm just like you—a soldier who follows orders even if my commander is an idiot."

"Your commander sank almost a half million tonnes of enemy ships."

"And you think he did that all by himself? There's more than thirty men on the average U-boat and you need everyone working together in order to sink an enemy ship. But do they get credit? No. Only the captain gets that credit. Even if one of those ships was sunk while he was sleeping soundly and I was on watch."

"Your commander deserves much more respect than that, Lieutenant Neuer. He served the Fatherland well."

"Koenig is stuck in the past. He is still reliving the happy time when U-boats ruled the Atlantic. And he still believes that it will come back, that one day we will be rescued by German forces and welcomed back as heroes and continue the fight for the Fatherland, ruling the waves with our wolf packs and torpedoes. But you and I both know that will never happen, don't we, Sergeant? There will never be a rescue. The only way we'll go home is when this damn war ends and based on what's happening in Europe now, there won't be many victory parades in our hometowns."

"Your commander has punished others for less traitorous words."

"Again, Sergeant, that was a long time ago. You forget that most of us submariners have been prisoners for several years and that is a long time to be sitting here doing nothing, twiddling our thumbs. In the early years, we still had spirit. Many of us still thought the Fatherland was the greatest country in the world, that we had the strongest forces and would, over time, overcome all our enemies. But as more and more prisoners like yourself kept arriving and we kept hearing stories of debacles and bad command decisions, we started to face reality. At least some of us did. I realized that even though there was no way I could leave the submariner group without facing some consequences, I had to plan for my future after the war. Because life is going to be very shitty when we get back home. You probably know that better than me, Neumann. I was only a kid after the First World War and from my view, things were pretty bleak during those times. And I'm betting it was worse for veterans who came back."

Neuer paused to see if there was a reaction. Neumann said nothing.

"Thought so. Anyway, when I started to think about my future, I found some people who were willing to help. You see, I don't want to go back to Germany after all this empty-handed."

"You sound like Heidfield. He made the same offer to me," Aachen said. "Is he part of those people you found?"

Neuer was briefly surprised at the mention of Heidfield's name. But then he shrugged. "So what if he is. At least he's looking to the future, unlike the rest of you."

"But how does the murder of Captain Mueller fit into your future plans? He was harmless."

"I didn't kill Captain Mueller. No one connected to Heidfield killed Mueller. And I know Koenig is trying to get control of the camp back somehow or at least get a more patriotic group in charge, especially because of the invasion—he believes there is too much disloyalty in the camp—but he is still pretty far away from that. There's no way he'd take the chance of sticking his neck out and killing someone like Mueller. He doesn't have the power yet, and I don't think he's going to get it."

"I don't buy it. You must have played a role in Mueller's death considering what you did to Aachen."

"The attack on Aachen was not connected to Mueller, at least not directly. In fact I didn't even wish to kill Aachen. Just to hurt him. But then it got out of hand."

"Why Aachen, then?" asked Neumann. "Why were you trying to scare him away from that investigation, if you weren't involved with Mueller's death."

"Attacking Aachen had nothing to do with Mueller. It was all because of the match, of course. The plan was to injure the corporal so he would withdraw from the match, or at least make him a weaker opponent."

"So you admit to being involved in Aachen's beating."

Neuer grimaced. "Only slightly. Personally, I didn't think it was necessary. I know I can beat him. He's strong and small, but I'm faster and have a longer reach. His only chance of winning was to drag out the match."

"If you think you could beat him fairly, why was he beaten?"

Neuer shrugged. "I had the impression that there were other considerations involved. Like I said, I didn't think Aachen had to be worked over so I could beat him in the match, but in the end I didn't make that decision. I was persuaded that it would be better for the future if we did this."

Neuer turned in his chair to face Aachen. "I'm truly sorry, Klaus. If it means anything, I only hit you once and even then I pulled my punch."

Aachen glared at Neuer and then turned away angrily.

Just then a large rock crashed through a window on the other side of the room. It was followed by another one, and then a third. The voices of the mob outside were becoming angrier and angrier.

Neuer shrieked and ducked under the table. One of the soldiers pulled him to another table. The rest of the soldiers, including Aachen and Neumann, gathered in the centre of the room, the best place to be in case of a storm.

Aachen looked about as a few more rocks came flying in and someone started banging on the door. "We're going to have to do something, Sergeant," he said. "Very soon or we're going to be in big trouble."

"Why not just give them Neuer? He's the one they want," Knaup suggested without any malice in his voice. "They'll probably just beat him up a bit."

"This crowd is out for blood. They'll probably kill Neuer. I don't think we'll come away without a few scars of our own, if we don't do something soon," Neumann said.

"You can't be suggesting we give him up?" Aachen asked as another rock came flying in, bouncing off the table under which Neuer was hiding and nearly hitting Neumann. He quickly stepped aside to avoid it.

"Why are you defending him?" Knaup asked. "I'd think you'd be keen on getting revenge. This is one way, don't you think?"

"No, it's not. If I'm going to get revenge on Neuer, I'll do it myself. I'm not going to give him to a crazy mob so they can tear him apart."

Neumann snapped his fingers as the shouting became louder and another window was broken. One prisoner tried to climb through the window but cut himself on the glass. He screamed and backed away.

"That's it. Brilliant idea, Aachen," Neumann said. "If it's a fight they want, it's a fight they'll get."

"Are you insane, Sergeant? If we fight this mob they'll kill us."

"We're not going to fight—Aachen is."

"But he's only one man. He can't tame this whole crowd."

"Don't be an idiot, Knaup," Neumann snapped. "Aachen's not going to fight the mob, he's going to fight Neuer."

"What the hell are you talking about?" Knaup shouted.

Neumann ignored Knaup and looked at Aachen who had turned to face him. Slowly, they smiled at each other. "So what do you say, Klaus?" Neumann asked.

Aachen nodded.

"You sure? He's a tough sonofabitch, wasn't going to be an easy fight in the first place. But now you're pretty beat up. Think you can beat him?"

Aachen's smile became brighter. "Always," he said. "Never a doubt."

28.

Aachen and Neuer stood in the middlfire of a dusty field normally used for football, just to the east of Recreation Hall 2,
about five metres away from the eastern perimeter fence.

Neumann had chosen the site himself after convincing the
mob outside the classroom to let the much-anticipated match
between Neuer and Aachen occur a couple of days earlier than
expected. To have it outside added even more to the drama. The
site was no chance selection, either; it was one of the football
pitches which had rafts of bleachers along the west and north
side, so while a good number of prisoners did crowd around
the wrestling area, many of them decided to use the bleachers so they could have a better view over the top of the heads
of those on the ground. The set-up also allowed for the east
side to be open, so the Canadian guards who were interested
in the match could watch from the fence or up in the nearby

towers. Neumann made a point of showing all those guards to Neuer.

"Take a good look at all those Canadians over there, Lieutenant," he whispered. "They are all watching the match, many of them with their Enfields loaded and ready to shoot."

"Yes, but they are always there with their guns. What difference would they make?"

"They make a lot of difference. I wish you well in your match, but you and I both know that when it ends, no matter who wins, this mob is going to come after you. I want you to understand that."

"I do. So why are we doing this, if it will end that way?"

"To help you escape, of course. When the match ends, win or lose, I want you to run as fast as you can, jump the fence, and go into No Man's Land. Don't stop until you get to the tall fence. And don't look back either. Keep looking at the Canadians."

"But they'll shoot me as soon as I jump over."

"No, they won't. Not if you have your hands in the air and you are yelling for help. Remember to yell for help, something like 'Save me, they will kill me. Save me.' And shout it like that in English. You can speak some English, can't you?"

"Of course."

"Good. The Canadians will help you and put you in protective custody."

"But that's for traitors and informants."

"You may be neither, but at the very least you'll be alive. And when this war ends, no one will care anymore who's a traitor or not. We'll all just go home."

"But why are we doing it this way, Sergeant," Neuer asked. "What's stopping me from running away to the Canadians now?"

"Your honour, of course," Neumann said, slapping the sub-mariner on the back. "Everyone's been looking forward to this match for a long time, especially you and Corporal Aachen. Don't you want to prove who's the better wrestler before you run over to the Canadians?"

Neuer smiled. It was the first time Neumann had ever seen him smile. "Why are you doing this, Sergeant?"

"Because I want to see the match as well."

"No. Not that. Why are you helping me?"

"To save your life, of course. Although before the match begins, I hope you will tell me who put you up to attacking Corporal Aachen."

Neuer looked about nervously and then leaned in close. When he whispered the name, Neumann nodded. "Not that much of surprise," he said.

29.

The match didn't last long. Neuer started with some passion, but that quickly faded as the crowd moved in for a better look. He made a few quick shots against Aachen, trying to use his speed and height for advantage, but they were only half-hearted attempts. His eyes were unfocused, darting back and forth between Aachen and the mob that surrounded him, the mob that stared angrily at him, accusing him of killing Mueller and calling out for his execution.

Aachen tried to return Neuer's focus to the match, slapping the submariner across the head a couple of times, whispering words of encouragement as well as jibes to keep him interested. But even though he did make some attempts to wrestle, everything Neuer attempted was half-hearted and ineffectual.

This lack of effort only further incensed the crowd which

began to inch even closer, jeering at the two men for turning a highly anticipated event into an anticlimactic one.

While the two of them were seemingly working to lock in, Aachen dropped to his knees, raising a small cloud of dust off the hard prairie ground. Neuer lost his balance, arms flailing at nothing, and fell forward against Aachen's shoulder. The corporal then tucked his head to get under the submariner's arms and wrapped his arms around Neuer, locking his hands together. He screamed with effort and pushed up.

Sensing what was happening, Neuer regained his balance, also wrapping his arms around Aachen and locking his hands. He pushed down with his weight, stretching his legs to keep his feet from leaving the ground.

But Aachen kept pushing up. Neuer tried to spin to get away from the lift and to throw Aachen off balance. It was too late. The corporal was in complete control; he simply moved with his larger opponent. They struggled for a couple of seconds and then Aachen screamed again. In one fluid movement, he arched his back, pushed up from his knees, and lifted the submariner off the ground, spinning into a half turn to throw Neuer to the ground.

The submariner fell first on his shoulder and then onto his back. An instant later, he pushed himself half up, but Aachen was on top of him. He released his grip around Neuer's waist, bringing his arms up to wrap around the man's neck, also locking an arm in a submission hold. He squeezed, his arm muscles bulging.

Neuer struggled, wriggling to break free, even slapping

against the bruises on Aachen's body, the reminders of his beating, but Aachen refused to let go, increasing the pressure of the hold. Neuer struggled only for a moment before relenting. He paused, tapped Aachen twice on the shoulder, and then went completely slack, the signal that he had given up.

A second later, Aachen released the submariner who fell to the dust gasping for breath. The corporal also gasped and sat back on the ground with his arms raised in victory, but only for a second, because he was unable to hold them up any longer.

Since the majority of the crowd was made up of Wehrmacht prisoners, the crowd cheered the win with approval. That joy, however quickly disappeared and crowd turned ugly. "Come on!" someone shouted. "Why did you let him go? You should have killed him!"

"Yeah, grab him again and choke him to death!"

There were more shouts for death and soon a chant started. "Kill him! Kill him! Kill him!"

Aachen gave Neuer a quick nudge to get him off the ground. But Neuer didn't move. He was looking around in fear, freezing at the sound of the crowd calling for his death, unable to get up, unable to catch his breath, unable to move. The Canadians also looked about in fear, bringing their rifles up, but unsure of what was going on and how they could stop it.

Aachen pushed himself up and moved to help Neuer get to his feet. "Get up, you fool, and run," he hissed at him, yanking on the man's arm and pulling him to his feet. Neuer was unsteady and almost fell back down again, but Aachen caught him and started pushing him towards the fence. "Run! Run! They'll kill you if you don't!"

Neuer began to run towards the fence but stumbled, landing on his hands and knees in the dust. He tried to get up again, but his arms were too weak and the dust was too loose for him to get his footing.

"He's trying for the fence!" someone shouted.

"Get him!"

"Kill him!"

Neumann tried to rush forward to help Neuer get up, but the crowd surged forward, knocking him back. Aachen again grabbed Neuer by the arms and pulled him up. He pushed him towards the fence and the submariner half-ran, half-stumbled forward. He frantically waved his arms in the air, shouting at the Canadians. "Help me, help me, they're trying to kill me!"

But he shouted in German and the guards pointed their rifles at the lieutenant as he fell over the three foot barbed wire fence. He flipped over and the back of his pants got caught, leaving him hanging.

A surge of prisoners rushed towards him. Aachen came to his rescue. He stretched his arms wide and roaring, grabbed a bunch of them in a massive bear hug, and held them back. But there were too many of them. They knocked him onto his back, a number of them kicking and punching him. Others simply ran over Aachen, pursuing Neuer. Still, the few seconds that Aachen held the crowd back allowed Neuer to free himself from the barbed wire and he started running for the fence again. His hands waved in the air and this time he shouted for help in English.

The mob surged towards the inner fence, pushing against it, screaming for Neuer's blood. A couple began to climb it and soon others figured they could too.

Neuer faced the outside of the fence, banging his hands and body against it, pleading for help as two Canadian guards pointed their rifles at his chest, their fingers on the triggers.

A shot rang out.

Neuer gasped and started to fall back, but one of the Canadians reached through the fence and grabbed the front of his shirt, pulling him up.

Another shot rang out from the same sentry standing high above on one of the towers. The prisoners froze, falling back from the inner fence. A few struggled against it, trying to move forward. There was a third shot, this one hitting the ground not far from the fence. The bullet ricocheted from the dirt striking one of the prisoners on the arm. He fell back screaming. It was only a flesh wound but it left a long strip of blood along the outside of his arm.

The crowd fell back, many of them scrambling away from the mayhem, their anger quashed by the shots. A few of the prisoners lingered by the fence, staring at Neuer. The Canadian who hung onto the lieutenant's shirt smiled at him.

"Don't worry, buddy. You're okay. No one's going to hurt you." He then turned to his colleague. "Hey, Mike, help me get this guy out of here."

"Sure thing, Dove. Let me cut a hole in the fence so you can drag him outta there."

Mike pulled out a pair of wire cutters and started slicing bits of the fence away.

"Jesus, McDonald, not that big of a hole will ya, the commander will have our asses as it is."

"Can't help it, he's a big fella. He's gonna need a big hole."

"Hurry it up, okay. Those Krauts are really pissed at this guy."

The Canadians pulled Neuer through the hole and then guided him to the south where the protective custody barracks were located. Slowly, the rest of the prisoners dispersed, some feeling sheepish for how they acted, others angry that Neuer evaded them.

A few others, Sergeant Neumann and Corporal Knaup included, didn't move. They were frozen to the spot, staring at the body of Corporal Aachen who lay unmoving in the dust of the Canadian Prairie.

30.

Almost every single prisoner came out for the funeral procession. They lined the roadway from Rhine Hall, where the actual funeral was held, to the front gate, all in dress uniforms—whether they were Wehrmacht, SS, Kreigesmarine, Luftwaffe, Foreign Legion didn't matter. The entire camp stood side by side watching the flag-covered coffin as it was pulled along on a wagon by a horse borrowed from a local farmer.

An honour guard of local prisoners, which included Sergeant Neumann, walked in front of the horse-drawn wagon. The Veterans Guards even had their own Honour Guard in front of the Germans, a piper playing "Amazing Grace", and bagpipe arrangements of "O Esca Viatorum" and Beethoven's *Funeral March*. Despite the strangeness of German music being played on something as un-German as bagpipes, it was a thoughtful contribution by the Canadians.

The Canadians also allowed the German national flag to be draped across the coffin. And all the German soldiers, no matter which service they were part of, gave the flag the Nazi salute, rather than the traditional salute favoured and still allowed for members of the Wehrmacht.

As the procession approached the inner front gate, it swung open, allowing them to pass. Not long after, the outer gate did the same and the entire procession, including the German Honour Guard, left the camp.

More Canadian guards stood outside the gate, doing their best to remain respectful, while still ensuring no members of the German Honour Guard made a run for it.

There was even a large group of civilians about ten metres down the road from the gate. And while they seemed more curious to see the German prisoners involved in the procession as well as a public display of the Nazi flag than anything, they did respectfully remove their hats or place their hands on their hearts as the coffin bearing the body of an enemy soldier passed them by.

Neumann and one of the other members of the Honour Guard looked over to the Canadians. They kept their eyes forward, following the Canadian Honour Guard and their bagpiper. Fifty metres out of the camp, the procession turned west and followed a short road to a fenced area—the cemetery for prisoners who had died in the camp. There were already five headstones in the cemetery and now there was a freshly dug grave where the sixth body would go. There was, as of yet, no headstone for the new grave.

The priest was already waiting at the top of the gravesite with his Bible and a trio of Canadian guards, each of them in their own version of dress uniforms and armed with an Enfield.

The Canadian Honour Guard entered the cemetery area, moved in unison to the far side of the grave, and stood about five metres away. Since the horse and wagon couldn't enter the cemetery, the Germans, led by Neumann, removed the coffin from the wagon and carried it to the gravesite. They walked in a slow march, then set the coffin down on the bed of ropes used to lower the casket into the grave and stepped back, standing at attention a couple of metres away from the site. The actual ceremony was short. The priest said a few words, the Canadian riflemen fired three shots to honour a fallen soldier, and the casket was lowered. The bagpiper played the "Last Post." Although it was a British tune and the dead soldier was German, it did not offend anyone.

Once the song ended and the Germans saluted the grave, they were slowly led back by a group of guards. Less than five minutes later, the gates shut behind them and they were all back in Camp 133.

The Honour Guard dispersed leaving Neumann to himself. The lines of Germans also dispersed, quietly going back to their duties or whatever they normally did. Neumann slowly made his way back to his bunk in his barracks.

No one approached him or acknowledged him in any way. No doubt some were still angry that he permitted Neuer to escape vigilante justice. But the rest were probably just ashamed of what happened to Corporal Aachen and their role in it.

Back at his bunk, Neumann slowly removed his dress uniform and all its accessories, gently folded it, and placed it back into his duffel bag. He put on his regular uniform, looked about for a moment, and then sat down on Aachen's bunk. He stayed there for several moments, just breathing.

"It's a terrible shame," a voice said. "I hate funerals."

Neumann looked up and at the end of the bunk was Staff Sergeant Nico Heidfield. He was still in dress uniform and looked very dapper.

"What do you want, Heidfield?" Neumann said with a deep sigh. "I'm not really in the mood for anything you have to say."

"I just wanted to express my sorrow for what occurred with Corporal Aachen. It was a terrible shame."

Neumann laughed, a reaction that surprised Heidfield. "That's quite ironic considering the fact that you were the one that had him beaten in the shower."

Heidfield stepped back and frowned. "Neuer told you, didn't he?"

"Yes, he offered me information in exchange for saving his life. You shouldn't be surprised because we both got an excellent bargain. That's how you operate isn't it, making deals?"

"I would disagree with your concept of an excellent deal. If you would have left Neuer to the mob, what happened to Corporal Aachen wouldn't have occurred. It's sad too. I didn't want to kill Aachen—he's a good man, tough and smart. But I made him an offer. Asked him to take a fall during his match because there were a lot of bets on him. But despite my best efforts to convince him, to make him think of the future, he spurned me. So I had to do something to protect myself. Unfortunately, one of the men took things a bit too far. He's new to the camp, used to a more violent way of doing things. I'll make sure he understands that we're a little more subtle here than in Camp 130." Heidfield narrowed his eyes. "But you knowing that I had Aachen attacked makes no difference. I can't be hurt by that."

"I wouldn't be too sure about that," Neumann warned.

"To be honest there's not much you can do with that kind of information," Heidfield said with a shrug. "The man who gave it to you is now in protective custody, a home for informants and traitors. So any testimony he would offer would be circumspect. No one with any pull in this camp would listen to it."

"At least I'm aware of it, which is important to me."

"So that's a kind of threat, I'm assuming. I'm not afraid of you, despite who you are."

"And I'm not afraid of you, despite your corruption."

"Then we're at an impasse, which is too bad. I was hoping we could work together, reach some sort of compromise, so that I could continue to function without interference."

"Does the expression 'Fuck you' mean anything to you?"

"Ahh, not surprising. You're a smart man, Sergeant, but you have no vision for the future."

"And fuck your future, too. Fucks like you, Heidfield, are nothing new. Jesus, there were even fucks like you in the trenches of the First War, always blabbing about their great plans for the future, their incredible ideas for how they would rule the world, or whatever tiny little empire they had their eyes on. Most of them didn't survive that war."

"So far I've survived this one. And will probably make it to the end. It only takes a great man to survive, we've all seen that."

Neumann laughed loudly. "Take it from me, Heidfield, you are not a great man. I've seen your type over and over again. You're a low-rent criminal and you may have some success after the war, but something bigger will come along and destroy you. That's how it always works."

"Maybe I'm different."

"Ha. Your type always thinks you're different. Thinks you're special. But you're just a piece of shit."

Heidfield shrugged and backed away. "I just hope you stay out of the way and don't bother my operation. That's all I ask."

"All I'm asking—" Neumann pushed himself off the bunk and stood over Heidfield "—is that you stay out of *my* way."

"So again, an impasse. Whatever shall we do about it?"

"Well, I was going to do something like this," said Neumann. His right hand flew up and grabbed Heidfield by the throat. He shoved and Heidfield fell back against the barracks wall. Neumann squeezed tighter, holding Heidfield against the wall.

A few prisoners in the barracks jumped at the sound and looked over to see the commotion, but when they saw what was happening, they left the area or turned away. Only Corporal Knaup, who had his bunk nearby, remained. A couple of large prisoners burst through the door. Knaup moved to cut them off, but Neumann raised his free hand.

"Stop where you fucking are or I'll snap his neck. You too, Knaup. Stay where you are."

Heidfield's bodyguards froze, almost falling over themselves to do so.

"And if you motherfuckers take another step towards me," Neumann said, pointing at the two bodyguards, "I will kill this piece of shit and then come over to do the same to you. If you think I can't kill you two idiots then just give it a try and see what happens."

The two bodyguards looked at each other and then backed away. Neumann looked to Heidfield who was struggling to break free, his face red, his eyes bugging out. "See, like I said, you can make all the plans you want for the future until someone stronger comes along and destroys you. Could be someone like me. I could kill you right now and no one would really care. Or it could be a rival criminal, could be the Ivans for all I know. But before I decide to kill you or not, I'd like you to answer me one last question, is that okay? One answer before you possibly die."

Heidfield tried to nod, but Neumann held his neck so tight, he couldn't move. But the effort was enough for the sergeant.

"I understand why you had Aachen beat up. Didn't like it but I understand the reasoning behind it. I've seen it before from criminals like you and it probably made sense to you," Neumann said. "But Mueller I don't get. Why did you have him killed? He was a threat to no one, especially someone like you."

"I, I, I didn't kill Mueller," Heidfield managed to croak.

Neumann leaned in close, his face only a couple of centimetres from Heidfield's. "I'm sorry, it sounded like you said you didn't kill him. Now, don't lie to me, Heidfield, or you won't take another breath. You'll probably wet yourself, but you won't breathe."

"I didn't kill Mueller."

"I said don't lie to me!" Neumann shouted, squeezing tighter and lifting Heidfield off the floor. The smell of urine filled the air as Heidfield's bladder let go.

"I didn't kill Mueller," he croaked. "I didn't."

Neumann held Heidfield in that position for several more seconds and then tossed him to the ground. Heidfield fell down at the feet of his bodyguards. They tried to pick him but he batted them away, cursing at them.

He slowly picked himself up and did his best to save his dignity. "This isn't finished, Neumann."

"No, it's not, Heidfield. I could come by and kill you in your sleep some night. So keep your eyes open."

Heidfield and his men scrambled away. Corporal Knaup slowly approached Sergeant Neumann. "Holy shit, Sergeant. I thought I had seen your bad side, but I guess I was wrong."

"That wasn't even close to my bad side, Knaup. Not even close." The sergeant clapped the corporal on the shoulder. "But thank you for trying to come to my rescue. I won't forget it."

Knaup flushed and shrugged. "I just thought it was something Corporal Aachen would do."

"It was. So thank you."

Neumann again walked over to Aachen's bunk and sat down. He sighed and rubbed his face with his hand. Knaup followed and stood leaning on the bunk.

"Have you visited him yet today?" Knaup asked quietly.

Neumann shook his head. "I was part of the Honour Guard for Mueller's funeral. Haven't had the time. Did you?"

"Yeah. I went before the funeral. I read a bit for him. The doctor says it's good if you read or talk to him while you visit."

"Any response?"

"Not yet. But the doctor said it's been only a couple of days. He could wake up any minute now."

"I should go visit him," Neumann said.

"You should. You want me to walk you over? In case those kinds of boys show up again?"

"No. I'll be fine," Neumann said with a smile. "I'm not afraid of those kinds of boys."

31.

Sergeant Neumann sat in an old wooden chair next to the hospital bed. Corporal Aachen looked a little bit like a mummy with bandages around his head and chest and a couple of casts, one on his right arm, the other on his left foot. Neumann sat there without speaking for a long while and picked up the book that was sitting on the table by the bed, the one Knaup had been reading. He opened it up at the bookmark, read a few lines to himself, but then set it back down.

"You know Klaus, I had a discussion today with Sergeant Heidfield. You know that prick. Looks like a movie star, acts like he's best friends with all the men. Well it got out of hand at the end with my hand against his throat, threatening to kill him." Neumann waved his hand at Aachen as if the corporal had responded. "I know, I know. I let my temper get the best of me. But I just couldn't take it anymore. He told me what he talked about with you. About him asking you to throw your match and you refusing. I can't believe he had the gall to do such a thing. He obviously knows little about your character."

Neumann laughed, instinctively looking to Aachen for a smile or any kind of response. His laughter ended quickly when he realized that none would come. He sat back in the chair, sighing. "Heidfield also admitted that he was the one who gave the order to have you attacked. Not killed but attacked. Konrad got out of hand. You probably knew Heidfield was behind it. I could tell from your questioning of Neuer that you figured that part out but at least you have some consolation that they really didn't want to kill. Though it makes little difference, I guess.

"And did you see me whispering to Neuer? I wasn't just telling him where to run if the crowd turned ugly, I was pumping him for information. I couldn't help it—I'm an old village policeman and it seemed like the right time. He was in the right mood to talk, especially since I told him we were saving his life and he owed us. So he told the truth. Heidfield also confirmed it, bragged about it to me, before I had my hand to his throat. Apparently he didn't like the fact that you spurned his offer, so he decided to take you out of the competition. Again, shows that he knows little of your character. Nor mine or he wouldn't have bragged so much to my face about it. Those bruises of my fingers on his throat are going to linger for a while.

"But while I had my fingers on his throat, I thought it would be a good time to ask him about Captain Mueller. It's an old and probably outdated interrogation technique. Although I bet some of our countrymen in black still enjoy using it. And I can understand why. It did feel good to have that fucker's life in my hands. I've killed many men in my time, you know that, Klaus, you've helped me kill them, but I've taken no joy in doing so. It's all part of war. But let me tell you, holding Heidfield by the throat, seeing him struggle to breathe, smelling his piss as he wet his pants in fear—that was quite enjoyable. In fact, later tonight I might pay him a visit and do it again, just to get out of this depressing mood. I know you're stuck here and I'm glad to see you, but this is a very depressing place. And it's been a bad day with Mueller's funeral and all. But I guess I shouldn't complain considering the state you're in."

Neumann stopped talking. He picked up the book again, but just held it loosely in his hands before setting it down. He sat up in his chair and leaned his elbows on Aachen's bed, next to the corporal's shoulder, and leaned his chin on his hands. He stared at Aachen's bandaged face.

"Heidfield didn't kill Mueller, you know. He told me and since I was choking him, I believed him. I should have known that, too, but since he had you attacked in a similar way, I assumed that he had Mueller attacked as well. But that really didn't make sense. Heidfield had no reason to kill Mueller. The man meant nothing to him; he wasn't part of his enterprise and didn't threaten it in any way. He barely knew the man, except by reputation. So, of course, Heidfield didn't kill Mueller. It just doesn't make sense. But who did?"

Neumann took his elbows off Aachen's bed and then rested his head on the mattress next to Aachen's shoulder. He shut his eyes. "It's got me perplexed, Klaus. It's obvious that Mueller didn't kill himself. And many men liked him. Sure, he may have said some things against the war, but would that be enough for him to be branded a traitor and killed? And if it was, why didn't the boys in black make a point of bringing it to our attention? When they catch traitors, they publicize their actions quite openly, don't leave any room for interpretation. And Mueller's death is quite confusing. While there is some indication that he was killed for his attitude, it's still all vague. It's not like them to act this way. If they did kill Mueller, then their message has been clouded. There's something missing here, Klaus. Maybe it's something about Mueller. But what? He's no different from the rest of us in the Afrika Korps. He drove a tank, commanded some men, did an excellent job by all counts. He was captured and shipped here like the rest of us in the hell holes of those ships. And then he settled into the camp, teaching boys like you to become better, so there's nothing—"

Neumann stopped, opened his eyes, and stared at the wall for several seconds. Then he slowly lifted his head and turned to look at Aachen. "There was a difference, Klaus. With Mueller. He wasn't…"

Neumann stood up quickly, almost knocking the chair over. He tapped the end of Aachen's bed. "Don't go away, Corporal. I'll be right back."

32.

Neumann threw open the door of the legionnaire hut and shoved past Hans, Philip, and all the other guards. He didn't really have to push that hard because he had been there before and he had the respect of Colonel Ehrhoff. Neumann walked past the bunks all the way to the area where Ehrhoff had his tent.

He pushed his way through the opening. Ehrhoff was sitting there with two older legionnaires, drinking tea and smoking tobacco from a hookah that looked to be made from a French horn or some other similar brass instrument.

Colonel Ehrhoff and the other legionnaires were surprised by Neumann bursting into the tent, but they did not get up.

"According to Bedouin tradition, Sergeant Neumann, a person must have an invitation to someone's tent," Ehrhoff said sipping his glass of tea. "Bursting into someone's tent in this manner is considered extremely impolite. It could even be seen as an act of violence."

"Good thing I'm a German and not a Bedouin. In the past few years, we've become quite known for bursting into places uninvited. And it's obvious that it's an act of violence because we've brought soldiers, guns, tanks, and planes that drop bombs." He pointed at Ehrhoff. "And no matter how you like to dress up, underneath all those robes is a fucking German. A little different, like one of those Indian hobbyists who like to read Karl May and dress up and live in teepees on the weekends, but you're still a fucking obnoxious German. If you weren't a German, you wouldn't have agreed to fight for Rommel. You would have gone over to the Free French side and fought for those bastards. But you didn't and here you are, right where you belong, in a prisoner-of-war camp for Germans."

Ehrhoff gave each of the other legionnaires in the tent an apologetic look, as if Neumann was an uncouth peasant interrupting a group of aristocrats having afternoon tea. He slowly stood up, adjusting his outfit as he did so. "Excuse me, gentlemen," he said to the two men and then walked over to Neumann. "Is it possible for us to discuss this outside?"

"No, this is fine. I won't be long so you can go back to your pretend Bedouin lifestyle—"

"—Please, Sergeant Neumann, there is no need to be insulting," Ehrhoff said, cutting him off. "I am quite aware of the difficulties you've had in the last few days, especially the horrible incident with Corporal Aachen, but there is no need—"

"—Mueller was a legionnaire, wasn't he? That's why he was

on your ship during transport. The Afrika Corps were in their own ships, except the Italians, some leftover Vichy diehards, and you legionnaires who fought for Rommel. That's why you were on the same ship as Mueller. It wasn't random, he was a fucking legionnaire."

At the mention of Mueller, the other two men in the tent quickly set down their tea glasses, stood up, and left without a word.

Neumann watched them leave and then turned to Ehrhoff. "Looks like I hit a sensitive subject. Am I right? Mueller was a legionnaire, wasn't he?"

Ehrhoff nodded.

"And because your precious Legion has some fucked up code about honour and loyalty, the fact that he didn't identify with you, that he turned his back on all that honour, wasn't acceptable to you and you had to do something, didn't you?"

"Are you intimating that we killed Captain Mueller?" Ehrhoff asked. His face was one of incredulity.

"Once a legionnaire, always a legionnaire, isn't it? If you turn your back on the Legion you're a traitor, a disgrace, and must be dealt with harshly."

Ehrhoff shook his head and backed away from Neumann. He returned to his spot in the tent and sat down. He picked up his cup of tea and sipped. "Please, Sergeant, sit down. Take some of that anger about Corporal Aachen and put it away."

"I prefer to stand, Colonel. Especially when I'm pretty much surrounded by people who could be my enemy."

"We are not your enemy, Sergeant Neumann," Ehrhoff said

with a sigh. "You have no reason to fear being harmed by me and my men."

"But others do, like Mueller, who turned his back on the Legion. Traitors must be made an example of."

"We didn't kill Captain Mueller."

"Don't get me wrong, I sort of understand. If anybody deserted my squad during combat, I'd shoot them. It's one of the difficulties of being in charge. Then again, none of my men would have done so during combat. One or two may go AWOL afterwards, but I'd punish them with extra work, not kill them. Much of my squad is still here in the camp, but I don't expect them to hang around with me like we did in North Africa. For the most part, no one's out to kill us here so there's no need for us to remain a squad. I'm not going to punish them for going their own way in the camp. That would be stupid."

"You're not listening to me, Sergeant. We didn't kill Captain Mueller. We had no reason to."

"But he was a legionnaire, wasn't he?"

"Yes, he was. But a long time ago. Mueller, like many of us, was lost after the First War. We just couldn't settle in. Civilian life seemed too simple after all those years of combat. And the mood of Germany was so downtrodden. We wanted to feel strong again, to go back into a fight. So that's why many of us joined the Legion. Surely you understand that?"

"Actually I don't. After losing my youth and almost all my friends in those trenches, the last thing I wanted to do was to find another fight. I just wanted to go home and live my simple life as a village policeman. Life was hard in those early years, but it was almost paradise when compared to the horror of the war. Hopefully it will be the same after this one."

"I surely doubt that, Sergeant. Germany and the rest of Europe's going to be in a terrible mess after this war."

"Germany and the rest of Europe have been in similar messes. We'll come out of it. But fuck the politics, tell me more about Mueller. He was a legionnaire after the First War?"

"Was a legionnaire. That's the operative phrase. After a time, Mueller realized that the Legion wasn't what he wanted. He, like you it seems, didn't want to return military life. So he left."

"Just like that, he left the Foreign Legion."

"People are allowed to leave the Legion, Sergeant, but only a few do. There's a bond that's created so people stay. But if you want to leave, all you have to do is put in your required five years and leave. That's what Captain Mueller did—he left after his first tour of duty, got his French citizenship, and left to teach. Which is why he was on the boat with us. Because of his dual citizenship, which he had plainly forgotten about, the Allies classified him as some sort of Vichy-German."

Ehrhoff set down his tea cup, picked up the pot, and poured himself another glass. "So you see, we had no reason to kill Captain Mueller. No reason at all."

Neumann looked at the colonel and saw the truth in his eyes. He rubbed his eyelids sighing deeply. Ehrhoff poured an extra cup of tea and reached over to hand it to Neumann. "Here, Sergeant, have some tea. It's very good. The Canadians have access to some fine leaves."

Neumann slowly sat down. He took the cup in his hands and

sipped. He closed his eyes, the tension leaving his body. He took another sip and looked at the cup.

"This is good," he said, looking up at Ehrhoff. "Very good."

"Some Bedouin traditions are very good, Sergeant Neumann, despite what you say."

"I would say this is more of an English tradition, considering what time it is. Apart from the crumpets and those silly sandwiches, we Germans could probably adapt it to our lifestyle. Add a few sausages to the menu."

"That's actually a great idea. I'll have to consider it."

"See, you can dress up all you want, but you're still a German." Neumann flushed slightly and set down his teacup. He stood up, adjusted his uniform, and saluted the colonel. "Thank you for your time, Colonel Ehrhoff. I'm sorry I burst in on you like this and accused you falsely."

Ehrhoff stood up and returned the salute.

"Don't apologize for doing your job to the best of your ability. I'm quite sure that Captain Mueller would be quite grateful for all the work you've gone through to find his killer. Hopefully it's not politically related so you can bring someone to justice."

"It's looking more and more like that may be the case, Colonel."

"Well, I'm pretty sure you'll find the solution. If you can't do it, then no one can."

"Thank you, sir. And again, thank you for the tea and your time." Neumann saluted again and Ehrhoff, smiling, returned it.

The sergeant left the legionnaires' barracks and made his way back to his own, winding through all the gardens between them.

There were more gardeners now, their backs hunched over, picking weeds, digging up the dirt. During his walk, he saw General Horcoff harvesting a few early berries and digging out some weeds with his trowel. Neumann thought of going over to report on his findings to the general and then thought the better of it. The general seemed happy in his garden, away from the stress of command.

Neumann also thought about going back to visit Corporal Aachen at the hospital, but couldn't imagine walking all that distance just to sit next to the bed helplessly. So he went to his bunk, undressed to his underwear, and climbed into bed. He fell asleep an instant later.

It was dark and all the other prisoners were in bed when Neumann's bladder woke him up. He tossed and turned, trying to fall back asleep, but the need to piss was too insistent. He got up, slipped on Aachen's special slippers, and padded to the toilet. He sat down on the toilet, but soon noticed that the toilet next to him was plugged, brown, disgusting water almost spilling over the edge. He would have gotten up but the pressure was too much and his bladder gave out. Neumann held his breath, but the stench coming from the toilet was overpowering, reminding him of those two weeks crossing the Atlantic from North Africa after being captured. He pushed as hard as he could without hurting himself so the piss would leave his body as fast as possible. Finally he finished and escaped, barely pulling up his underwear. When he managed to reach the sinks, he quickly washed his hands and splashed cold water on his face to get rid of the smell. It still lingered. So he quickly walked to a door and stood outside.

There was no one out there and the sky was clear, the stars sparkling. From where he stood, he couldn't see any towers so it was almost like he was back home. He pulled out a cigarette and lit it, taking a deep drag. He let the smoke leave his lungs, inhaling the smoke that left his mouth through his nose. A few more French inhales and the scent from the stuck toilet left his nose.

A second later, the scent triggered something in his brain, reminding him of his trip across the Atlantic, and then of someone who said they were on the same ship as some Italian prisoners.

"Fuck," he said as the cigarette fell from his mouth. His legs gave out from under him and he sat down hard on the steps. He didn't move for a long time.

33.

Neumann watched the sun rise, watched the sky turn from black to dark blue, then mixed with reds, pinks, and oranges before becoming the daily bright blue that stretched from horizon to horizon. As the sun rose and the day came to light, the camp also changed. The bright spotlights that covered the area soon faded. The prisoners who baked bread through the night trudged back to their bunks while the morning cooks and their helpers took their places. Even though Neumann's hut was not next to the mess, he could pick up the scent of baked bread and frying bacon and sausages.

The scent woke some of the prisoners, but then the Rouse, the Commonwealth bugle used to wake their troops, sounded and the entire camp was awake, prisoners dashing about here and there, and those scheduled for the first mess rushing to get a good seat before all the best bits of food were gone. Even though Neumann sat on the steps at the entrance of his hut and was partially blocking the way, no one complained. They just moved around him like he was a large rock that had always been there and always had to be navigated around in order to leave the building.

Neumann let the prisoners move around him, let the camp come alive as he smoked cigarette after cigarette, adding to the pile of discarded butts that he had started so many hours ago.

Only when he ran out of cigarettes, when he finished his daily ration of two packs, did he finally stand up. He reached his arms into the air, stretching his body like a man waking up from an afternoon nap. He adjusted his uniform, wiped his mouth, and stepped away from the hut.

Neumann strolled through the camp and found General Horcoff where he expected to find him, on his knees, working in his garden. He greeted the general the way he always did, with a quick clearing of his throat. This time, though, he did not stand at attention.

The general spotted him. "Sergeant Neumann, good to see you again," Horcoff said with a smile.

Neumann didn't smile back. "We need to have a talk, General."

Horcoff's smile immediately faded, and when he saw the serious look on the sergeant's face, he frowned. He slowly stood up, using a piece of the fencing as leverage to push himself to a standing position. Every movement the general made coincided with a grunt of effort.

"Is there something troubling you, Sergeant? You seem quite reticent at the moment, even more so than you did following that ugliness with that submariner the other day. Is everything okay with Corporal Aachen? His condition hasn't worsened, has it?"

Neumann shook his head. "Corporal Aachen's condition is unchanged."

"That's good to hear, although we're all hoping he can recover from these injuries. Terrible thing to get trampled by a crowd but he's a strong boy," Horcoff said wiping his brow. "So what is the reason for this visit?"

Neumann looked about. "It would be best, General, if we talk about this privately," he said softly. "The camp is very crowded."

The general stared at Neumann for a few seconds and then nodded. "Yes, okay, I know the perfect place." He gestured for Neumann to follow him and the sergeant did. They weaved their way through the barracks, ignoring all the salutes and nods of greeting from the other prisoners they passed. Horcoff took Neumann to an open space near the western edge of the workshops. There stood a small shed about five metres squared, surrounded by piles of sand, soil, manure, discarded vegetables peelings, and other foodstuffs—all materials the gardeners would use in their work.

As he walked up to the shed, Horcoff pulled out a key. He used it to open a lock that hung off the door. "One of the Luftwaffe navigators built this after they erected the camp and he started gardening. He needed a safe and secure place to store all his gardening tools to ensure they wouldn't be stolen and used to dig tunnels for escapes," the general said, as he worked the lock. "The Canadians are very strict with us. They check with us every day, making us sign our tools in and out so that each and every one is accounted for."

He continued talking as he opened the door and stepped in, gesturing for Neumann to follow. "If we lose a tool, we must have a good explanation and find it very quickly or they close us down, which is why none of us has ever lost a tool. Our gardens are too important to us and to the camp."

The shed was small, but well-organized, the smell of dirt and manure lingering in the air. Gardening tools of various types hung from wooden pegs on the western wall or leaned in tidy stacks near the two corners of that wall. There was a small table on the far wall directly across from the door on which sat a ledger and a pencil. Along the entire length of the eastern wall was a metre-high stack of sandbags, each bag about twenty-five centimetres long. Horcoff noticed Neumann looking at the sandbags.

"Ah yes, Corporal Aachen's weightlifting sandbags. When the other gardeners noticed how well they kept the weeds out of my beddings they had to have their own," Horcoff walked over and hefted one in his hands. "The Canadians were quite happy to give us our own supply once we explained what we needed them for. The guards have asked for a share of our spoils, but that's a small price to pay because we'll more than triple our harvest due to the lack of weeds."

The general turned to face Neumann. "But I'm guessing you don't care much about gardening. Still, this is a suitable and quiet place to talk in private. So please, Sergeant, feel free to tell me your concerns."

Neumann gave the shed a quick once-over and then looked

at the general. "I believe I may have determined who killed Captain Mueller."

"I don't understand," Horcoff said, perplexed. "I thought Lieutenant Neuer killed him. Wasn't he the one that tried to kill Corporal Aachen in the shower?"

"He was part of the group involved in that incident, yes. But he wasn't the instigator."

"And have you determined who that instigator is?"

Neumann nodded.

"So he is the murderer then?"

Neumann shook his head.

"How could that be? He instigated an attack on Corporal Aachen which was almost identical to the attack on Captain Mueller."

"While he admitted he was behind Aachen's attack, he denied being involved in Mueller's murder."

"Of course he would deny that. He's lying."

"No, he wasn't. I'm sure of it."

"You sound quite confident of that, Sergeant," General Horcoff said. "Who is the person we are talking about, anyway?"

Neumann hesitated, but then told the general.

"Heidfield! The man is a criminal, no doubt about it, regardless of how he fought on the battlefield," the general scoffed. "He was involved in such activities in Africa and hasn't changed his ways. In fact, it seems lack of battlefield action has made him an even more notorious criminal, especially considering his actions against Aachen and Mueller."

"Sergeant Heidfield did not kill Mueller. I interrogated him myself."

"I'm sorry, Sergeant Neumann, I don't mean to disparage your abilities but in the end, you are only a village policeman while Sergeant Heidfield is from Berlin. His urban sensibilities and criminal sophistication are far above your abilities."

"Heidfield is nothing but a small-town crook with big-city fantasies. He hid nothing from me," asserted Neumann, his voice rising slightly.

"I beg to differ, Sergeant. You may be a good policeman but you are also a good man, too good in some cases. There are others in this camp, who would be much more … compelling in their interrogations of Heidfield. And no doubt they would be able to use their skills to get a confession out of him. It wouldn't be pretty but they would get results."

"Which would be incorrect and allow Mueller's actual murderer to go free."

"I insist you allow me to report your findings to command so that they can deal with Sergeant Heidfield. You, of course, will get credit for weeding him out in the attack on Corporal Aachen and leading us down this path. But leave the interrogation to the more experienced."

Neumann took a step towards the general. "I may not be Gestapo. I may not be willing to use various forms of thumb-screws on people. But my interrogation techniques get much better results, more honest results. Heidfield did not kill Captain Mueller."

"Please, Sergeant Neumann, this should not be a question of professional competence. You must allow—"

"—When did you join the Legion, General?" Neumann

asked, cutting off Horcoff and taking another step forward. "Was it directly after the war, or a few years later?"

Horcoff froze, staring at Neumann with disbelief. "I beg your pardon?" he asked after a moment. "What are you talking about?"

"You became a legionnaire sometime between the wars, didn't you? Civilian life wasn't what you expected, especially for someone of your standing. You were probably blamed in some way for the Fatherland's defeat in 1918 so you decided to redeem yourself through the Legion. Which is understandable—many veterans of the First World War did so."

"This is preposterous, Sergeant Neumann. You have really crossed the line here. The incident with Corporal Aachen has severely affected your abilities. And only because of that am I willing to forget this conversation and—"

"—and then when Rommel came to Africa and was looking for men experienced in desert fighting, he turned to German legionnaires, especially ones he probably knew from the previous war. And again, here was another chance to redeem yourself, to fight for the Fatherland again, this time for victory. Also understandable."

"Sergeant Neumann, you are bordering on insubordination if you—"

"But you decided to keep your Legion past a secret from the rest of us. Rommel no doubt knew but didn't care. You could effectively lead men, you could fight. Most of the legionnaires could. But only he knew, or a few others, like Colonel Ehrhoff, who also didn't care. But Captain Mueller. He must have known, somehow. Possibly you served together—"

"—I was not a legionnaire!" Horcoff shouted. "I am no soldier of fortune out for faded glory. I am a general of the Wehrmacht. A winner of the Iron Cross First Class with two clusters. I've been in briefings with the Führer himself. And if you continue in this manner, I will have you brought up on charges."

Neumann looked at the general who was gripping the sandbag quite tightly with his fingers. "When they shipped us out from North Africa after we were captured, there were a number of troop ships. Most of them carried soldiers like me and Aachen, members of the Wehrmacht," Neumann said. "However, there was another ship, a single ship that carried other soldiers—Italians, some Vichy French who refused to fight for Free France, and a group of Wehrmacht soldiers who were different from the rest. Legionnaires who had fought for our side. Men like Colonel Ehrhoff and the group in his hut. Mueller was also on that ship, but he wasn't really part of the group. He had been a legionnaire, but retired after his five years and went back to teaching. Only when war started again did he sign up.

"And then there's you, General Horcoff. You were on that ship as well. You said so yourself. You mentioned Italians and how their cooking and lazy attitude bothered you. But the only ship that had Italians was also the one that had legionnaires. No other ship of German prisoners had Italians. Only yours. Which means you were a legionnaire."

Horcoff stumbled back against the stack of sandbags, face white.

"And that's been the common theme in all of this: the Legion. Mueller was a legionnaire; Pohlmann, who came to view Mueller's body and ran, deciding to escape rather than face an interrogation from me, was a legionnaire; Ehrhoff is a legionnaire and remains one, as do all his men. The only other legionnaire left is you. But for some reason you don't want to be considered a legionnaire; you want everyone to think you are a regular Wehrmacht general. But why, General? It's not a big problem. Rommel knew who you were, the Leader probably did as well, but they didn't care. All they saw was an experienced German soldier, experienced in desert warfare, who was willing to fight for their country. There was no reason to—"

Horcoff sat down hard on the top of the stack of sandbags, blinking quickly, sweat forming on his brow, looking like an old man about to have a heart attack. Neumann stopped his tirade and leaned in close. "General Horcoff? Can you hear me?"

Horcoff's breath came out in staccato gasps. He looked at Neumann but a second later his eyes rolled back in his head. His breath stopped for a second.

"Are you okay? General Horcoff? Can you hear me?"

After several seconds, Horcoff finally let out a long gasp. His eyes returned and looked at Neumann. He looked as if he was about to faint. But a second later, life had returned and with it, a look of anger, like an animal readying to attack.

Neumann raised his arms quickly as the general swung the sandbag in an arc towards the sergeant's head. Though he managed to partially block it with his forearm, the blow hit him on the top of his head, filling his vision with a spray of sparks, followed by a short-lived blackness. Neumann quickly regained his bearings, but his vision was blurred and his head and his forearm throbbed with pain. He took two stumbled steps backward, but the general moved forward, swinging the bag again. This blow caught Neumann on the shoulder, dislocated the joint, and then bounced up, grazing his head just above the ear. This time he was knocked to the side, colliding into the wall, and knocking a number of tools off their pegs to the dirt floor.

Neumann raised his injured forearm again, but Horcoff's third blow came low, connecting fully with the side of Neumann's body where the ribs curved toward the back. The bag burst, sand erupting, spraying all over Neumann's body and throughout the shed. The sound of his ribs breaking echoed in Neumann's head and that was quickly followed by an explosive pain that radiated in and around his entire torso. His breath was knocked out of his lungs and he collapsed to the dirt, his body jerking for oxygen and every jerk an eruption of agony.

In a daze, he tried to get away from the attack, his arms and legs scrambling against the dirt and the side of the wall. Yet he only managed to trap himself in one of the corners farthest away from the shed's door. He banged against the wall, but quickly those attempts became weaker and weaker. He looked at Horcoff approaching as he lost the ability to move his arms. He could not raise them and protect himself. Neumann closed his eyes and waited for the next blow.

34.

"You're a fool, Sergeant Neumann. A complete fool."

General Horcoff stood over the sergeant, his back facing the door, shaking his head. "I thought Captain Mueller was foolish but you ... well, Sergeant, I expected better of you. I expected you to be smart enough to realize that it was good enough to have Lieutenant Neuer take the blame for Mueller's death. But you had to push harder, to discover the truth. No doubt something to do with honour."

Horcoff dropped the expended bag of sand on the ground beside Neumann and started looking about. "Unfortunately, honour, as you and I used to know it, has been dead for a number of years. It's been disassembled and demolished like my grandfather's manor by that short, little piece-of-shit corporal from Austria." As he talked, Horcoff glanced over the various gardening tools hanging from pegs, like a farmer searching for a substitute for a lost ax to euthanize an injured animal—something to put it out of its misery.

"I know it's traitorous to say such things about the Führer, to criticize his actions because he was a great man who put the Fatherland back in its rightful place as the ruler of Europe," Horcoff said, reaching out for various gardening tools, picking up one or two, before setting them back on their pegs. "But Hitler is a terrible strategist. He has no concept of the proper tactics, of how to implement a military plan of action to achieve the proper results and honour. All the military victories of the Reich, the ones he takes credit for, are the result of brilliant plans of his great generals, Rommel and Guderian, while our greatest blunders, Russia and now this invasion of the continent, are his fault entirely. He is only a corporal, a smart one to be sure but not smart enough to realize that he should allow his generals to plan and fight the wars instead of him."

Neumann looked about, groaning in pain as he did, his eyes searching for something to use. Underneath a small pile of sand, he found a pair of shears. He struggled to tuck them into his hand. Horcoff noticed his movement and reached down to slap him once across the face. Neumann's head snapped back and his eyes faded away for a moment or two. The general took that moment to grab the sergeant's hand, pry open his fingers, and remove the shears. He tossed them aside.

"Still acting foolishly, Sergeant? Still think you can win this battle? Unfortunately, you are dead. They will find your body and wonder who killed you. Many will assume you were punished by somebody for letting Neuer escape or for asking too many questions. And though they will wonder, they will not pursue it. Your death, and of course Mueller's, will be seen as warnings, telling them not to ask questions, telling them not to speak out."

Neumann blinked. "Mueller," he groaned as he slowly and painfully tried to push himself up. But Horcoff pushed him down with a boot to the chest.

"Yes, I killed Captain Mueller; he left me no choice. Somehow he found I had served with the Legion before Rommel came to Africa," Horcoff said. And then he laughed. "The captain wanted us to be comrades of all things. He even belonged to a cadre of former legionnaires who did not join with the larger group in the camp but still were honoured to be associated with the Legion. And he asked me to join them. He was keen on telling his fellow members about me. Well, I couldn't have that. I spent too long removing that association from my record, proving that I was a true German, a genuine member of the Wehrmacht who had put aside his past to fight for the Fatherland. Reputation will be everything once we win this war and move forward with the thousand year Reich. Only true and loyal Germans will be part of the Reich, all the traitors will be removed. I couldn't let Mueller ruin that.

"I asked him to meet me before sunset that morning, here in the shed, so we could discuss it in private," Horcoff sighed and shook his head. "But he didn't understand. He said the war was over, Germany had lost. Hitler had ruined the country."

Horcoff turned around and grabbed another sandbag from the pile. "I must admit those words angered me and I panicked, striking him with the only thing I had on hand," he said, hefting the bag. "An amazing piece of weaponry, this thing. We used a similar type of bag, filled with rotten fruit, to punish any revolutionaries we captured in Algeria, most of them hapless Blacks or smelly Arabs. We would beat their bodies so they would turn to mush on the inside but on the outside, nothing. So their compatriots or families would find them dead but with not a single mark on them. Many of them believed we had a secret weapon that could kill a man from the inside. Like them, Mueller tried to protect himself but I just beat through his defenses just like we used to do in Algeria.

"Once he was unconscious, I realized I couldn't leave him in the shed to wake up and tell everyone what I did. Fortunately it wasn't light yet, so I stuffed my handkerchief in his mouth to keep him quiet in case he woke and took him to his classroom where I hung him from a pipe to make it look like a suicide— another German soldier distraught over the invasion of the continent and the state of the war."

Horcoff slapped the top of the sandbag with his open hand, a cloud of dust flying off of it. "But you, Sergeant, I will not hang. I'll kill you here, leave you, and one of the other gardeners will find you. They'll assume that you were killed by those angry at you for letting Neuer escape. And since I've been a strong supporter of you, no one will suspect me this time. Even if they do for some reason, no one will be asking questions anyway because they'll realize that if someone can get to you, they can get to anyone. That's the one good thing about German soldiers: they know when to shut up and not ask questions. Except for you of course, which is why you are in this position."

Horcoff slung the bag over his shoulder preparing to bring it down on Neumann. The sergeant looked up, eyes wide with fear. "Goodbye, Sergeant Neumann. I'm sorry this has to happen because you were a good soldier and an excellent squad leader, but you let foolishness get the better of you."

Horcoff grunted and started to swing the bag down. But a body came flying into the shed, tackling the general like a rugby player. The sandbag flew out of the general's hand and crashed to the ground on top of Neumann's boot. It burst apart, the sand exploding into the air like a cloud.

General Horcoff crashed against the back wall of the shed, his arms flailing, the front of his face erupting into blood as his nose hit the wall. Several teeth burst out of his mouth and his breath gushed out in a loud "Ooofff."

Through the cloud of dust, the general and his tackler crashed to the ground, the general's body limp. His attacker jumped to his feet, grabbed the unconscious and bloody general by the scruff of his neck, dragged him across the floor of the shed, and tossed him out the door. There was a sound of a struggle outside, of several other men shouting in alarm. The attacker then turned to Neumann, bending down on one knee. He took the sergeant's head in his hands and slowly turned it this way and that.

"Are you okay, Sergeant?" a voice asked. It was a voice he did not recognize. Neumann groaned in pain.

Through blurred vision, Neumann saw the prisoner. He had seen the face before but it took him several seconds to realize who it was.

"Pohlmann," he groaned, the burst of pain hitting as he breathed. "I … thought … you escaped."

"I just pretended to escape because I was worried I might be next, and hid in the camp. It's a big place—lots of great hiding places," Pohlmann said with a nod.

"I … wanted to … talk to you…"

"I know. And I thought about coming to you to talk but knew if I showed myself too much, the Canadians would find me. But I was still able to keep an eye on Horcoff."

"Horcoff … you knew?"

"Not directly. I thought he might be involved because I was the one who told Mueller about Horcoff being in the Legion and knew they were meeting that morning. Mueller told me about it, was pleased the general agreed to meet him." Pohlmann paused for a moment. "You see, Sergeant, before we were captured Horcoff ordered me to destroy his file, which had information about him being in the Legion. Which is why I ran away from you … sorry Sergeant, I was worried I might be next, that you were working for the general, you were so close that I…" Pohlmann trailed off.

Another face came into view and this time a voice he did recognize spoke to him. "Is he okay, Corporal?" asked Colonel Ehrhoff.

"He looks to be in bad shape, Colonel, but he'll live. Although he probably won't like it. Those broken ribs are going to hurt for a long time."

"Better get the doctor, then," Ehrhoff said.

Pohlmann nodded, stood up, and left the shack. In the

distance, Neumann heard people questioning him, but he couldn't hear what was being said.

"Hold still, Sergeant Neumann," Ehrhoff said. "The doctor will be coming."

Neumann looked up, his face full of questions. "Pohlmann … you knew?"

"Save your strength, Sergeant. Don't speak. But to answer your question, Pohlmann even fooled me. I thought for sure he was long gone. But when he saw that you were talking with General Horcoff, he came to me, and told me that a legionnaire who had harmed another was about to harm someone else. Took a bit of convincing, but once he told me about General Horcoff, I came. Horcoff even had me fooled—I had no idea he had been a legionnaire, thought it was a mistake he was in the same ship as us. But Pohlmann knew because it was Pohlmann who looked after all those records. In fact, it was Pohlmann who first told Mueller…"

Neumann tried to listen, but couldn't keep his eyes open any longer. As Ehrhoff told the story, Neumann let the black embrace him.

35.

When Neumann woke up, he was racked with pain. Every inch of his body hurt and he loudly groaned. A hand cupped the back of his head and raised it slightly. Even that movement almost knocked him out.

"Drink this," said a familiar voice.

A cup of cool water touched his lips. It hurt to swallow, but even that small amount gave him the strength to open his eyes. He looked over and saw Corporal Aachen still dressed in a hospital gown, his face less swollen but still covered in bruises. He seemed to have lost some weight as well.

"You look like shit, Corporal."

Aachen smiled. "You should talk, Sergeant. But based on what you were beaten with, I'm betting you feel a lot worse than I do."

Neumann nodded. "Like the time I was buried alive after that artillery barrage in Tunisia. I remember telling you to put me back in the hole because it hurt so much."

"Your injuries are worse now than they were then. You'll be here for a while, says the doctor."

Neumann nodded. He looked over at the pitcher of water. Aachen read the look and helped the sergeant to another drink, this time a longer one. Neumann sighed as Aachen set his head back onto the pillow.

"What happened with the general?"

"Dead," Aachen said with a blink. "Some cooks found him hanging in a supply building."

"When?"

"A day or so ago. The note said he was disappointed in Germans and our failure."

"Note? What note?"

"His suicide note. He said we bungled the war and because of it he didn't want to call himself a German anymore."

"Do you believe it?"

Aachen shrugged. After a moment of hesitation he said, "I didn't figure the general as a traitor. Since he was so busy making the camp ready for the Führer, I didn't think he was one to support that kind of thing."

Neumann pushed himself up, fighting past the pain as he did so. "What are you talking about, Corporal?"

Aachen's eyes opened wide with realization and he nodded. "Sorry, Sergeant. You've been unconscious for a number of days so you're unaware of the developments in Germany."

"What developments?"

"The assassination attempt on the Führer's life."

"Someone tried to kill Hitler?"

Aachen nodded. "They planted a bomb at a meeting but fortunately, it was placed far enough away from the Führer that he wasn't killed. He suffered some minor injuries but is still alive. Of course, there is much retribution going on. It seems the assassins had many supporters. And based on the general's note, he was one of them. He wrote that their failure means that Germany will suffer greatly and he couldn't live to see that."

Neumann sighed and let himself fall back onto the bed.

Aachen looked at him. "Do you believe that, sir? Do you believe that Horcoff killed himself? The SS says it looks pretty cut and dry, that the general was a traitor and they won't allow a military burial because of it. But is this something we should look into when you're better?"

Neumann waved at Aachen. "No, Corporal. It's best not to annoy the blackshirts, especially now that they are dealing with the fact that someone tried to kill the Führer. Best just let it be."

"Are you sure, Sergeant?"

"To be honest, I don't care how the general died. Or even Captain Mueller, anymore. They're both dead, goddammit. A lot of people are dead and no one really worries too much about them. So why should we?"

"That doesn't sound like you, Sergeant. Maybe you should sleep on it?"

"Yes, sleep would be good. That's what I'll do, Corporal, and based on your looks, I think you should do the same. Maybe we'll get lucky."

"Lucky? I don't understand, Sergeant."

"Maybe we'll sleep long enough so that when we wake up, we can go home. That's all I'm hoping for at the moment. Just to go home."

Acknowledgements

I wish to thank the Canada Council for the Arts and the Alberta Foundation for the Arts for their help in completing various drafts of this book. More thanks go to the folks at Ravenstone and my editor Allan Levine. I also read a ton of articles and historical documents to help in the research of this book but to list them all here would take too much space. But these books were most helpful: *Canadian Escapades: The True Story of the Author's 3 Escapes from WW2 POW Camps* by Klaus Conrad; *Prairie Prisoners: POWs in Lethbridge during Two World Conflicts* by Georgia Green Fooks; *POW—Behind Canadian Barbed Wire* by David J. Carter; and *Soldaten, On Fighting, Killing, and Dying: the Secret World War II Transcripts of German POWs* by Sonke Neitzel. And please note, even though this book is set in an actual location during historical times, it is a work of fiction, not a historical document.